Eric Wilder

Cycles
of the
Moon

Edmond, Oklahoma

# Other books by Eric Wilder

Ghost of a Chance
Murder EtoufFée
Name of the Game
A Gathering of Diamonds
Over the Rainbow
Big Easy
Just East of Eden
Lily's Little Cajun Cookbook
Of Love and Magic
Bones of Skeleton Creek
City of Spirits
Primal Creatures
Black Magic Woman
River Road
Blink of an Eye
Sisters of the Mist
Garden of Forbidden Secrets
New Orleans Dangerous

This book is a work of fiction. Names, characters, places, and incidents either are products of the author's imagination or are used fictitiously. Any resemblance to actual events or locales or persons, living or dead, is entirely coincidental.

© 2021 by Gary Pittenger

All rights reserved, including the right of reproduction, in whole or in part in any form.

**Gondwana Press**
1802 Canyon Park Cir. Ste C
Edmond, OK 73013

For information on books by Eric Wilder
www.ericwilder.com

Front Cover by Gondwana Graphics

**ISBN: 978-1-946576-11-8**

## Acknowledgments

I wish to thank Donald Yaw and Linda Hartle Bergeron for beta reading, editing, and providing valuable input involving timeline and character development.

*for Marilyn*

# Cycles of the Moon

A novel by
Eric Wilder

## Chapter 1

Aura Hartel couldn't believe her luck. Though she'd participated in digs in South America, Southeast Asia, and even the Sahara Desert, none had been as physically uncomfortable as the one where she now found herself. August is hot in most of the United States. In New Orleans, it's both warm and almost unbearably humid. Though she'd been in New Orleans for only a few days, she already hated the weather and the first assignment with her new job.

Both an archeologist and anthropologist, Aura loved the study of ancient cultures. While over three-hundred years old, New Orleans was young even by European standards. Seth Daniels, Aura's boss and the head scientist on the dig, didn't seem any happier.

"What the hell, Seth! We should be working in Egypt. Does anyone give a damn what we find here?"

"If someone didn't care, then we would be in Egypt," Seth said.

Seth was forty-something though his longish hair helped maintain his boyish looks. Bouncy brown waves failed to produce his desired look, and he usually wore a broad-brimmed hat to compensate for it. Seth had never married, the career that often took him from continent to continent, precluding any long-term relationship. He made up for it in other ways.

Seth was the head of the UNO archaeology department, and Aura found herself in New Orleans because of him. After meeting at a national convention, the two had enjoyed a wild albeit brief affair. Aura thought that was all there was to it until a job in the department had opened, and Seth called her to fill it. Though she still had feelings for the attractive older man, she quickly learned the sentiment wasn't mutual.

Aura had tied her brown hair in a bun, an Army-green Boonie hat like the ones worn by jungle soldiers covering her head. The cap was soft. In the heat of New Orleans, she used it to wipe the sweat dripping down her face.

Though not startlingly beautiful, the young woman had expressive green eyes and sparkling teeth. Aura had never been in a serious relationship and wasn't over the short fling she'd had with Seth Daniels.

Aura and Seth were only supervising four

grad students doing the digging and heavy lifting. None of them looked particularly happy. Seth pointed to the nearby Creole townhouse that had partially collapsed because of the weight of time.

"Most of the property in the French Quarter is privately owned. When an owner allows you to dig, you take the opportunity," he said.

"Seems a bit random to me," Aura said.

"At least we have a wall around us and don't have to contend with gawking tourists staring over our shoulders," Seth said.

Aura glanced at the eight-foot-high masonry wall enclosing the courtyard where they were digging. Spanish moss-draped to the ground from the live oaks and a large butterfly was flitting in a hedge draped with blooming honeysuckle. Bushes and flowering vines that had gone untrimmed for decades had all but overgrown the open space.

Aura's tone was sarcastic when she said, "Thank God for small favors."

"Get over it," Seth said. "We won't be here long. The water table is only five feet deep, and that's as far as we can dig."

"What was this place?" Aura asked.

"The New Orleans home of some rich sugar planter who probably had a plantation on River Road. Overseers and slaves did most of the work. Plantation owners spent much of their time in New Orleans socializing and leading the good life."

The grad students had staked out two eight-foot by eight-foot excavation sites and were using shovels and sifters. Work came to a halt when a young grad student named Amanda squealed. Seth sprang off his portable chair and hurried to the hole.

"What is it?" he said. "A snake?"

Amanda was from Australia, petite, with honey-blond hair and a killer body. Everyone participating in the dig, including Aura, knew she was sleeping with Seth.

"Found something, Professor Daniels," she said.

The other three grad students called the two supervisors by their first names. Seth loved the young woman's Aussie accent, her loving attention, and was oblivious to the talk going on behind their backs. Grabbing Amanda's hand, he helped her out of the hole. Aura joined them.

"An old coin," Amanda said. "It's heavy."

Seth took the coin, practically unrecognizable from its coating of encrusted dirt, to a work table erected beneath an open canopy. Aura and Amanda watched as he used a microscope to view the coin and a descaling tool to remove the grime.

"We got this," Aura said. Catching Aura's tone, Amanda gave her an angry look before returning to her excavation site. "What is it?"

"An 1811 gold Napoleon. Now we know what timeframe we're dealing with," Seth said.

"That's eight years after the Louisiana Purchase," Aura said. "What's a French coin doing here?"

"Gold," Seth said. "You can buy anything with gold no matter which country issued it."

Seth dropped the coin when a grad student called out. "I've found something."

Seth and Aura stood at the edge of the excavation. The hole was almost five feet deep, groundwater seeping up over the grad student's boots. Water, turning the loamy soil into mud, continued to rise.

"What is it, Beau?" Seth asked.

Beau and a red-headed Irish exchange student named Sean had doffed their sweaty shirts. Beau was from France and also an exchange student. His dark hair, eyes, and deep tan seemed the antitheses of Sean's pale complexion and blue eyes. Both he and Sean spoke with accents.

"Don't know yet," Beau said.

Sean's shovel struck something with a thud.

"What is it?" Seth asked.

"A skeleton," Sean said.

The excavation site had become a mud hole as another grad student named Joey jumped in to help. Joey was a local African-American. Like Sean and Beau, globs of mud-coated his chest, pants, and boots. When they finally broke the suction, the three filthy grad students began pulling parts of a skeleton out of the hole, laying it to rest beside the canopy.

Joey returned to where he was working as Beau and Sean began assembling the skeleton. Mud coated the bones, an arm poking through the mire. Amanda was taking pictures.

"Wash the mud away and let's see what we have," Seth said.

Joey called from the other hole before they could begin the task. "I've hit water," he said. "What now?"

"Found anything?" Seth asked.

"An old bottle and another skeleton," Joey said.

The four grad students, though unpaid, were receiving extra college credit for their work in the dig. Seth would be bestowing grades, the reason the other students weren't happy with Amanda. Seth turned to Aura.

"This little project just got bigger," he said. "Hope our workers don't mutiny on us."

"No one was expecting to find human remains," Aura said. "Should we contact the authorities?"

"This is private property, the new owner planning to put in a boutique hotel with a pool. The skeletons need to be moved and reinterred elsewhere. Meanwhile, we can classify the bones and find out who and what we are dealing with."

"Why weren't the remains buried in a cemetery?" Aura asked.

"Don't know," Seth said. "There were aboveground cemeteries in New Orleans in 1811. Maybe we'll get a handle on it before we finish the dig."

Seth's answer failed to satisfy Amanda's curiosity, and she commented in her Aussie accent.

"Perhaps it was a slave."

"Everyone in New Orleans, even the slaves, was Catholic and received proper Catholic burials. There must have been a reason someone buried these skeletons below ground."

"What reason?" Amanda asked.

"We may never know."

Seth glanced at Aura when she said, "Maybe the deceased wasn't from New Orleans."

Joey interrupted their thoughts. "Seth, you better come see this," he said.

The students had washed all the mud off the two skeletons. They were staring at the jumble of bones as Seth and Aura arrived to take a look.

"What you got?" Seth asked.

Joey gestured with the palm of his hand. "Two skeletons. This one's an adult African-American male," he said. "There's no skull or hands."

"That's not all," Beau said.

Seth gave the two men an assessing glance. "What?"

"The hands and skull aren't just missing," Joey said. "Looks like someone lopped them off."

"Maybe with an ax," Sean said.

Seth got on his hands and knees to get a better look.

"You're right," he said.

"What's it mean, Professor Daniels?" Amanda

asked.

"Don't know," he said. "What about the other one?"

"The skeleton of an older, African-American male. Look at the skull."

Seth gazed at the skull as he held it in his hand. "Jesus! Looks like this poor bastard took a bullet to the head at point-blank range." He blinked and rubbed his forehead. "Ninety degrees in the shade, and this is a problem I didn't need."

Seepage of water into the holes had effectively ended the digging. Mud coated Sean and Beau as they helped each other out of the growing mudhole.

"I've got one more for you," Joey called from one of the holes.

"Another skeleton?"

"A body," Joey said.

"What the hell!" Seth said.

Aura, Seth, and the grad students watched as Joey handed the nude body of a small woman to Beau. After helping Joey out of the hole, they brought the body to Seth. Beau laid the human remains on the ground and waited for directions.

Seth was frowning when Joey joined them. "You found it in the hole?" he asked. "It's barely muddy."

"Where else would it have come from?" Joey asked.

Their attention returned to the woman with long dark hair and light green skin with an almost inner glow. The woman's eyes were closed, her arms folded across her chest. She looked to be perhaps mid-twenties, quite beautiful and completely naked. Despite being beneath five feet of dirt for more than two hundred years, the body showed no decomposition signs.

"Good God!" Sean said.

Seth touched the woman's neck. "The body is

warm though I don't feel a pulse."

"Impossible," Joey said.

One of the woman's hands was clenching something. Seth began working her fingers, trying to loosen the grip.

"What is it?" Aura asked.

"Her hand is frozen, and I can't get it open. It'll have to wait for now."

"How can she still be so perfectly preserved?" Amanda asked.

"Voodoo," Joey said.

"Why do you say that?" Seth asked.

"I'm a homeboy, born and raised right here in New Orleans," Joey said. "I know."

"We need to get her to a hospital," Aura said.

Seth gave Aura a glance. "She's been buried for more than two hundred years. She can't be alive."

"How can you be so sure?" Aura said. "We need to get her someplace where they can check her out."

"No," Seth said. "Whatever's going on here is important. It's our discovery. I'm not turning her over to the whims of the City of New Orleans."

"Then what do you intend to do?" Aura asked.

"We have a refrigerated room for storing bodies at the university. Call and have them bring a van. The skeleton also needs to go."

Though Aura wasn't smiling, she began punching in a number on her cell phone. Late afternoon shadows covered the courtyard when the van arrived from UNO to pick up the skeletons and the body.

The grad students had erected a makeshift shower attached to a branch of a towering live oak. Sean, Beau, and Joey had stripped down to their boxer shorts and were washing away the mud beneath the slow spray.

Not to be outdone, Amanda stripped to her

red thong panties and joined them. Aura turned away when she noticed the look of jealousy on Seth's face as he watched the grad students showering together. Joey was drying his hair when he approached Seth and Aura.

"I'm taking Beau and Sean club hopping. We'd love to have you join us."

"Thanks," Seth said. "Other plans."

"Aura?"

"Not tonight," she said. "I have notes I need to edit."

"Suit yourself," Joey said.

The three male grad assistants waved as they exited the gated compound. Seth's broad smile spoke volumes about how he felt when Amanda appeared in a leather miniskirt and low-cut blouse, dramatically emphasizing her ample cleavage.

"Amanda and I are having dinner at Antoine's," Seth said. "There's a quaint old bar on Chartres Street called Bertram's. After dinner, we're heading there for drinks. Will you meet us?"

"Are you sure?" Aura said.

Seth gave her a wink and a peck on the cheek.

"Of course, I'm sure."

Seth didn't wait for an answer. Aura agonized over the invitation as she spent time working on her notes. The sun was low, shadows creeping over the courtyard when she stripped off her clothes and stood beneath the makeshift shower, washing away the day's grime.

The once beautifully manicured French Quarter courtyard had become overgrown with native weeds and vegetation. The lily pond, which had played host to golden koi, was cracked and devoid of water. None of the fountains worked, and the branches of the live oaks extended to the brick masonry. Aura jumped when something peeked around the corner of the abandoned Creole townhouse.

The creature had the snout of a dog, although its teeth were longer and crooked. Brown was the color of its hairless body that had the look of old leather. A fin extended down its back to its bony tail. It was standing on its hind legs. When Aura screamed, the beast ran behind the house. She didn't know what to think as she hurriedly pulled on a fresh set of khaki shorts.

"What in holy hell was that?" she said.

## Chapter 2

Sometime during the night, a gust of wind blew open the door to my French Quarter balcony overlooking Chartres Street. I was lying in bed, awake, or else dreaming I was awake. It seemed like the latter because I wasn't surprised when a wispy cloud floated through the door.

Aglow with ephemeral radiance, the cloud wafted to the foot of my bed, the translucent image coming into focus of a person I knew. A voodoo woman so old, she transcended time. I somehow found my voice.

"Is that you, Madam Aja?"

"Who else would it be?"

The image continued to flash in and out of clarity.

"Are you real?" I asked. "You look like a ghost."

"Because I am a ghost," Madam Aja said.

"Then, this is just a dream, right?"

"Sometimes, life is nothing more than a dream," she said. "Or a nightmare. This is one of those times."

"What are you doing here?"

"I have left this world. Before I move on, I need your help."

"To do what?"

The ghostly figure of the ancient woman Madam Aja extended her hand toward me.

"You're a Traveler, a special and privileged person. With privilege comes duty, and sometimes that duty is deadly serious."

Still groggy from having just awoken, I rubbed my eyes to assure myself Madam Aja was really at the foot of my bed.

"You're confusing me," I said.

"There has been a discovery in the Quarter that has exposed the city's dark past. If I were still alive, I could help. I am not and I have no place to turn except to you."

"I'm happy to help," I said. "Tell me what you want me to do."

Madam Aja had something in her hand, a glow emanating from her closed palm as she extended it toward me. "Take this," she said.

Madam Aja's touch was cold when she dropped a gold pendant into my palm. Several milky crystals dangling from the chain reflected a prism of color emanating from the flashing neon outside my open patio door.

"What is it?" I asked.

"A moonstone pendant that was once magical."

"Once?" I said.

"One of the moonstones is missing. It caused the pendant to lose its power."

"What happened to it?" I asked.

"Someone who wanted to prevent the pendant's magic took it," Madam Aja said.

"Can you tell me who that person is?"

"They are no longer alive the moonstone removed centuries ago."

"And you want me to go back in time and find

it?"

"Yes, and then restore it with the pendant and return it to its rightful owner."

"Is there more you can tell me?" I said.

"I wish I could help you more than I am but I've told you all I can. You'll have to figure it out for yourself."

The glimmering image of Madam Aja flickered and died as I passed my hand through an icy mist. My fingers were still cold when the cell phone on the night stand beside the bed rang and woke me.

A cool breeze was blowing the white linen curtains of my balcony door. It was daylight, a mule snorting as the carriage it was pulling passed on the street below. Mama Mulate spoke when I answered the phone.

"Wyatt," she said. "Madam Aja died last night."

August, with all its heat and humidity, had arrived in the Big Easy. Three in the afternoon, the temperature was almost intolerable. I felt every bit of it as Mama Mulate and I waited on a Basin Street curb for a jazz funeral to begin.

Mama Mulate, my sometimes business partner, was a tall, quite attractive African-American woman. She had a Ph.D. from the University of South Carolina and taught English lit at Tulane University. She was also a practicing voodoo mambo.

I'm a private investigator. Years before, when a client had hired me to help him lift a voodoo spell he thought his wife had placed on him I'd formed a partnership with Mama that had proven lucrative. We'd created a loose association to assist people with questions concerning the paranormal, a subject not uncommon in the Big Easy. Since then, I'd developed a close friendship with the intelligent and eccentric woman.

One of the people whom I'd met through my friendship with Mama Mulate was an ageless voodoo woman named Madam Aja. It was Madam Aja's funeral we were attending and the reason we were on the side of the street with hundreds of well-wishers also waiting to celebrate the woman's long and illustrious life.

Mama wore a bright yellow African tribal dress complete with a flowing necklace of pink coral. Out of respect for her departed friend and mentor, a traditional Creole tignon covered her long, Afro-style tresses. Like almost everyone else at the funeral, I was dressed casually in khakis, bright Hawaiian shirt, and sandals with no socks. We were there to celebrate Madam Aja's life and not to mourn her death.

Because of our close friendship with Madam Aja, Mama and I were part of the procession's first line comprised of family and friends. A small band of old black men, dressed in matching caps, white shirts, and dark pants waited to lead the procession to the cemetery. Soon, the little drummer removed his hat, raking a bony hand through his snowy hair before tapping his drumsticks on the edge of his snare drum six times. Another band member began playing a slow dirge on his trumpet. Trombone and tuba joined in.

I was one of the many honorary pallbearers charged with carrying Madam Aja's wooden casket on the short distance to St. Louis Cemetery Number 1. Vehicle traffic, in deference to Madam Aja's funeral, had ceased as we paraded down the middle of Basin Street.

Elaborate crypts were visible over the top of the masonry fence surrounding the graveyard. Though I'd visited the oldest cemetery in New Orleans on many occasions, I'd never been quite so aware of the finality I now felt. The front gate was open, and we carried the coffin to a honeycomb vault where an empty rectangular space awaited Madam Aja.

Inclusion in the task was an honor and there were at least a dozen pallbearers. Everyone wanted to help ease Madam Aja's coffin into its spot some seven feet above the ground. Once the box was securely in place, gentle rain that seemed to evaporate before getting you wet began to fall.

The temperature dropped, and clouds covered the sky as a fiery preacher said a few final words about Madam Aja's life and her family. Like the rain, the sermon didn't last long. Smiles had suddenly replaced the tears and solemn expressions as the band struck up a Mardi Gras marching song and started toward the entrance.

Mama Mulate, accompanied by a woman I knew well, joined me. It was Senora, Madam Aja's daughter. Senora was as tall as Mama. Though only forty-something, her hair had gone prematurely gray. No one knew Madam Aja's age. From the looks of her when she was alive, she must have been well over a hundred. It seemed more likely that Senora was her granddaughter, or maybe even her great-granddaughter. I'd never asked her.

Senora's dress was red and equally as festive as Mama Mulate's. She lived in a small house in Faubourg Marigny. While Madam Aja performed voodoo spells for the locals, Senora provided herbs, tribal medicines, and secret potions that Mama Mulate and other voodoo practitioners used to assist in employing their craft. Together, along with the hundreds of well-wishers, we marched out of the cemetery and proceeded up Basin Street.

The noise and number of participants

marching in the second line had grown as we started through the French Quarter. More musicians playing horns and keeping time with drums joined us. The street was crowded with locals and tourists as the procession continued up one road and down the other. Hours had passed when we paraded by Senora's house in Faubourg Marigny.

Mama, Senora, and I broke away from the march. The Creole cottage had a front porch facing the street. Mama sat in the swing, and I sprawled on the porch, draping my legs over the edge.

"Come inside, and I'll get us something to drink," Senora said.

"This swing feels good," Mama said. "I'm so tired I can hardly move."

"Then wait on the porch," Senora said. "I'll get the drinks."

Senora's smile had disappeared when she returned with a glass of iced tea, a bottle of whiskey, and two empty glasses. I grabbed the tray as Mama arose from the swing to give Senora a comforting hug.

"It's okay," Mama said.

"This is going to be so hard," Senora said. "I've never lived alone. I don't know what I'm going to do."

"Get a man or a pet," Mama said. "Either one will work."

Mama's suggestion returned the smile to Senora's face. "I'm going to miss the old woman."

"I know you will," Mama said.

I set my tea on the porch and poured whiskey in their glasses. A smile transformed Senora's gloom as Mama held the pungent liquid to her lips and let her taste a sip.

"Old Crow, Madam Aja's favorite alcoholic beverage," Senora said.

Mama made a face. "Horrid!" she said. "Don't know how she drank this swill, much less liked it."

"I know," Senora said. "There's only a bit left in the bottle. It seemed like a good idea to toast Madam Aja with her favorite drink."

"You got it, sister," Mama said. "Wyatt? You can at least take a sip."

I obliged with a taste from Mama's glass. "Damn!" I said. "If Old Crow was all there was to drink in New Orleans, I'd have never become an alcoholic."

Senora was feeling better, her smile turning to laughter as she joined Mama on the swing. We were soon recounting tales about the old lady as sounds of the jazz funeral disappeared in the distance.

The bottle of Old Crow finally empty, the sky was growing dark. Senora's tears had returned, and Mama used her yellow tignon to wipe them away. Both Mama and Senora had a tolerance for alcohol, and neither of them showed the least signs of inebriation.

"Do you mind sharing with us how Madam Aja passed?" Mama asked.

Senora pointed to a rocking chair, Madam Aja's favorite orange shawl still draped over it.

"Madam Aja was an early riser. Sometimes, she never went to bed. The sun was coming up, and she was sitting in her chair when I came out to the porch."

"She loved that rocker," Mama said.

Senora folded her arms. "Yes, she did. She didn't answer when I asked if she wanted coffee."

Mama hugged Senora when she started crying again. "It's all right, baby."

"When I realized she wasn't breathing," Senora said, "I ran next door to get help. The neighbors called 9-1-1. Paramedics arrived, but they couldn't revive her."

There was a sip of whiskey left, and Senora drank it straight from the bottle. Mama took it from her and set it on the porch.

"I need something else to drink besides Madam Aja's Old Crow," Mama said. "Let's go to Bertram's and have him make us some of his famous martinis."

"I'd better stay here," Senora said. "It's been exhausting since Madam Aja passed. I've been so depressed that yesterday I slept the entire day away."

"You need to be with warm-blooded humans and not ghosts," Mama said. "You are coming with us. I'm not taking no for an answer."

"I'm sorry," Senora said. "I can't get my head around Madam Aja's passing. I never thought she'd die and leave me alone."

"You know she isn't gone," Mama said. "Madam Aja's a Traveler.

"While it's true she's still out there someplace, it doesn't matter because I'm going to be so lonely in that house all by myself," Senora said.

"Then get out of the house and socialize. Maybe meet that man I mentioned," Mama said.

"Oh, Mama, I just don't know," Senora said.

"Nonsense," Mama said. "There's a club in Bywater where I go every Wednesday night. They have wonderful local talent, and occasionally big performers stop in to jam with the regulars. You'll love it."

"Maybe," Senora said. "I'll have to see how I feel about it."

"Good," Mama said. "Let's go to Bertram's. You can stay the night at my house and I'll bring you home tomorrow."

Senora shook her head as she hugged Mama.

"I'm going to be alone from now on. I'll get

used to it and I'm starting tonight," Senora said.

"Then I'll call you tomorrow," Mama said.

"I look forward to it," Senora said.

We left Senora sitting in her front porch swing.

"What now?" I asked.

"With or without Senora," Mama said. "I need one of Bertram's martinis."

Mama's vintage Bugeye Sprite was parked down the street. I held on to the door handle as she raced away toward Jackson Square.

## Chapter 3

Not far from Jackson Square is Bertram Picou's Bar. The rain had lowered the temperature but left lung-popping humidity in its wake. As a result, foot traffic on the sidewalk was almost nonexistent. We found Bertram's almost empty as the weather had caused a similar effect there.

Probably the most eclectic watering hole in the French Quarter, Bertram's was also one of the oldest. The building measured its age in centuries and not decades. Crisp air and Bertram's booming Cajun-inflected voice greeted us when we entered the double doors.

"Look what the cat done drug in," he said. Bertram crawled through the opening in the bar and gave Mama a big hug. "Where the hell you been?"

"Rafael got me a gig working a voodoo cruise on a riverboat sailing from here to St. Louis. I've never had so much fun in my whole life," she said. "I can't wait to do it again."

"So sorry to hear about Madam Aja," he said. "I had lots of customers after the parade honoring her. This damn Nawlins' heat wave sent them all home early."

"Some things never change. August in the French Quarter is one of those things," Mama said.

"Me and Miss Lady are shutting down this place next August and going somewhere cooler," Bertram said.

Mama laughed. "You've never been farther north than Mississippi, and it's just as hot there in August."

"I might fool you. Me and Lady could spend the summer fishing in Alaska and surprise you."

"That would surprise me," Mama said.

"If you go, take me with you," I said.

Bertram flashed his Cajun grin. "Grab some stools at the bar. I'll fix us some drinks."

Lady was Bertram's beautiful collie. She remained behind the bar, her tail drumming the hardwood floor when she heard her name.

Except for the lissome brunette with a sullen expression sitting beside me, the bar was empty. Her little-bit-of-nothing black dress and stylish heels drew my attention to her long legs. Though I knew I wasn't the person she intended to impress, I was wishing I was. She was sipping a soft drink through a straw, her tanned shoulders and big green eyes the only things keeping me from staring at her legs. For a moment, I had a problem suppressing a wolf whistle.

When I smiled and nodded, the young woman gave me a dirty look and moved over a stool. Not everyone in New Orleans is as friendly as are the locals. I returned my attention to other things when Bertram arrived with our drinks.

Mama was enjoying her martini and talking to Senora on her cell phone. I made do with lemonade as Bertram gave the brunette an assessing glance.

"Can I mix you something stronger than that

soda pop you're drinking?" he asked.

"No, thanks," she said.

"You ain't from around here, are you?" Bertram asked.

"What difference does it make?"

"If you're sightseeing, you can party tonight and sleep in tomorrow," he said.

"I'm not sightseeing."

"Then what are you here for?" Bertram asked.

"You're a nosy one," she said.

"I'm a bartender. Being nosy is part of my job description."

Bertram's blunt reply and Cajun-inflected accent brought the hint of a smile to the young woman's pretty face.

"I'm working in town," she said.

"Okay, then," Bertram said. "If you just moved here, your next drink is on the house,"

"I arrived in town last night," she said. "I can't afford to lose my job on the first day at work."

"You won't, Bertram said. "Everyone in New Orleans drinks. Well, except for Cowboy here. Where you working?"

"I'm an associate professor of archaeology at UNO."

"If you're gonna be living in Nawlins, you gotta loosen up. You'll get the hang of it. I'll whip you up one of my lime mojitos, and it's still on the house."

"I'll try it," she said.

Bertram had no other customers and was working hard to keep the ones he had. He hurried away to mix the mojito before the young woman could refuse his hospitality or request her tab.

"Don't drink that thing too fast," he said when he returned with the colorful drink. "The rum will go straight to your head."

"And I have to be at work at five tomorrow morning."

"I'm Bertram. What's your name, pretty lady?"

"Your comment is sexist," she said.

"I'm Cajun," he said. "My mama didn't raise no priest."

"Aura," she said.

"This is the Big Easy," Bertram said. "It's okay to party all night, put in a full day's work the next day, and then do it all again tomorrow night. Where you working that you have to be there at five?"

Though Bertram was nosy, he had a way about him that kept people from becoming offended by it. Still, the woman hesitated before answering. When she did, she drew Mama's attention, pivoting on her stool to listen.

"I'm helping supervise a dig in the courtyard of an old Creole townhouse here in the quarter."

"The Old François Place?" Mama asked.

"You know about it?" Aura asked.

"I know it's haunted," Mama said.

"I don't believe in ghosts," Aura said. She pushed the mojito toward Bertram. "Though your drink is lovely, I'd better pay my tab."

"May as well drink it," he said. "You ain't digging tomorrow."

"How do you know that?" Aura asked.

"Raining outside. Gonna rain all night, and all day tomorrow. Your dig'll be one muddy mess," Bertram said.

Before Aura could react to Bertram's announcement, her cell phone rang. It was Seth.

"Plan to sleep in tomorrow," he said. "I just watched the weather report. It's going to rain all day. I'll meet you at the department around one."

"Damn!" she said as she sat the cell phone on the bar. "I was hoping to finish the dig this weekend so I could concentrate on finding a place to live." The tropical storm had intensified. Wind whistled down the street and blew open the door. "How often does it rain like this?"

"Sometimes every day," Bertram said, pushing the mojito toward her. "At least take a sip. I guarantee it'll relieve what ails you."

Mama and I were still listening as Aura sipped the mojito.

"This is good," she said.

Bertram held up a palm. "Like I said, not too fast. I put an extra pour of 151-proof rum in it. It'll knock you on your ass if you ain't careful."

Ignoring his warning, Aura downed the drink. "Bring me another."

"You sure?" Bertram asked.

"I can hold my liquor," she said.

"You the boss, pretty Miss Aura," Bertram said as he began mixing another mojito.

Uninterested in our company, Aura turned away from Mama and me as she began working on her second mojito. As if remembering I was also at the bar, Mama turned her knees toward mine.

"Sorry about the long phone call," she said. "I'm worried about Senora."

"She'll be fine," I said. "She's a strong woman."

"You've been amazingly quiet," Mama said. "Is there something you want to tell me?"

"Your perception never ceases to amaze me," I said.

"I'm listening," Mama said.

I leaned against the back of the stool and sipped my lemonade.

"Madam Aja visited me the night she died."

Bertram stopped what he was doing and leaned on the bar.

"What the hell you mean by that?" he asked.

"Maybe you better bring us another round," I said.

"Your tab?" he asked.

"Isn't it always?" I said.

Mama was tapping her long fingernails on the bar, glaring at me as Bertram mixed a fresh martini.

"This better be good," she said.

"Don't know how good it is, but you asked. Madam Aja appeared to me in a dream the night she died," I said. "At least I thought it was a dream until I woke up the next morning with this in my hand."

Mama and Aura watched as I placed the pendant on the bar. Bertram was also gaping.

"What is it?" he asked.

"A gold necklace with a moonstone pendant attached," I said. "One of the moonstones is missing."

Aura grew suddenly animated. "Where did you get that?"

"It was in my hand when I awoke. Why do you ask?"

Aura was facing me, her arms clasped around her chest and her legs tightly crossed. Her face was pale, her neck glowing with a crimson blush. She didn't answer my question. Mama took the necklace.

"I'm calling the police," Aura said. "You stole the necklace from the Old François Place."

"Now wait just a minute," Bertram said. "Cowboy's lots of things. Thief ain't one of them."

"I saw a picture of that same necklace at the dig," Aura said.

Bertram glanced up at one of the slowly rotating fans.

"A picture?" he said.

"An old portrait in the upstairs hallway."

"Moonstone necklaces have always been popular," Mama said. "Perhaps the necklace you saw simply looks like the one in the portrait."

"It's the same necklace," Aura said.

"Wyatt's been with me since early this morning," Mama said. "Are you saying your crew dug up that necklace and someone stole it?"

Feeling the warm effect of Bertram's mojito, the young woman's face was flushed.

"That's not what I said."

"Then what did you say?"

"I saw that necklace in a portrait at the Old François Place. It belonged to the woman in the portrait. I have a trained eye for art. That pendant is one-of-a-kind and likely very valuable. Where did you find it if not at the Old François Place?"

"The necklace Wyatt has isn't the same as the one you think you saw," Mama said. "Madam Aja gave it to him the night she died. Bertram's alcohol is affecting your perception."

Aura uncrossed her arms long enough to sip the mojito. "Maybe."

I glanced at her. "What did you find at the Old François Place?"

"A naked woman buried in the courtyard."

"I don't think you better be calling the police," Bertram said. "If you tell them what you just told us, they'll probably lock you up in the insane asylum."

Mama grinned. "There are no insane asylums any longer."

"Well, you know what I mean," he said.

Aura also seemed to understand. "Please, bring me another mojito," she said.

"You already had two," Bertram said. "I done told you they was strong."

"I'm not driving and my hotel is only a few blocks from here," Aura said.

Bertram was already pouring her next mojito. "You got it, pretty Miss Aura."

"How do you explain finding a perfectly preserved body that had been buried for two-hundred years?" I asked.

"Joey, the grad assistant who found the body blamed it on voodoo."

"I doubt it," Mama said.

She smiled when Aura asked, "How in hell would you know?"

"She's a voodoo mambo," Bertram said. "She knows."

"Then what's the answer?"

"If you dug her body out of the mud after two-hundred years and it wasn't decomposed, I'd say she's supernatural," Mama said.

"No one is supernatural." Aura looked at Mama and asked, "What are you laughing at?"

"Your disbelief," Mama said.

"I don't believe in myths," Aura said.

"Do you believe your own eyes?" Mama asked.

Aura gave Mama a pointed glance. "What do you mean?"

"How do you explain digging a warm body buried two-hundred years out of the mud?"

"I'm sure there's a scientific explanation," Aura said.

Mama snickered. "You need to wake the hell up. There is no scientific explanation for what you just told us."

"I believe in science and not the supernatural," Aura said.

"Doesn't matter what you believe," Mama said. "The world is what it is."

"Bullshit!" Aura said. "There's a scientific explanation for everything."

Mama shook her head. "No, there isn't. People see what they want, and believe what they want to see. Everything else they disregard."

Aura raised a finger, motioning Bertram to hurry with her drink. The rum had begun affecting her brain, and she rocked unsteadily on her stool.

"Maybe you're right," she said. "Before leaving the dig tonight, I saw something that scared the holy hell out of me."

"Like what?" I asked.

"A creature. It looked a little like a big dog except its skin was leathery and it had no fur. Its teeth were long, jagged, and crooked. An appendage that looked like a fin extended down its spine. There was something else about seeing the creature."

"Like what?" I asked.

"I had the strange sensation that not only had the creature recognized me, I can't stop thinking I'd seen it somewhere before. Maybe in a dream."

Two men walking in the door had caught Aura's description of the beast.

"What you saw was a chupacabra," the first man said. "Perhaps tomorrow, you can take us to the place where you saw it."

## Chapter 4

Our eyes were all on the two men. They weren't alone and had a film crew with them. The crew began unpacking their gear. The two pulled up stools beside Mama Mulate as the crew began filming.

That someone was shooting our location surprised none of us as New Orleans is a Mecca for the film industry. People who lived in the Quarter were used to seeing famous actors roaming the streets, and directors making documentaries and feature films.

"Hope you don't mind my crew," one of the men said. "We're filming in the French Quarter."

Resting his elbows on the bar, Bertram eyed the person dressed in designer jeans, tailored white shirt, and expensive snakeskin boots. A handsome man, his stylishly-cut prematurely-gray hair and John Lennon-style glasses made him appear younger than he probably was.

"You look real familiar," Bertram said. "How do I know you?"

The second man answered for him. "You kidding me? He's Jake Huntington, the Cryptid

Hunter, the star of the most popular reality show on television."

Bertram's solemn expression morphed into a big, Cajun grin. "My favorite TV show. What the hell you doing in New Orleans?"

"Looking for Wyatt Thomas," he said. "We were told we might find him here."

"Sitting one stool down from you," Bertram said.

Jake Huntington reached behind Mama and shook my hand.

"How can I be of service, Mr. Huntington?" I asked.

"Just Jake. This old war hawk with me is Colley Hornbeck. "Colley's one of the best pilots to come out of Desert Storm. He's my chopper pilot and we're here doing preproduction for an episode to air this fall."

Colley didn't look old enough to have served in Iraq. Long hair covered the tops of his ears. Unlike Huntington's, Colley's was light brown, as was his trimmed beard and mustache. His cowboy boots were well-worn cowhide accenting his faded Levis, western shirt, and black leather vest. He had the good looks of an aging movie star. From the way he was smiling at Mama, he knew it.

"I don't watch much television, Jake," I said. "How exactly can I help you?"

"I'm a cryptozoologist. I travel around the world looking for cryptids like the Loch Ness Monster, Sasquatch, rougarous, and the Congo River Basin's Mokele-mbembe. Though we've never found one, we've spent time looking for the chupacabra such as the young lady described."

"You're looking for a chupacabra?" I said.

"New Orleans is quite possibly the most haunted city in America, maybe the world. We're interested in the chupacabra and always curious about ghosts and spirits. My people told me you know a few things about voodoo."

"Not as much as my business partner," I said.

"And who might that be?" Jake Huntington asked.

"You're sitting beside her. Mama Mulate has a doctorate in English literature from the University of South Carolina. She teaches English lit at Tulane and she's a practicing voodoo mambo."

Jake didn't miss a beat. Grabbing Mama's hand, he stared into her eyes.

"I mistook you for a college coed out on the town."

"You're a liar, Mr. Huntington," Mama said. "But I love it."

"Just Jake," he said. "A lie has never issued from my lips. Is it true you're a voodoo mambo?"

"I am," Mama said. "My friend Senora is an herbalist and the daughter of the greatest voodoo woman in New Orleans since Marie Laveau. Wyatt and I helped her lay Madam Aja in her grave today. Senora is home but we're here continuing to celebrate Madam Aja's life."

Jake patted Mama's hand. "Let me offer my condolences. I heard about Madam Aja when I was prepping for our French Quarter episode. She's a legend."

"Cryptid Hunter was one of Madam Aja's favorites. Senora told me they never missed it."

"Then I'm doubly honored," Jake said, turning his attention to Bertram. "What's your name, good sir?"

"Bertram Picou," Bertram said, pumping Jake's hand. "I can't believe I got Jake Huntington hisself in the house. Your drinks are on me."

"Nonsense," Jake said. "Put everyone's drinks on my tab. Cryptid Hunter is buying."

"Don't argue with him," Colley said. "Jake's

the richest man in Oklahoma, a billionaire oilman even before he started chasing creatures of the night."

Billionaire was all Bertram needed to hear as he began mixing fresh drinks for everyone.

"What are you two drinking?" he asked.

"Straight whiskey with a beer chaser for me," Colley said. "Boss man here likes Bombay Gin. Kinda goofy if you ask me, but hell, he pays the bills."

"With Fentiman's Tonic Water, if you have it," Jake said.

"You bet I do," Bertram said.

Aura was still sitting two stools away from me. Bertram's mojitos were working on her and she was swaying on her stool. Jake walked past me to introduce himself.

"Jake Huntington," he said. "What's your name and claim to fame?"

Not even the aloof young woman was immune to Huntington's charm.

"Aura," she said. "I'm an archaeologist."

"In town for a holiday?" Jake asked.

"A project," she said.

"Aura's helping supervise a dig in the courtyard of an old Creole townhouse. The Old François place here in the quarter. It's haunted," Mama said.

"Really?" Jake said. "Is that where you saw the Chupacabra?"

"I don't know what it was I saw," Aura said.

"They dug a body out of the mud," Bertram said.

"You mean a skeleton?" Jake said.

"Pretty Miss Aura here says it was a woman," Bertram said.

"You mean like a mummy?" Jake asked.

Aura shook her head. "Seth said her body was warm."

"Seth?"

"Dr. Seth Daniels, the lead scientist on the dig," Aura said.

"Who are you conducting this dig for?" Jake asked.

"The University of New Orleans," Aura said. "Their archaeology department just hired me."

"Dammit, Colley!" Huntington said. "Seems as if we just walked into the Twilight Zone. I must be dreaming because this is too good to be true."

"You're not dreaming," Mama said.

Aura wobbled on her stool when Jake grabbed her shoulder.

"You need to cease operations until my crew is ready to begin filming," Jake said.

"You're crazy," Aura said. "My superiors wouldn't allow the filming of a reality TV show at our location."

Colley Hornbeck slammed his shot of whiskey, chased it with a slug of Abita straight from the can, and motioned Bertram to bring him another.

"Never say no to Jake Huntington. He knows everyone from the President of the United States to the Queen of England. If he wants to make something happen, he generally gets it done."

"He won't get this done," Aura said.

Unperturbed, Jake asked, "Where is this perfectly preserved body of the woman you found?"

Aura's words were slurred when she said, "It was transported to UNO, along with a mutilated skeleton."

"How far away is UNO from here?" Jake asked.

"Not far," Mama said. "The campus is on the south bank of Lake Pontchartrain, about twenty minutes away."

"You found a mutilated skeleton along with the body?" Jake asked.

"Yes," Aura said. "The skeleton of an African-American male with missing head and one of his hands. Lopped off, we think."

Jake pulled his cell phone from his pocket. "Hi, Angie. Colley and I stumbled onto a possible episode. Call the president of UNO and arrange a meeting with him or her, and the head of the archeology department about an hour from now. Can you handle it? Thanks, sweetie. I'll be waiting for your call."

Aura snickered. "You can't be serious."

"As a heart attack," Jake said.

"There's no way you'll arrange a meeting with the president of UNO and the head of the archeology department in an hour, especially at this time of night."

"Want to lay a little bet on it?" Jake asked.

"And what exactly are we betting?" Aura asked.

"Whatever you're willing to lose," Jake said.

"You're bluffing," Aura said.

Jake's phone rang before he had a chance to answer her.

He listened, and then said, "Thanks, Angie. You're a doll."

Aura snickered again when Jake returned the phone to his shirt pocket. "You expect any of us to believe you can just make a random phone call in the middle of the night and arrange a meeting with the president of a university who you've never met?"

"We're meeting President Tower and Professor Daniels in an hour," he said.

"You are so full of shit!" Aura said. "Seth will never stand for this."

"You and Dr. Daniels are working for me now." He was smiling when he said, "You're coming with us."

"I've had too much to drink. I'm not going

*Cycles of the Moon*

anywhere except back to my hotel," she said.

"Yes you are," Jake said.

"Seth will fire me."

"Not gonna happen," Jake said. "You're now an adviser on this project and Dr. Daniels is copasetic with it."

"But. . ."

"No buts," Jake said. "You can call me Boss Man from now on."

Colley had a mile-wide grin as he downed another shot of whiskey with a beer chaser.

"Jake's just bullshitting you. You can call him asshole if you want to. He's the best boss on the planet and he don't care what you call him."

"I think I like this man," Mama said.

"Good, because you're part of the team," Jake said.

"How much does this gig pay?" Mama asked.

"Let's just say you're going to be very happy when you get your paycheck," Colley said.

Jake pulled a roll of cash out of his pocket and began counting out hundred dollar bills for Bertram.

"While I'm here in New Orleans, this is going to be my official bar. I anticipate we'll shoot several scenes here and you'll have a speaking part. You'll be well compensated not to mention all the national exposure you'll get."

"You mean I'm gonna be in an episode of Cryptid Hunter?" Bertram asked.

"You, your bar, your gorgeous collie, and all of your customers," Jake said.

"I teach at Tulane," Mama said. "I don't think the administration even knows I'm a practicing voodoo mambo. I'm unsure how they'll react to one of their professors appearing on a reality television show."

"Not just appearing," Jake said. "Starring. Trust me when I tell you Tulane will have donors and alums coming out of the woodwork to make hefty contributions. They'll probably make you a dean."

"Are you sure about that?" Mama asked. "I love my job and wouldn't want to lose it."

"That won't happen, I promise," Jake said. "Even if I'm the only one who makes a hefty contribution. Bertram, I think we have time for another round before we have to leave for UNO."

Jake's crew had already packed their equipment and left the premises. Jake and Colley remained at the bar.

"Want me to call a couple of cabs?" Bertram said.

"I have a vehicle waiting outside. We'll all fit in it nicely," Jake said. "Where's the men's room?"

Bertram pointed. "Down that hallway. First door on the right."

Aura slid off her stool to follow him. "Please bring me a cup of strong coffee," she said. "Despite what Mr. Huntington says about my job security, I'd like to be a bit more sober when we arrive at UNO."

"Gotcha covered, pretty Miss Aura," Bertram said.

"Jake's cute," Mama said. "Is he married?"

"Don't go there," Colley said. "He's coming off a bad divorce and he's a long way from being over it."

"Maybe he needs a little help," Mama said.

"Trust me," Colley said. "He needs lots of help. You're mighty quiet, Wyatt. You okay?"

"Still thinking about Madam Aja," I said.

"I'm so sorry," Colley said.

"You're fine," Mama said. "Madam Aja would want us to have a good time. Wyatt's a teetotaler."

"Guess that about explains it," Colley said.

"I wasn't always a teetotaler," I said. "Not that long ago I would have been leading the charge.

Not everyone from New Orleans can hold their liquor and I'm right there at the top of the list."

"That's a fact," Bertram said as he began delivering our latest round of drinks. "I've yanked this one out of the gutter more than once."

"Bertram saved my life," I said. "If it weren't for him and his lemonade, I'd probably be lying on the sidewalk drinking Mad Dog 20-20 with the other derelicts on Camp Street."

Aura and Jake were laughing when they returned from the restrooms.

"Let's finish our drinks," he said. "We've got work to do and we need to get on the road."

## Chapter 5

Mama squealed when we walked out the door. Parked in front of Bertram's was a limousine, pulsating neon light from the window's sign reflecting off its sleek black exterior. As heavy rain beaded off of the vehicle's polished hood, Mama grabbed Jake's hand.

"Is this for us?" she asked.

Jake smiled and nodded as he gave the driver exiting the car, the high sign. The young man dressed in a black suit, tie, and chauffeur's cap carried a large umbrella and hurried through the downpour to the overhang protecting us.

"Where to, Boss Man?" he asked.

"UNO campus, Bradley."

The chauffeur, standing at least six-foot-six, was enormous. I guessed he was packing from the bulge beneath his coat and that he probably doubled as Jake's bodyguard. That Jake needed a bodyguard was somewhat disconcerting. Using the umbrella, Bradley ushered us into the limo.

When Mama caught me ogling Aura's tanned legs as she climbed in, she frowned and elbowed me.

I smiled and shrugged when she said, "Try to

keep your eyes in your head."

The big vehicle was cozy and dimly lit. Despite Bradley's best efforts with the umbrella, we were all damp as we settled into the posh leather seats. We didn't have long to dwell on our dampness as Jake began dispensing drinks from the bar. Mama, Jake, and Colley had no trouble handling their alcohol. Aura looked at me as if her eyes were about to cross.

"Please don't let them give me another drink," she said.

She nodded when I took the tumbler Jake handed to her and stowed it in a compartment built into the seat.

"You aren't dressed like an archaeologist," I said.

"I was supposed to meet someone," Aura said.

"They stood you up?"

"Not the first time," Aura said, folding her arms tightly across her chest and turning her knees away from me.

Mama and Jake were engaged in a flirty discussion, so I shifted in the comfortable seat, giving the intoxicated young woman her space.

"The driver seems to know you," Mama said.

"Jake only travels one way," Colley said. "First class. Bradley drove the company limousine down from Tulsa yesterday,"

"Is the main studio of Cryptid Hunter located in Tulsa?" Mama asked.

"My hometown," Jake said. "Ever been there?"

"I haven't," she said.

"Like to go sometime?" Jake asked.

"Never know," Mama said with a grin. "What's it like?"

"Used to be the oil capitol of America. Like New Orleans, it's situated on a historical river and has beautiful old neighborhoods. And like

New Orleans, it's had a checkered racial past."

"Sounds interesting," Mama said.

Jake squeezed Mama's hand. "Perhaps, when we get to know each other better, you'll allow me to give you an in-depth tour."

"You're not married, are you?" Mama asked.

"Until a month ago when my divorce went through. Colley and I have been celebrating ever since."

"How long were you married?"

"Too long," Jake said.

"Children? Mama asked.

Jake's grin spread across his famous face. "I thought you were a voodoo mambo. Are you also an attorney?"

"Girls have to guard against broken hearts," Mama said.

"Then you're in trouble," Jake said. "I was married almost thirty years. I'm ready to break a few hearts."

"That's what I like to hear," Mama said. "I'm too old and set in my ways for just one man."

"Then maybe you've never known a man like me," Jake said.

"You have my attention," Mama said.

I was trying unsuccessfully not to listen to Jake and Mama's racy conversation. I couldn't see through the darkly tinted windows as persistent rain drumming the roof blended with the ambient music playing in the background. Mama and Jake were holding hands when the limousine stopped, and Bradley opened the door for us.

When we stepped out of the limo into a dimly lighted parking garage, we found we weren't alone. A young woman with dark eyes, chocolate complexion, and long wavy hair like Mama's greeted us. Lights flooded the room as cameras began filming.

"Welcome, Cryptid Hunter," the woman said. "We've been waiting for you."

Jake hugged the attractive young woman. "Hi, Angie. How was your trip?"

"Uneventful," Angie said. "The crew arrived twenty minutes ago. What took you so long to get here?"

Jake glanced at Mama and said, "I had Bradley take the scenic route."

Angie noticed his glance. "I'll bet you did," she said. "President Tower and Professor Daniels are waiting in the president's office upstairs."

Unhappy about the attractive young woman named Angie, Mama was no longer smiling. When I put my fingers to her lips, reminding her to smile, she quickly took the hint.

Cameras followed us up the stairs and even more greeted us when we entered the conference room on the upper level. Though the hour was approaching eleven, the man behind the executive desk was dressed in tie and pinstripes, pumping Jake's hand as cameras continued to roll. Mama whispered something in my ear.

"This seems almost like a setup."

"Same thing I'm thinking," I said.

"I'm P.D. Tower," the man said. "As president of UNO, I want to welcome you to our campus."

Tower was short and overweight, his jowls bulging from beneath his blue tie. From the way he continued pumping Jake's hand, he was happy to see him.

"Thank you, President Tower," Jake said. "We're honored to help any way we can."

The large office was noisy and filled with people. Mama cupped her hand to my ear again.

"Help with what?" she asked.

"Don't know," I said, "though it looks as if Jake and President Tower do."

Tower gave a short, scripted summation of

UNO's history and accomplishments. Jake was quick to reply.

"Today, there's no more interesting place in America. We're happy to be here and glad to help," he said.

"I'd like to introduce Dr. Seth Daniels, head of our archaeology department," Tower said.

Instead of shaking his hand, Jake hugged Dr. Daniels.

"We've met," Jake said. "Seth was my first roommate at Duke."

Dr. Daniels, his long hair tied in a ponytail, wore khaki shirt and shorts. President Tower hadn't stopped smiling for the cameras.

"That's great. Seth is supervising the French Quarter dig. He'll be your liaison."

Still, photographers began snapping publicity photos of Jake and President Tower. Their pictures, most likely, would soon be displayed across the Internet. The publicity shoot completed, we followed Professor Daniels as the cameras continued rolling.

I couldn't help but notice the visual exchange between Aura and Professor Daniels. Her frown was apparent when he said, "Love your dress," and then whispered something in her ear. Daniels beckoned us to follow him down the hall and into an open room.

"This is the anthropology and archaeology lab," he said. "UNO's grad students have offices in this building. This room serves as storage for artifacts and antiquities before they become exhibits in the university's museum."

Except for the cubicles used as offices by the grad students, the large room was open. Artifacts, relics, and skeletons littered the rows of shelves on one end of the room. Dr. Daniels led us to a table where someone had laid out two skeletons. Three young men waited by the table.

"Sean, Beau, and Joey," Seth said. "Grad students assisting Aura and me with the dig. Sean and Beau are foreign exchange students." Everyone laughed when he added, "Joey here is from New Orleans, and that's almost like being from another country."

"What is it we're looking at?" Jake asked.

"Skeletons of adult African-American males," Seth said. "We found their remains earlier today while excavating in the courtyard of the Old François Place in the Quarter."

Seth handed a skull to Jake, a gaping hole replacing nose and eye sockets.

"What the hell?" Jake said.

"Appears the poor fellow took a point-blank bullet to the face. The back of the skull is all but gone. The other skeleton's even creepier."

"Why are the skull and hand missing from this one?" Mama said.

"We don't know," Seth said. "My grads seem to think someone with an ax chopped them off."

"The remains need to be reinterred and a ceremony performed," Mama said.

"It's the property of UNO and is going nowhere," Seth said.

"They were human beings," Mama said. "Not your property simply because you found them."

Seth glanced at Jake and then back at Mama. Jake didn't mince words as the cameras recorded his every inflection.

"As Dr. Mulate said, we must reinter these remains. After you take your pictures and measurements, Mama and I will take care of the burial details. Right now, we want to view the body of the woman you found."

"It's this way," Seth said.

A young woman with blond hair walked beside Seth as we followed him down a hall to a locked door.

"Who is she?" I asked Aura.

Aura's arms were clasped tightly across her chest again.

"A grad student. She and Seth are sleeping together."

Aura's voice had deepened, her neck and face growing flushed.

"Cozy," Mama said.

Amanda stayed close to Seth as he opened the refrigerated room door and switched on the overhead fluorescent lighting. Condensation poured into the hallway. The young grad assistant shivered as she entered the room.

Amanda wasn't the only one shivering. The rest of us, all dressed for a hot summer day in New Orleans, were ill-prepared for the meat locker temperatures accosting us. Seth led us to a gurney with a blue rubber sheet covering something we all anticipated as the woman's body dug up at the Old François place. Seth pulled back the sheet revealing the naked body of a young woman. Bright lights ignited, and cameras began rolling.

"This won't take long," Seth said.

Jake rested his hand on the edge of the gurney, gazing intently at the body resting on it as the mike on the boom above us recorded every word.

"This body is perfectly preserved," he said. "Are you telling me you found it buried beneath five feet of dirt and mud?"

"Exactly what I'm telling you," Seth said.

The body of the woman was tiny, probably less than five feet tall. She had long dark hair and translucent skin with a light green tint.

Jake revealed a large eye the color of a sparkling emerald when he opened one of her eyelids with his finger. The body bore the breasts and shape of a woman, though it seemed somehow otherworldly. I wasn't the only one to notice.

"Is she . . . human?" Jake asked.

The question took Seth by surprise. "What else would she be?"

Mama brushed the hair back from her ear. Amanda gasped. Instead of a normal human shape, the woman's ears were pointed, like an elf or a fairy.

"The Nunnehi are a race of immortal spirit people in Cherokee mythology. The Sioux called them Mialuka, the Wild People. The Shoshone tribe dubbed them the Nimerigar. This being doesn't look quite human because she isn't. She's a fairy."

"That's preposterous," Seth said.

Mama glanced away from Seth's glare. "Turn her over," she said.

"For what purpose?" Seth asked.

"Do it," Jake said.

Joey helped Seth flip the body over onto its stomach. Mama touched the stubs protruding from the shoulder blades.

"What the hell!" Seth said.

"Wings," Mama said. "At least where they once were before someone chopped them off."

Aura's hand went to her mouth. "Who would do such a thing?" she said.

Jake wasn't looking at the wing stubs on the strange woman's back. She had something in her hand, and he was working deftly to see what it was. Finally, he pulled the rubber sheet back over the woman's body.

"That's it for tonight," he said. "We'll worry about this later."

The film crew extinguished the camera lights and began packing away their equipment when Angie said, "That's a wrap."

Jake squeezed Mama's hand.

"My helicopter is waiting outside," he said. "Colley, Angie, and I have more work to do. Bradley will take you home, and we will meet again tomorrow."

"My car's outside," Seth said. "Amanda and I will take Aura to her hotel."

Bradley appeared at the door. The hour was late, and we followed him to the sleek limousine in the dark parking garage.

## Chapter 6

It was late when we reentered the limo and started away.

"That bastard," Mama said.

"Who are you talking about?" I asked.

"Jake, leading me on and then flying off to who-knows-where with a younger woman."

I'd witnessed Mama's snits before and was determined not to get entangled in this one. Instead, I changed the subject.

"There's more to the body we saw. Lots more," I said.

"What about it?" Mama asked.

"The lights and cameras," I said. "Seems like everything that happened tonight was somehow orchestrated."

"Hello!" Mama said. "Cryptid Hunter is reality TV. What did you expect?"

"It's almost as if everyone except us was following a script," I said. "I've never really watched reality TV. If tonight is any indication, there isn't much reality to it. The woman was naked. It didn't stop the cameras from rolling. How does Jake's series square that with network censors?"

"Everytime the cameras pan the body, they distort the picture electronically," Mama said. "Viewers can tell the body is naked though they can see no private parts. It's great for ratings because it renders the scene even more salacious than if they'd shown an actual naked body."

"Interesting," I said. "Was the woman even real?"

"Don't know how they could have faked it if she weren't," Mama said.

"Neither do I."

"Then stop worrying about it. Even if Jake is a bastard, he's paying us quite handsomely."

"At least he could have let us in on the charade."

"If he had, we would have treated the scene like actors," Mama said. "Instead, we reacted with honest shock like any other person would have after being involved in such a bizarre scenario."

"You're probably right," I said. "When the cameras panned our faces, we were staring at the body, our mouths open in disbelief."

"Real people witnessing the seemingly unexplainable," Mama said. "No wonder their ratings are through the roof."

"What about the archaeologist Aura Hartel," I said. "She's either the world's best actress or else as surprised about the whole affair as we were."

"Maybe she was," Mama said. "I could see she has feelings for Seth Daniels."

"You think?"

"Written all over her face," Mama said.

"If she wasn't in on the setup how did she happen to wander into Bertram's?"

Mama grinned as rain continued to pound the roof of the limousine.

"Pretty girls are often manipulated by older men."

"I need to find out what she knows or doesn't

know."

"What difference does it make?" Mama said. "Reality TV isn't based on truth."

"More like professional wrestling," I said.

"Watch it," Mama said. "You know MMA is my third favorite sport."

She grinned again when I quipped, "Reality TV and professional wrestling; two peas in a pod."

"Like I said, what difference does it make? I'm enjoying this gig, Wyatt Thomas, so don't mess it up for us."

"I don't intend to mess anything up," I said.

"Then what's your problem?"

"A few unanswered questions."

"Madam Aja's moonstone pendant?"

"It's somehow connected to the body and the skeleton they found at the Old François Place."

"It has been a long day," Mama said. I'm going to have Bradley take me home. I'll catch a cab tomorrow and retrieve Baby. What's your plan?"

"Return to Bertram's."

Through the glass separating the driver and the passenger seats, we could see the back of Bradley's head. The limo drew to a halt and our driver interrupted us when his deep voice resonated over the intercom.

"There's been a change of plans," he said. "We're at the SuperDome."

The limo began to rock as the drone of a landing chopper overcame the sound of the impending rainstorm. Rain blew in the window when Mama lowered it. Bradley had rushed through the downpour with his umbrella to help someone exiting the helicopter. They hurried to the limousine. Bradley held the door as Jake Huntington joined us. Mama grabbed his hand.

"Bradley told you we have a change of plans."

"Such as?" Mama said.

"My son was in a auto accident," Jake said. "He's in a hospital in Tulsa. I have to go there."

"I'm coming with you," Mama said. "I sense you'll need my help."

"This isn't a pleasure trip," Jake said.

Mama clutched Jake's hand. "I'm not expecting one."

Jake gave me a glance. "Angie is in charge until we return. Will you work with her?"

"Of course," I said.

"There's something I need to give you. It was clenched in the woman's hand. I haven't told anyone else about it," Jake said. "Take it."

Jake handed me a finger bone bearing a gold wedding ring.

"What the hell!" Mama said.

"Digitus quartus, also known as the ring finger. That seems to indicate the piece of antique gold jewelry is a wedding ring." He added, "If it were the digitus quartus. It's not. It's the bone of a man's little finger."

"You found it in the woman's hand? What does it mean?" Mama asked.

"Maybe Wyatt can tell us when we return from Tulsa."

Mama put her hand on mine. "Will you be okay?"

"I'm good," I said.

"Then see what you can find out about this," she said, folding the finger bone and ring into my hand.

Bradley, beneath his large umbrella, hurried through the rain with Angie. She piled into the backseat, climbing over Jake and Mama. She was wet and I could smell her intoxicating perfume. She scooted close to me and smiled. Bradley waited outside the door, heavy rain spraying off the umbrella as Jake and Mama climbed out of the limo.

Angie and I watched through the open door as the chopper lifted up and disappeared in the driving rainstorm. The quiet resumed when Bradley shut the back door, his voice resonating again through the intercom.

"Where to, Angie?" he asked.

"My hotel," she said.

"Mr. Thomas?" Bradley asked.

"Bertram's bar on Chartres," I said.

Though the seating in the limo was spacious, Angie continued sitting close to me.

"I didn't have time to talk to you at the university," She said. "What's your take on the fairy woman?"

She laughed when I asked, "Are you taping this?"

"Off the record."

"I believe we are dealing with something supernatural," I said.

"Really!" She grabbed my hand and winked. "Don't take this gig too seriously," she said.

Before I could reply, the limo pulled to a stop. Bradley opened the back door.

"Your hotel," he said.

Angie slid out of the big vehicle, stood on her tiptoes, embraced the tall chauffeur and kissed him.

"Sweet dreams," she said to me before hurrying away up the sidewalk.

It wasn't far back to Bertram's, rain pelting the building overhang when Bradley opened the door for me to exit.

"You don't happen to have an extra umbrella, would you?" I asked.

"I can take you anywhere you need to go," he said.

"This is good," I said.

"Then take my umbrella," he said. "I won't need it again tonight."

I stuffed the finger bone in my pocket and watched the lights of the limo disappear down the street. Unless I missed my guess, back to Angie's hotel. A half-block away from Bertram's, I thought I heard someone calling my name. It was Aura, wringing wet and still wearing the same short skirt I'd last seen her in. I hurried back to where she was waiting. Even through the rain pelting her face and matted hair, I could see she'd been crying.

"What in holy hell?" I said.

"I was hoping Bertram's might still be open."

Her expression darkened further when I said, "I thought Professor Daniels was taking you to your hotel."

"Long story," she said.

"I have all night. Let's go back to Bertram's."

"Where were you going?"

"What does it matter?"

"The dig, weren't you?"

"Why would you think that?"

"It's not far from here. Where else would you be going?"

"Like I said, it can wait until tomorrow."

"I'll go with you," she said.

"My room at Bertram's is at the top of the stairs. Here's my key. You can shower, change into a bathrobe and get some sleep until I return."

Aura shook her head. "Either you come with me or else I'm going with you."

"Don't be stubborn. You need to dry off and get warm."

"I can't get any wetter than I already am."

"Sure about this?" I asked.

"It's creepy as hell out here. Take me with you."

"It'll be even creepier at the Old François Place."

Rain had momentarily ceased. It didn't stop Aura from huddling close to me.

"Cold?" I said.

"Shivering," she said.

"If I had a sweater or jacket, I'd give it to you."

"I'll live. Why didn't you have Bradley drop you off in front of the dig?"

"I think he has a thing going with Angie, Jake's assistant. I didn't want him knowing where I was going."

"Why the secrecy?" she said.

"Character flaw," I said. "Besides, I know a shortcut through the alleys."

I couldn't help but feel the warmth of Aura's body as we started down the street to the Old François Place. The rain started again, slowly at first and then in a blinding torrent. Water flowed down the deserted streets, no sane person out in this unusual August weather.

A strong breeze blowing up from the river whipped the street lights, adding to the psychodelic effect of rain and flickering neon. When we reached the time-worn masonry wall surrounding the Old François Place, a howl penetrated the surreal silence. Aura squeezed my arm.

"What was that?" she said.

"Strange sounds are common in the Quarter, especially this time of early morning. Do you have a key?"

"Not with me," she said.

Fumbling in my pocket, I found the set of lock picks I sometimes carried and used them to open the heavy cypress door.

"Are you also a cat burglar?" Aura said.

"Never know when these things might come in handy."

Aura didn't quiz me on how I'd learned to use the picks. The old iron hinges screeched as I pushed open the wrought iron gate, leaving it ajar as Aura followed me into the courtyard.

We were woefully prepared to visit an abandoned French Quarter house in the darkness. The only light I had was a tiny flashlight attached to my keychain. Shining it at my feet, I found a flagstone pathway probably leading to the frontdoor of the townhouse. Slippery from the rain, I grasped Aura's hand.

The little light kept flickering. Though I didn't know exactly what I expected to find, I hoped the batteries would last long enough to give us time to look around. The flagstones led us past two water-filled holes dug by the archaeologists. I released Aura's hand when I bumped into the statue of a gargoyle, the eyes of the stone creature looking almost alive in the flashes of overhead lightning. I had to touch it to assure myself it wasn't.

I didn't need the lock picks. The heavy cypress door of the townhouse was open. Swaying in the breeze, its creaking hinges imitated eerie sound effects straight from a circus fright ride. After entering the house and lowering the umbrella, I quickly reopened it. My flashlight told me why Aura and I were still getting wet.

Rain, pouring through a hole in the roof, watered the room and the large tree growing up through the floor. A candelabra complete with candle stubs resided on the mantle of a masonry fireplace. The fireplace was out of the rain and the candles illuminated the room when I lit them. As our eyes adjusted to the light, we gazed at the ruined remains of a once regal living area.

Whoever had owned the townhouse must have treasured books. A bookcase stretched from the floor to the ceiling. Hundreds of volumes filled the shelves. When I examined one of the books, I realized the damp and moldy library had become a repository of ruined literature.

Broken furniture evocative of a different era lay strewn across the floor. The cypress flooring, cracked and displaced, outlined the tree growing up through it. The tree's highest branches reached almost to the large hole in the roof.

A once magnificent circular staircase led to the darkened second floor. Movement seen from the corner of my eye caused me to wheel around. Whatever it was, was gone, leaving me to wonder if my mind was playing tricks.

"Did you see that?" I asked.

"See what?" Aura said.

I didn't bother answering her. Well after midnight, the old Creole townhouse was likely sated with ghosts and spirits moving around us. Even if they weren't, I didn't feel as if Aura and I were alone.

"Wait for me. I'm going to check out the second floor."

"Not without me, you aren't," Aura said, latching on to my elbow.

When I clutched the candelabra and started up the stairs, I realized we really weren't alone.

An unusual-looking tiger-striped cat lying on the steps was watching us, its big head following our every movement. When I reached to touch it, the feline shrieked and bounded past us. The shriek propelled my heart, and apparently Aura's from her reaction, into a faster rhythm. Clutching the banister with my free hand, I started up the damp stairway. A surprise awaited us as we neared the top of the stairs.

Hanging crookedly on the wall was a large painting. Rather than a proper portrait of the patron or matron of the manor, it was a painting done mostly in green of an unclothed, winged fairy. The eyes of the fairy seemed to follow me as I moved the flickering candle light.

There was something about the portrait that riveted my attention. The face of the fairy was someone I recognized, though the realization didn't instantly occur to me.

"Look at the necklace she's wearing," Aura said. "It's the exact one you have."

"You've seen this painting?" I asked.

"I told you so, at Bertram's. Why do you think I thought you had stolen the pendant?"

"It does look like it," I said.

"Exactly like it, and that woman is the fairy we dug up in the courtyard."

"Maybe," I said.

"Seth and I toured the building before we began digging. I'd had too many of Bertram's mojitos and didn't remember where I'd seen the portrait when I accused you of stealing the pendant."

"I see now why you did," I said.

I was staring at the portrait when something else caught my eye. Aura saw it too and clutched my arm tighter.

"Oh, shit!" she said.

What had grasped our attention was the light pouring from the keyhole of a door.

"Transients," I said. "Probably some homeless person."

"What are you going to do?" Aura asked.

Before I could answer, the candelabra grew hot in my hand. We found ourselves in total darkness when I dropped it to the floor. Aura lost her footing causing both of us to end up on the floor. Not wanting to tumble down the stairs, I grabbed Aura's arm and started crawling.

"I can't see shit," she said.

"Neither can I."

"Where are you going?"

"Trying to keep from taking a tumble down the stairs," I said.

Aura wasn't the only one who was disoriented. When I moved forward, searching for the stairs, I bumped into a wall. Even more disconcerting, I heard footsteps.

"Did you hear that?" I said in a whisper.

"Shit, Wyatt, there's someone up here with us."

Fumbling in my pocket, I found my little flashlight. The battery was almost dead, only enough power left to reorient me. The stairs were behind us. When I stood to reach for the railing, I slipped and tumbled headfirst down the circular stairway. Still clutching my arm in a deathgrip, Aura came with me. We landed in heap at the bottom of the stairs.

"You okay?" I asked.

"Let's get the hell out of here," she said.

The front door of the townhouse was still ajar. lightning directing my steps as I pulled Aura to her feet and hurried for the opening. When I exited the door, I realized I'd dropped my flashlight and keychain. It didn't matter. I had no intention of returning to the house to try to find them.

A dim glow emanated from the top of the masonry wall. We didn't make the front gate, slipping on damp flagstone and plunging into the muddy water of one of the archaeological excavations. The wail we heard from the open door caused Aura to dig her nails into my arm. When a sudden incandescence lighted the courtyard, I wondered if our luck had finally run out.

## Chapter 7

Few things are more spectacular than a moonlight chopper ride over a major city. Mama Mulate had never ridden in a helicopter and realized what an epic experience she was in for as Jake Huntington's jet-powered aircraft powered up from the pad. She took in the spectacle, turning away from the window when Jake squeezed her hand.

"What do you think?" he asked.

"I'm entranced. I've never ridden in a helicopter," Mama said. "It's nothing like a plane."

"Not the same at all."

"How long will it take us to get to Tulsa?"

"Less than four hours. Don't worry, there's a bathroom in back and lots of booze on board."

"Then it'll be dawn when we get there," Mama said.

"No better time to see Tulsa from above. It's about the same size as New Orleans, and resides on a river. What are you drinking?"

"Though I love martinis, vodka will work. Are you planning to get me drunk and have your way with me?"

Jake smiled. "I'll try though I have a feeling you can hold your liquor better than I can."

"Is that a bet?" Mama asked.

"My guess is you've never been in a situation you weren't in control of."

"Does that intimidate you?" Mama asked.

"Not at all. I like strong women who know their own minds."

"Are you pulling my leg?"

Mama laughed aloud when Jake said, "No, but I'd like to."

Moving blips of light marked the terrain below them as they turned north and left the neon glow of New Orleans behind. Jake exhaled, resting his head on the chopper's comfortable upholstery.

"You're worried about your son," Mama said.

"Very much so. He's my only child. I don't want to lose him."

"Tell me about him," Mama said.

"He's tall, his hair dark and wavy. His name is Jeff."

"Sounds like a good-looking kid, just like his dad. Is your wife with him?"

"Ex-wife. Almost thirty years was more than enough for both of us."

"You fell out of love and got divorced?"

Jake nodded. "Something like that."

"You must have loved each other if your marriage lasted nearly thirty years," Mama said.

"Sometimes it's easier to stay married than to make a change."

"Please explain."

Jake sipped his chilled glass of Bombay Gin before answering.

"Like my father, I grew up with the so called silver spoon in my mouth. I'd seen most of the world before I was twelve and was given anything I asked for."

"Must be nice," Mama said.

"Money doesn't make you happy. I soon realized I was sorely cut out for the oil business. Though I didn't know it then, I wanted to be the Cryptid Hunter. I spent lots of time and energy wasting money, chasing women and being an all around horrible father."

"But your wife stuck with you."

"We were a power couple. Belinda's a former Miss Oklahoma and from one of the state's richest families. Her dad was into oil, entertainment, and publishing and not necessarily in that order. No one, neither my family nor hers, wanted to see us divorce."

"Then why now?"

"I'd been especially unhappy for awhile. Colley told me he was going to kick my ass unless I filed the papers."

"You divorced your wife because of Colley?"

Jake poured himself more gin before answering. "Except for the bedroom, Belinda and I never had much in common. She had her special friends, charities, and social functions. I had my obsession with cryptids."

"An obsession you continue to have."

Jake drained his gin and poured himself another. "My dad was a second-generation Tulsa oil baron. Granddad was a wildcatter and Dad's hero. When I bailed out of Huntington Oil, I left my family and most of my friends in a lurch. My old man never quite forgave me for not embracing the family business."

"Your dad is dead?"

"Both mom and dad. They were Tulsa socialites and I was a change-of-life baby. Mom drank herself to death. Dad ran a red light coming home from a bar and was tee-boned by an oncoming vehicle. He died on the way to the hospital."

"So you sold the oil company?"

"Still have it, though I don't care how many wells it drills every year or how much oil it produces."

"Who runs the company?" Mama asked.

"Sam Jones, Belinda's longtime lover."

Jake nodded when Mama said, "Belinda your ex? Who is Sam Jones?"

"My former best friend. We were roommates at OU until I transferred to Duke. He grew up in a wealthy Tulsa oil family that went bust in the eighties. He never forgave me for not bailing them out." Jake laughed. "He got even by taking my wife, my oil company, and my son."

Mama refilled her own drink and topped up Jake's.

"Explain," she said.

"Belinda and I have lived apart for the past several years. We have a sprawling ranch-style house on a lake east of here. She started spending time there without me and it eventually became a permanent arrangement."

"I'm so sorry," Mama said.

"Nothing to be sorry about. She did her thing. I did mine. I've been away from home more often than I've been in Tulsa. Sam is more of a father to Jeff than I am."

"And you resent it?"

"Yes. I wanted Jeff to follow in my footsteps; become a Cryptid hunter like me. My television empire is now worth far more than Huntington Oil. I saw to it Jeff had his own silver spoon but he spit it out when he was a boy. He grew up mowing lawns and tossing newspapers. Wanted to be his own man."

"And?"

"He graduated from Oklahoma University with a degree in geology. He has always wanted to be in the oil business. He works for Sam."

"You broke away from your father's wishes," Mama said. "Why is it so hard to understand your son's desires?"

"Because it makes me my father," Jake said.

"Then embrace your differences and your similarities."

"And do what?" Jake asked.

"Make peace with your son and move on down the road."

"That's pretty much what Colley told me."

"Colley's a smart man."

"He's my best friend," Jake said.

"Take his advice," Mama said.

"Is it also your advice?"

"If you need a second opinion. I don't believe you do."

Jake grinned. "Please hit me with it anyway."

"Give your oil company to your wife and make amends with Sam Jones and your son."

"Sounds drastic to me," he said.

"You just told me your television fortune is worth more than Huntington Oil. You'll never spend a billion dollars if you live to be a hundred, much less two billion."

"Jake sipped his gin. "Might be fun to try."

"You created Cryptid Hunter," Mama said. "It's yours and yours alone. Can't you just let go of Huntington Oil?"

"It's hard to give up a billion bucks."

"I wouldn't know," Mama said.

"Sam would end up with it all," Jake said.

"So?"

"He didn't earn it."

"Didn't he? Maybe there's more than one reason for your animosity."

"He stole my wife," Jake said.

"You didn't love her."

"He stole my son."

"I don't think so," Mama said. "Did you love your dad?"

"He was my hero."

"But you took different paths."

"Because I hate the oil business," Jake said.

"And your own son loves it. Don't you see the analogy?"

Though Mama didn't know it, they were flying over the Ouachita Mountains of Arkansas, the ground below them almost totally dark. The sky wasn't dark, the light from a near-full moon illuminating the passenger compartment of the helicopter.

"None of this will make any difference if Jeff is dead when we reach Tulsa. I don't think I can survive if he is," he said.

Mama squeezed Jake's hand. "He'll be fine. Did you bring me to counsel you on what to do?"

Jake shook his head. "Among other things," he said.

"Such as?"

"My home in Tulsa is known as Huntington Manor. It's on a bluff overlooking downtown Tulsa, a mansion that's three stories tall and sits on ten acres of well-kept landscaping."

"Sounds wonderful," Mama said.

"It's not," Jake said. "It's haunted by my grandfather's ghost."

"Have you seen him?"

"The people who worked there have. They won't' stay after dark."

"If you haven't seen him, how do you know he's there?" Mama asked.

"I've felt his presence. Noticed things like missing objects, broken glass, and doors opening unexpectedly."

"I've seen many ghosts," Mama said.

"I know you have. That's not the reason I wanted you to come to Tulsa with me."

"Then what?"

Jake kissed Mama square on the lips, a passionate kiss though barely a touch.

"I fell in love with you the moment we met," he said.

---

The sun was rising in the east when Mama opened her eyes and realized she was leaning against Jake's shoulder.

"Sorry," she said.

"You weren't bothering me a bit," Jake said. "That's Tulsa up ahead."

Mama could see skyscrapers and church steeples in the distance as Colley banked, changing course slightly.

"Are we almost there?" she asked.

"Another fifteen minutes. There's a landing pad near the emergency room. Colley's taking us straight to the hospital. Jeff's in intensive care upstairs."

As they approached the city, Mama saw the river that bisected it.

"It's beautiful," she said. "It does remind me of New Orleans except this river is blue and not red like the Mississippi."

"The Arkansas River, navigable from here all the way to New Orleans. There are parks along the river and festivals held there throughout the year."

"You're a horrible liar, Jake Huntington," Mama said.

"About the Arkansas River?"

"About telling me you love me," she said.

Mama changed the subject when Jake said, "Guess I'll have to prove it to you."

"Hiking trails?"

"Pardon me?" Jake said.

"Are there hiking trails along the river?"

Jake nodded. "And bike and jogging paths. From your gorgeous legs, I'm guessing you're either a biker or a jogging enthusiast."

"A runner, not a jogger. I've participated in hundreds of 10-Ks."

"What's your fastest 10-K?"

"Just under 31 minutes," Mama said.

"Whoa! That's world class. Are you telling the truth?"

"I had a track scholarship at the University of South Carolina." Mama showed Jake a gap between her thumb and index finger. "I came that close to going pro but decided to pursue my doctorate instead. I have trouble breaking 36 minutes these days."

"That's still less than 6 minutes per mile," Jake said.

Though his hair was almost white, Jake's physique was slim and sleek. Mama guessed his age at five to ten years older than she was."

"Did you run track in college?"

"Dabbled in it," he said. "I was more of a book nerd."

"Nothing wrong with that. How did you become interested in cryptids?"

"Granddad Hunt. I was Mom and Dad's only child, Hunt's solitary grandchild. Hunt doted on me and told me tales of mythical creatures, elves, leprechauns; you get the picture. My mom thought he was scaring me and told him to quit."

"But he didn't?"

"We all lived in the Huntington Manor. My grandmother passed away when I was young. Hunt never remarried. He read to me almost every night. He broke Mom's rule once and told me while golfing in Scotland he'd actually seen the Loch Ness Monster."

"You believed him?"

"With all my heart. I've visited Scotland more times than I can count though I've never seen Nessie."

"Please tell me some of the things you have seen," Mama said.

Engine noise changed as the helicopter began to descend.

"Love to," Jake said. Right now, we're landing at the hospital."

## Chapter 8

Up to our necks in muddy water, I found my footing unsure as I clutched Aura's wrist and tried to wade to the edge of the excavation. The suction was intense and I soon lost a shoe in the mire. Holding my breath, I dunked my head into the water, sifting my fingers through the goo. Aura threw her arms around me when I burst to the surface.

"Dammit, Wyatt! What the hell are you doing? You just scared the holy hell out of me."

"Lost my shoe. I was trying to find it."

"Screw your shoe. Let's get out of here."

With darkness and muddy water combining to scare the hell out of both of us, I began dog-paddling to the edge of the pit.

"Don't get stuck in the mud," I said. "It's like quicksand."

We heard the wail again, as I struggled to climb out of the mud hole. Aura was crying and I was about to hyperventilate when what seemed like a disembodied hand grabbed my wrists and pulled me out of the muddy hole in the ground.

"Who is it?" I said.

"Wyatt, get me the hell out of this mud hole," Aura said. "There's something crawling up my legs."

I managed to yank her out of the excavation without falling back into it myself. Aura was screaming and slapping at her legs.

"Oh my God!"

"What is it?" I said.

"Worms, they're crawling all over me."

Barely able to see, I grabbed a wooden shingle that had fallen from the roof and began scraping masses of worms off Aura's legs as she held her skirt out of the mud. When I removed the last handful, she grasped her arms around my neck and began to sob.

"It's okay," I said.

Who or what had pulled me out of the hole was gone. I listened to Aura's labored breathing as pouring rain and distant thunder kept me from hearing anything other than the drumming of my own heart. When lightning flashed, a glint of green at my feet caught my attention. I dug it out of the mud, kicking my remaining shoe into the hole as I clutched Aura's arm and pulled her toward the gate.

Like my keys and flashlight, Bradley's umbrella was somewhere in the old townhouse. I wasn't going back for them. Lightning flashed across the dark sky as rain washed away the mud coating our clothes.

We hurried toward Bertram's, the mud gone by the time we reached the bar on Chartres Street. Bertram had closed for the night, the main lights extinguished, and only a dim glow radiating from the bar area. The Cajun bartender was alone behind the counter.

"What the hell!" he said. "Where you been, dripping water all over the place like two wet hound dogs."

"Don't you ever sleep?" I asked.

"Now and then."

"Got any coffee in this place?" I asked.

"Been sitting on the burner awhile. Tell me what the hell you two been doing and I'll whip up a fresh pot."

"I need to change clothes first," I said.

Bertram turned his attention to Aura, her little black dress dripping wet. Wet hair draped her bare shoulders, her arms clasped tightly around her chest. Bertram herded her toward the bar.

"Baby, what in hell you doing out in the rain this time of night with the likes of Wyatt Thomas? Didn't your mama teach you no better?"

Without waiting for an answer, he directed her to sit on a bar stool, ducked under the counter and disappeared.

"I think you need a cup of Bertram's coffee," I said.

Grabbing the pot, I poured Aura a cup. Like Bertram had said, it had been sitting awhile. I laced it with milk from a silver creamer. It was raining again, thunder rattling the front windows. Aura held the cup to her lips, letting steam waft over her face. Before she'd had two sips, Bertram returned from the back with a terrycloth bath towel and began drying her hair and face as if she were a child.

"That pretty little dress of yours is drenched," he said. "I got a guest room nobody ever uses. They's a bathroom with towels, soap and shampoo. Go get out of them wet things and take a hot shower. I got a warm robe hanging on the door for you. We'll worry about getting you some clothes later."

"Can I take the coffee?" she asked.

"Course you can," he said. "Follow Lady. She'll show you the way. If you ain't too tired when you finish, come back here. I'll fix some food for your belly."

We watched as she and Lady disappeared into the area in back where Bertram lived. Once they were gone, Bertram topped up my coffee.

"You the private eye," he said. "What's up with her?"

"If you can wait until I run upstairs and change clothes, I'll tell you," I said.

The door to my covered balcony overlooking Chartres Street was open, my cat Kisses asleep in the old recliner. Without waking her, I changed her water and food bowl and then hit the shower to wash the grit out of my hair. After pulling an old LSU sweatshirt over my khakis, I returned to the bar.

"Where you were?" Bertram asked.

"The Old François Place," I said.

"In the rain?" he said. "Couldn't you have waited till tomorrow?"

"I'm working for Jake now and I had a premonition."

"What premonition?"

"After what Mama and I saw at UNO, I wanted to visit the dig alone."

"Quit talking gobbledygook and tell me what the hell you and Mama saw?"

"You won't believe it if I tell you," I said.

Bertram took the steaming mug out of my hand. "If you want some of this ol' Cajun's coffee, then you better quit yapping and start explaining," he said.

"Like Aura said earlier, they dug up a skeleton and a body at the Old François Place. A hand and the head were missing on the skeleton. One of the graduate assistants who found it commented it appeared as if they'd been chopped off."

"Because?" Bertram said.

"No clue."

"And the body?"

"You know what a fae is?"

"Hell no."

"It's a fairytale creature; in this case, an actual fairy."

"You been hitting the bottle?" Bertram asked.

"Nothing stronger than this mud you call coffee."

Bertram reached for the cup. "You don't like my coffee?"

I grabbed it out of his hand. "Even if it is near-lethal, you make the best Cajun coffee in New Orleans."

"Don't sound like much of a compliment," he said.

"Just saying."

Bertram handed me the silver creamer. "Wussy," he said.

"Is that Cajun?"

"I said it, didn't I? Now tell me about this fairy."

I'd brought the bottle I'd found at the edge of the dig and handed it to Bertram.

"You're an expert on all things alcoholic. What do you know about this?"

Bertram took the bottle and twirled it in his hand.

"Where'd you find it?"

"In the mud beside the hole a disembodied hand yanked me out of."

Ignoring my comment, Bertram made a face. The green bottle had a paper label revealing a half naked woman with fairy wings surrounded by lush vegetation. The woman was also green and she was holding a bottle labeled absinthe. The words La Fée Verte written in ornate script was inscribed across the top of the label. Though the glass seemed very old, the label was undamaged.

"An old absinthe bottle," he said. "Haven't seen one like this in a long time." Bertram set the bottle on the bar. "What's up with Miss Aura?"

"Man trouble," I said.

"How do you know that?"

"She doesn't strike me as the type to be trolling the French Quarter in that little black dress of hers. She was supposed to meet someone here earlier. He stood her up. My guess is it's her boss."

"What makes you think that?"

"I'm not blind. His name is Seth Daniels, the head of the UNO archaeology department. Mama and I met him when we went with Jake to view the body."

"And?"

"He has another girlfriend; one of his grad students. They were supposed to take Aura back to her hotel. I suspect Aura confronted them and the evening ended badly. She was crying when she returned here in the rain."

"She's got a PhD," Bertram said. "How can she be worried so much about a man?"

"She may have a PhD but she's young and probably felt as if she were in love," I said.

"Hell, we all go through that once or twice. My grits and eggs will take her mind off of it."

"I'm hungry, too," I said.

Though my cup didn't need it, Bertram topped it up with the pot.

"Hell, you stay needy."

Bertram was firing up his stove when Aura returned to the bar dressed in a puffy bathrobe. A white towel covered her long hair like a turban and she had a smile on her face.

"I feel better," she said.

"Sit beside Wyatt, baby," Bertram said. "If he bothers you, I'll whup his ass."

The savory aroma wafting from the stove rendered us silent. Aura and I remained that way until Bertram returned with heaping platters of bacon, eggs, and homemade Cajun biscuits. Aura quickly took a bite.

"This jelly is wonderful," she said. "What kind is it?"

"Where you from; New York City?" Bertram said.

"I'm serious," she said. "It's good, sweet, with just a hint of tartness."

"Mayhaw jelly. The berries grow wild in the swamp."

"You picked them?" Aura asked.

"Aunt Betty from Thibodaux sends me a few jars every year."

"I've never heard of a mayhaw," Aura said. "What is it?"

"A variety of hawthorn berry that grows wild in wetlands all over the south," I said. "They ripen in May, thus the name mayhaw."

Aura smiled. "You're a fount of trivia, aren't you?"

"I think you have me pegged," I said.

"Bertram, you're coffee is wonderful," she said, "Though unlike any I've ever tasted."

"Chicory," I said, pushing my plate and coffee cup across the bar. "Another Louisiana tradition." "As usual, Bertram, you've outdone yourself."

Aura grinned again, shook her head, and then sat her cup on the bar. The green bottle I'd found at the dig was on the counter.

"What's this?" she asked.

I handed it to her. "An old absinthe bottle. I found it beside the mud hole we fell into."

"Does La Fée Verte mean what I think it means?"

"The Green Fairy," I said.

"The fairy on the label is the woman in the painting at the top of the stairs at the Old François Place."

"And..."

"The woman we dug up," Aura said.

Before I could reply, someone began knocking on the door. It was still dark outside, Bertram grumbling as he ducked under the bar.

"What the hell!"

We heard the rattle of keys followed by the resonant voice of a person I recognized.

"I couldn't sleep and thought I might find kindred spirits here," the man said. He hastened to the bar and began pumping my hand.

Bertram was grinning as he ducked back under the bar and began pouring scotch.

"I thought my night was gonna be a bust," he said. "Now, who shows up but my best customer?"

The handsome man was Rafael Romanov, tall, slender, and always dressed, even at four in the morning, in expensive and stylish clothes. He had dark hair and complexion, a regal, aquiline nose befitting his Romanian heritage, and smoky-gray eyes I'd only seen in one other person. Rafael was standing behind Aura's stool and he grinned after I'd introduced them.

"Having a slumber party?" he asked.

"Pretty Miss Aura here got caught out in the rain," Bertram said.

Aura smiled when Rafael said, "Glad you didn't melt."

"I'm not sweet, much less sugar," she said.

Seeing where the conversation was heading, I said, "Still sailing out of the Port of New Orleans?"

"Yes, but I'm not working the islands in the Caribbean anymore."

"Where you working?" Bertram asked.

"On a luxury riverboat cruising up the Mississippi River. I recently got Mama a gig as resident mambo on a voodoo tour."

"Heard all about it," I said. "She loved it."

"What's not to love?" Rafael said. "The work is easy, the people friendly, the perks out of this world, and the shipping company pays extremely well."

"What exactly do you do?" Aura asked.

"I'm a rent-a-priest."

"Excuse me?" Aura said.

"I perform marriages, hear confessions, and counsel lost souls."

"You're a priest?"

"Technically, yes," he said, "though I've been ex-communicated from the Mother Church."

"Then how can you still be a priest?" Aura asked.

"Once a priest, always a priest, my dear."

Aura turned on her stool to get a better look at the tall man behind her.

"Why were you ex-communicated?"

"My mother's a witch," he said. Aura let the remark drop as Rafael spotted the green bottle sitting on the bar."

"May I?" he asked.

Aura handed him the bottle. "Wyatt was about to tell us where he found it when you knocked on the door."

Aura gave me an incredulous look when I said, "The Old François Place here in the Quarter."

"We had no business going there," she said.

"Yes we did," I said. "Jake Huntington hired us to do just that."

Aura started to say something but turned to Rafael instead.

"Any ideas about this bottle?" she said.

"Absinthe," Rafael said. "A cocoction of

various botanicals, including anise which gives the distilled spirit a green tint."

"There's a fairy on the label. What does absinthe have to do with fairies?" Aura asked.

"Absinthe has a high alcohol content," Rafael said. "It was once a favorite drink of artists, musicians and authors who believed it provided them with artistic inspiration. The absinthe muse was known as La Fée Verte. Absinthe contains wormwood and was banned in countries around the world because many believed it induced hallucinations, and perhaps even death."

Aura stared at Rafael, her mouth open. "Does it?"

"Oscar Wilde reportedly said, 'After the first glass of absinthe you see things as you wish they were. After the second you see them as they are not. Finally you see things as they really are, and that is the most horrible thing in the world.' I've had it many times. I've never experienced hallucinations and I'm still very much alive."

"Wyatt, do you believe in fairies?" she said.

"Why do you ask?"

"Because, like I said, the woman on the label is the same person we dug up yesterday in the Old François Place courtyard. Right now, I'm dog-tired and plan to sleep a few hours in Bertram's guest bedroom."

After kissing me, Rafael, and Bertram, she disappeared behind the bar.

"Beautiful and intelligent woman," Rafael said when Aura was gone. "Too bad I'm leaving New Orleans shortly after dawn."

"Time for one more?" Bertram asked.

"Why not?" Rafael said, glancing at his watch. "But duty calls so put it in a go-cup."

"What now?" Bertram asked as we watched Rafael depart.

"I can't remember the last time I slept. I'm going upstairs and spend some time under the covers."

# Chapter 9

I lay on the bed for all of ten minutes. The rain had ended, at least for the moment, light beginning to splay through the open door of my balcony overlooking Chartres Street. Kisses was off tomcatting when I got out of bed, pulled on my pants and refilled her water and food bowls.

My clothes from the trip to the Old François Place were a mess. Too wet to throw in my clothes hamper, I put them in a pile in the corner of my little kitchen. After grabbing a fresh shirt and pair of pants from my closet, I retrieved the ghoulish object Mama had received from Jake.

It gave me a lump in the throat when I placed the finger bone and ring into the pocket of my khakis. Not wanting to explain my actions to Bertram, I climbed over the railing of my balcony and dropped to the sidewalk. My sudden appearance startled two elderly tourists taking pictures. Sensing they might be thinking I was a cat burglar, I pointed at the balcony I had dropped from and said, "Angry husband."

I was a half-block down the sidewalk before turning around and heading in the opposite direction. Something at the Old François Place had me by the throat. I wasn't going to get any sleep, no matter how tired I was, until I dealt with the problem. The rain had stopped, at least for the moment, as I headed toward the Old François Place to have another look around.

Except for me, there was no one else on the street. After pushing open the heavy door, I saw the courtyard for the first time in the light of day. Perennial flowers, untended for decades, were blooming, their perfume wafting in the damp air. Though now overgrown, it was apparent the large courtyard had once been a French Quarter showplace. It crossed my mind I knew nothing about the family who had once lived there. It was a deficiency I needed to rectify.

Flagstone covered much of the courtyard. Aura and her grad students had taken advantage of an uncovered area to do their excavating. What else might be hidden beneath the flagstone? I didn't dwell on the thought as I followed the pathway to the front door of the Creole townhouse.

Statuary ranging from fountains, birdbaths, angels and cherubs occupied the courtyard. The gargoyle, unlike any other I had ever seen guarded a spot near the front door of the townhouse. This particular stone creature had the head of an angry dog, complete with jagged and crooked teeth. A fin ran down its back, ending before it reached its bony tail.

From Aura's description, I wondered if the statue was the creature she thought she saw that Jake called a chupacabra. The unholy wail we had both heard the previous night somehow belied that theory.

The sky remained overcast. When I entered the townhouse, I regretted not bringing a flashlight. Except for dim light coming through the hole in the ceiling, much of the floor and walls were cloaked in dark shadows. Sensing something was staring at me, I turned to see the large tiger-striped cat sitting on the stairs. It didn't move when I approached.

"Here, kitty," I said, extending my hand to pet it.

Before I could touch the spot where the gorgeous animal's head had been, it disappeared in a wisp of damp vapor. A ghost; I should have expected no less as I looked around for a candle to light my way up the stairs.

The stairway to the second floor of the Creole townhouse was almost as creepy as it was the previous night. The steps were still slick with rain. I held on to the banister with one hand the lighted candle with the other. One of the reasons I'd returned was to study the portrait at the top of the stairs. I'd seen the same thing as Aura. I just wanted to make sure my eyes hadn't played tricks.

Even with the shadows, the portrait at the top of the stairs was easier to see. I have a photographic memory and never forget a face. The portrait was identical to the label on the absinthe bottle I'd found; the woman, as Aura had said, was the same person we'd viewed at UNO. I fished in my pocket and pulled out the ring and skeletal finger.

The woman in the portrait was indeed wearing a ring. There was no mistaking it was the same ring as the one in my hand. The finger bone wasn't hers, both of her hands I'd viewed at UNO's refrigerated room intact. She'd died with an amputated finger clenched in her hand. If she were actually dead.

I had little time to mull the thought as the sound of a creaking door behind me garnered my attention. When I wheeled around, I saw a man standing in the unopened door where Aura and I had seen the light coming from the keyhole. As I watched, the man's image flickered and disappeared. Another ghost. Putting the ring and finger bone back in my pocket, I checked the door.

The room was unlocked. Not knowing what I might find, I entered with caution. It was a master bedroom complete with a four-poster bed. The bedding was still intact though the aqua-colored blanket had faded, as had the matching curtains. A window was open, a damp breeze causing the curtains to dance. The cypress flooring was intact, though slick from the rain. There was no sign of the man I had seen.

Except for the damage of water and time, the bedroom, like the area below, was likely little changed from when it had been occupied. The owners hadn't packed and moved. Something else had happened. Judging from the ghosts of the cat and the man I had seen, it had been a traumatic occurrence.

There was no sign of transients in the room leaving me to wonder about the light through the keyhole Aura and I had seen. There was also no chupacabra, at least inside the house. I decided to take a closer look at the expansive courtyard. I was looking at the cracked stone of what must have been a majestic koi pond when I heard a voice I recognized. It came from the branch of a tree and I glanced up at a large bird.

"Hello, I'm Wyatt," the bird said.

It was Calpurnia. The raven lived in the French Quarter courtyard owned by Rafael's mother, Madeline Romanov. Even though ravens can talk, they don't really understand English. She was simply repeating the first words I had ever spoken to her.

"Hello, I'm Wyatt," she said again.

"What are you doing here, Calpurnia?" I asked.

"Buried alive," the bird said.

"What?"

"Buried alive," Calpurnia repeated.

The regal bird flew away in a flurry of beating wings as I stood beneath the tree, wondering if she'd really said what I thought she'd said. Again, sensing something or someone staring at my back, I turned to see the eerie eyes of the stone gargoyle gazing at me. I touched it just to make sure it wasn't real, an unexpected iciness chilling my fingers. I'd seen enough. Leaving the heavy gate ajar, I hurried out of the courtyard.

It wasn't far to the French Quarter shop known as Madeline's Magic Potions. Madeline, Rafael Romanov's mother, was a witch, a real witch and possessed powers I have never fully comprehended. More than a year had passed since the last time I'd visited her shop. I felt somehow guilty as I stood outside the locked establishment, ringing the doorbell. Madeline was smiling when she opened the door.

"Wyatt, please come inside. What brings you here?"

"Questions," I said.

"We all have questions," she said. "Few of us have answers."

Madeline's long hair had turned white since the last time I'd seen her, her dark dress dragging the floor and covering her feet. I waited as she placed a closed sign in the window and then locked the door behind us.

The little shop crowded with eerie objects had changed little since the first time I'd visited. The room was dimly lit and possessed the distinct odor of age and incense. An antique fan created a tinkling crescendo when its breeze encountered a wind chime decorated with gargoyles. And then there was Jinx, Madeline's black cat. When I rubbed her head, she arched her back, luxuriating in my caresses.

A familiar Gregorian chant issued from hidden speakers. Nothing much had changed. Old wooden display cabinets, filled with candles, incense, and colorful crystals bisected the room. Fire-breathing dragons and art deco prints of Elvis and Marilyn Monroe dominated the shop, along with a suit of armor standing alone in a corner.

I followed Madeline through the maze of eerie objects to a dark room in back lined with jars filled with various secret potions. Jinx came with us, winding between our legs. Madeline sat at a small table.

"How did you know why I came?" I asked.

"You said you have questions. My cards hold the answers."

"But I came because. . ."

"Because of Calpurnia?"

"She told you?"

Madeline smiled. "Calpurnia is many things; human isn't one of them. She flew into the courtyard just before you arrived and said your name. Tell me why you're here."

Madeline nodded when I said, "You knew that Madam Aja died? She visited me in my room that very night."

It was my turn to nod when she said, "Her spirit? Please sit." She pointed to the chair across the little table from her. "Tell me about Madam Aja's visit."

"She woke me from a fitful sleep. At first, I thought I was dreaming. I soon realized I wasn't."

"Go on," Madeline prompted when I hesitated.

"Madam Aja reminded me that I'm a Traveler. She said a grave injustice in the past had been committed. She said we all have our bridge to cross."

"What do you think she meant?" Madeline asked.

"Maybe that I have a debt to repay for something that happened in another lifetime," I said. "She gave me this."

I dropped the moonstone pendant into her hand. Madeline held it away from her body, as if its magic might burn a hole straight through her heart.

"Madam Aja gave you this?" she asked.

"Yes. Mama Mulate said it looks Wiccan."

"It's magical though not Wiccan," she said. "Madam Aja gave you this to return to its rightful owner."

"Who is?" I asked.

"Perhaps your cards will give us the answer."

Madeline began shuffling her deck of tarot cards, placing them on the table as Jinx continued rubbing against my legs. When Madeline lit the two candles bordering the little table, flickering light began melding with must and muffled chants from outside the door. After tapping the deck once with her gnarly index finger, she handed it to me.

"Shuffle the cards and then cut them into seven stacks."

I did as she said, and then watched as she arranged the stacks into a unique shape, flipping over the top cards of each. She studied them and then stared at me with disturbed eyes as if trying to see what answers my mind possessed. *Dies Irae*, a chant I recognized, began playing.

Madeline's silky white hair flashed in the candle light when she said, "The hanged man."

"What does it mean?" I asked.

"You're here by your own accord. You seek answers even though there are risks involved."

"What risks?" I asked.

"Your health, sanity, and perhaps even your life. Are these risks you are prepared to take?"

"Are you sure about that?" I asked.

"The cards never lie," Madeline said.

"I was at the Old François Place in the Quarter when I saw Calpurnia. She said something that caused me to come here."

"What did she say?" Madeline asked.

"Buried alive," I said.

## Chapter 10

Madeline spread the cards across the little table. "Calpurnia's words mean something to you." When I nodded, she said, "What were you doing at the Old François Place?"

"The current owners intend to turn the townhouse into a hotel. They asked the UNO archaeological department to see if there was anything of historical value that needed to be preserved before construction begins."

"What did they find?" Madeline asked.

"A mutilated skeleton and the body of a woman Mama says is a fairy.

"A body?"

"Long story," I said. "I'll explain as we go along."

"Where were the skeleton and body found?"

"In the courtyard, beneath five feet of dirt," I said.

Madeline cast me a skeptical look. "The skeleton and the body?"

"Yes."

"How long had they been buried?"

"More than two-hundred years," I said.

"A fairy is a magical being," Madeline said. "Do you think the moonstone pendant belonged to her?"

"There's a portrait of the woman in the townhouse. She's wearing the same necklace. The picture is identical to the label of an old absinthe bottle I found at the excavation. The woman in the portrait has wings and is portrayed as a fairy."

"Interesting," Madeline said.

"That's not all. Mama and I viewed the body of the fairy-like woman at UNO. She had no wings but she did have bony stubs where wings may have been before someone cut them off."

"Oh, my!" she said. "What monster would do such a thing?"

"I was hoping you could tell me."

Madeline's dour expression told me she wasn't happy about the Hanged Man card I'd revealed.

"What does it mean?" I asked.

"Time has stopped for you. Only you can answer the questions you have asked. The path you ultimately take may not be the one you would normally choose, but take it you must."

"How will I know?"

"Suspend your fears and prepare to surrender your soul."

"Is it that dire?"

Madeline didn't answer me. Instead, she handed me a business card with the name of the bar La Fée Verte. It was located in Pirate's Alley.

"Calpurnia dropped this in the courtyard. I'm quite sure she meant it for you."

Smoke wisped up from the table when Madeline licked her fingers and extinguished the two candles.

"Is that all you can tell me?"

"I gave you no answers, only the path to take

to find them," she said. "Tread cautiously."

It was midmorning when I left Madeline's little shop. There was someplace I wanted to go before visiting the bar on Pirate's Alley known as La Fée Verte. I needed to know the history of the Old François Place and the two people who could tell me weren't far away.

Allemands is a hole-in-the-wall bar situated on the edge of the French Quarter. It served as the office of two people who know more about New Orleans than anyone alive. It was often their counsel I sought when I had questions I couldn't answer.

Jake the bartender high-fived me when I came in the door, the ubiquitous odor of stale beer and cigarettes accosting my senses. The regulars at the bar didn't bother turning around. Someone was playing pool in back, breaking balls sounding over Fats Domino's crooning voice on the jukebox. The couple I'd come to see had a table of their own, and were almost always there.

Armand and Madam Toulouse Joubert were a power couple, both smiling when they saw me.

"Damn!" Armand said. "Where you been?"

Returning his smile, I said, "Here and there."

I'd never heard Armand's last name and didn't know if he even had one. A throwback to the beatnik era, he always wore black shirts, pants, and expensive sandals with no socks. His black hair had grown over his shoulders since the last time I'd seen him and he sported a bushy mustache. Unlike his constant companion Madam Toulouse, he wasn't black.

Madam Toulouse was also a reversion to an earlier time, her beehive hairdo decades out of style. She was almost a foot taller than Armand and her hair exaggerated their height difference. Her royal blue miniskirt was hiked well up over her linebacker thighs, one of which Armand had his hand on. She gave me a bear hug when I scooted in beside her.

Jake interrupted us with a fresh scotch for Armand, a red sugary cocktail for Madam Toulouse, and a pitcher of lemonade for me.

He smiled when I said, "Drinks are on me, so keep them coming."

"It's been awhile," Armand said. "What's up?"

"Questions, and you two are the smartest people I know."

Madam Toulouse was smiling when she said, "Flattery will get you everywhere."

I wasn't lying. For answers about New Orleans, I'd come to the right place. Madam Toulouse had worked at the Notarial Archives, a repository for practically everything that had happened in New Orleans since the establishment of the colony.

The French were sticklers for information and had meticulously recorded every transaction that had ever occurred in New Orleans. Though the Notarial Archives had changed hands and location after Hurricane Katrina, it was a trove of facts that no one in the world knew better than Madam Toulouse.

An expert on all things New Orleans, Armand also knew a thing or two. In a city as racially divided as it was, the white elite rarely if ever socialized with people they regarded as below their class. That didn't stop them from taking advantage of Armand's knowledge as an appraiser of practically anything to do with the old city.

Rarely ten minutes went by without Armand's cell phone ringing. Nameless clients never crossed him, and always sent cash for his and Madam Toulouse's valuable advice. Armand and Madam Toulouse didn't take checks.

For me, it was different. Madam Toulouse and Armand would help me for no charge. It had never prevented me from occasionally taking Armand an expensive bottle of scotch or giving Madam Toulouse a piece of jewelry from my mother's collection. Today, because I hadn't planned to stop by, I'd brought nothing except myself. From their smiles, Madam Toulouse and Armand didn't mind.

"Sorry I didn't bring you anything," I said.

"You know better than that, Cowboy. You're family. What you got that's so important?" Armand asked.

"Have you ever heard of the Cryptid Hunter reality TV show?"

"You kidding?" Armand said. "Madam T and I never miss it. Why do you ask?"

"I'm working on an assignment for Jake Huntington, the Cryptid Hunter."

"He's here in New Orleans?" Madam Toulouse said.

"He had to return to Tulsa because his son was in a car wreck. He'll be back, though."

"Things just changed," Armand said.

"What do you mean?"

"Madam Toulouse and I won't be able to help you today, unless. . ."

"Unless what?" I asked.

"Unless you introduce us to the Cryptid Hunter," Madam Toulouse said.

"I think that can be arranged," I said.

"Good," Armand said. "Then tell us what you need to know."

"I just came from the Old François Place. I'd like to hear the story about it."

Armand gave Madam Toulouse a wink and said, "If you been there, you already know it's haunted. Does the Old François Place have something to do with your Cryptid Hunter assignment?"

"My interest started before that; the night Madam Aja died. She gave me this."

I handed Madam Toulouse the moonstone pendant. After a close look, she handed it to Armand. With a jeweler's loupe he had in his shirt pocket, he gave the pendant a thorough examination.

I nodded when he said, "There a missing moonstone. "What did Madam Aja tell you about this?"

"Find the moonstone and then return the pendant to its rightful owner. What's wrong?"

Madam Toulouse took the necklace from Armand. "It's quite possibly the most valuable piece of jewelry you've ever touched. It's well known among potential collectors here in the city and it has a name," she said.

"Do you know who Erato is?" Armand asked.

"The muse of poetry?" I said.

Armand nodded. "This piece is known as the Moon of Erato. The moonstone is brilliant, unlike any other I've ever seen. Its spectacular colors are caused in part by microscopic flaws in the surface of the stone. Take a look."

Armand gave me his loupe and Madam Toulouse handed me the moonstone pendant. When I put the loupe in my eye and studied the stone, I saw what Armand was talking about. Tiny flaws pitted the surface of the otherwise perfectly polished stone.

"The flaws produce a visual anomaly. Such stones are exceedingly rare, and some say magical," Madam Toulouse said. "Collectors call the cyclical bands of fiery light Cycles of the Moon."

"There are people in this town who wouldn't hesitate to kill you to possess this piece," Armand said. "What do you intend to do with it?"

"Like I said, return it to its rightful owner. Know who that person is?"

"That's why we love you, Cowboy," Armand said with a grin. "You'd never let a few million dollars compromise your ethics."

"Then you'll help me?"

"I never expected to actually see the Moon of Erato, much less hold it in my hands," Madam Toulouse said.

"Of course we're gonna help you," Armand said. "Madam Aja would have us all burning in hell if we didn't." He waved to Jake at the bar. "But you're gonna have to buy more than a few drinks."

"Put it in your pocket and don't let anyone else see it, not even Jake," Madam Toulouse said.

"The walls have eyes," Armand said. "Don't trust anyone."

My pitcher of lemonade was still full. Jake took it anyway, leaving me another with fresh ice.

"Shots from now on," Armand said after killing his scotch.

When Jake had left the booth, Armand said, "The Old François Place was owned by a French nobleman named Felix François. He fancied himself a poet but he spent most of his time at a bar called La Fée Verte."

"You kidding?" I said.

"Not at all. Why do you ask?"

I showed him the business card Madeline had given me.

"Madeline Romanov's talking raven Calpurnia dropped this in her courtyard after saying something cryptic to me," I said.

"Like what?" Madam Toulouse asked.

"Buried alive."

Armand and Madam Toulouse exchanged a glance.

"Felix's wife disappeared, her body never found. Though the authorities couldn't prove it, they suspected he killed her," Armand said. "Along with a slave he owned whose body was also never found."

"Felix was a cruel master. Rumor had it he tortured his slaves and violated Code Noir." Madam Toulouse said.

"Code Noir?"

"A French law enacted by the Sun King, Louis XIV that prevented slave owners from murdering or torturing their slaves," Armand said.

"The Americans purchased Louisiana in 1803, Code Noir no longer in effect when Felix's wife disappeared," Madam Toulouse said.

"Felix might still have paid for the crime," she said.

"If the authorities could have found him," Armand said.

"He disappeared?"

"Off the face of the earth," Madam Toulouse said.

"Why did he kill his wife, or does anyone really know?" I asked.

"The woman wasn't from the colony and was supposedly a Native American," Madam Toulouse said.

"Supposedly?"

"From her description, she looked more like a fairytale character; petite with bouffant hair and big green eyes," Madam Toulouse said.

"Like this?" I asked, showing them the label on the absinthe bottle I had in my pocket.

Armand glanced at the label and then handed it to Madam Toulouse.

# Eric Wilder

"That's her," Armand said. "Felix commissioned a Paris artist to paint that picture. It hung in the hallway of the Old François Place."

"Her name was Maurelle. Some people said she was a forest fairy," Madam Toulouse said.

"Felix had a nickname for Maurelle. He called her Erato because he said she was his muse."

"What makes the moonstone pendant magical?" I asked.

"Felix's touts," Madam Toulouse said. "Most people thought the magic was in its beauty."

"What got her crossways with Felix?" I asked

"Felix was a drunk," Armand said. "Even then Maurelle's moonstone pendant was considered priceless. A visiting royal supposedly offered him a fortune for it."

"Felix sold the pendant?" I asked.

"Maurelle never removed the pendant from her neck and wouldn't have allowed Felix to sell it," Madam Toulouse said.

"But she did?"

"It went missing," Armand said. "Felix believed Maurelle was hiding it from him. Maurelle thought Felix had taken it from her."

"What happened to it?" I asked.

"You have it," Armand said.

"Madam Aja gave it to me. I have no idea where she got it, but now I know who the rightful owner is. One more thing; any idea what this means?"

I handed Armand the severed index finger with the wedding ring.

"Where'd you get this," he asked.

"Jake Huntington found it when we were viewing Maurelle's body. It was clutched in her hand."

After removing the ring from the skeletal finger with some difficulty, Armand studied it with his loupe.

"There's an inscription," he said.

"What's it say?" I asked.

"Pour toujours, Felix and Maurelle."

"Forever," Madam Toulouse said. "It's their wedding ring."

"Returning the moonstone to Maurelle won't mean much to her if she's dead," Armand said.

"Then there's something else involved," I said. "Madam Aja didn't give it to me to return to a dead woman."

## Chapter 11

Colley landed the chopper on the bullseye pad, rotor blades revolving as Jake and Mama hurried away from the aircraft. Still dressed in her colorful African dress, Mama caused quite a stir when they entered the emergency room door. After checking the front desk, they walked through an elegant hallway decorated with expensive works of art.

"Very nice," Mama said. "I hope their care is as good as their artwork."

"Better," Jake said. "I would have flown Jeff somewhere else if it wasn't."

The hallway was empty, morning sun beginning to filter through the windows when they reached the upper floor where Jake's son was located. The nurse at the registration desk pointed to a room down the hall. The door was cracked and Jake held Mama's hand as he pushed it open. Though neither uttered a word, the two people on opposite sides of the bed stared at them. Jake responded with his own silence.

Jeff's eyes were closed, his head bandaged, face puffy, black and blue. The sound of the instruments measuring his vital signs only amplified the palpaple tension between Jake and the two people standing by the bed. When Mama realized no one was going to speak, she folded her arms and backed against the wall.

The two were likely Jeff's mother Belinda and her boyfriend Sam Jones. Belinda was probably a few years older than Mama. She was a stunner, her blond hair bouffant and flowing like a movie star waiting for a key scene. Her stylishly short designer dress highlighted expensive high heels and a pair of killer legs. Her eyes were almost unnaturally blue.

Sam Jones was the Ken to Belinda's Barbie, a smattering of gray in his otherwise perfectly coiffed, dark hair. Not an extra pound of fat demeaned his athletic body. Like Belinda's outfit, his tailored jeans, monogrammed shirt, snakeskin cowboy boots, and flashy Rolex watch told Mama all she needed to know about his net worth.

Jake ignored them, bending over the bed to rest his hand on his son's head. As he did, Jeff's eyes opened.

"Dad, is that you?"

"It's me, son," Jake said.

Jeff moved his head with difficulty, blinking to clear his eyes.

"Where am I?" he asked.

"St. Francis," Jake said.

"What happened to me?" Jeff asked.

"Car wreck. You're pretty well banged up."

When Jake moved away from the bed to grab Mama's hand, Belinda and Sam draped themselves over Jeff's bed.

"Oh, baby, I've been so worried," Belinda said.

"You scared the hell out of us," Sam said. "What the hell were you thinking?"

"Leave him alone," Jake said.

"Don't tell me what to do," Sam said. "Where

the hell have you been for the last ten years?"

Jake didn't answer. Instead, he led Mama to the bed. "Jeff, this is Mama Mulate."

Pleased to meet you, Mama," Jeff said with a smile."

"Jake hasn't stopped talking about you since we left New Orleans. He didn't tell me what a good looking young man you are or what beautiful blue eyes you have."

Belinda and Sam had backed away from the bed, frowns on their faces and their arms tightly crossed around their chests.

"Did you meet Sam Jones and my mom, Belinda?" Jeff asked.

"We haven't had the pleasure," Mama said.

Sam and Belinda recoiled, neither of them responding to Mama's offered hand. Jake didn't say anything. Someone hurrying through the door interrupted Jeff's unspoken comment.

Belinda and Sam's frowns turned to smiles when Colley pushed through the door. Colley pumped Sam Jones's hand and then patted Belinda's back when she embraced him.

"You okay, baby?" he asked.

Belinda sobbed without answering Colley's question. Colley finally managed to break free. Grabbing their elbows, he hustled them outside into the hall.

Jeff had closed his eyes, his head cocked at an acute angle, his breathing labored. Jake touched his son's forehead again.

"Oh, my God!" he said.

"He's going to be okay," Mama said.

"How can you possibly know?" Jake asked.

"If he was critical, he'd be in the ICU and not in a private room," she said.

Colley reentered the room alone and quickly confirmed Mama's prognosis.

"He'll be okay," he said. "He's banged up but

has no broken bones or internal injuries. You two stressed out Belinda and Sam pretty good though."

Tears appeared in Jake's eyes when he draped himself over his son.

"Screw them," he said.

"Sam and Belinda went home. They were here all night. I told them we'd stay with Jeff until they returned. There's coffee across the hall. I'll get us some."

One recliner and two regular chairs occupied the hospital room. Though Jake made a point of offering the recliner to Mama, he was soon asleep in it without touching his coffee. Mama scooted her chair closer to Colley's.

"He's exhausted," she said. "You were up all night and you must be too"

Colley pulled a flask from his pocket and handed it to Mama.

"I'm used to it," he said. "A little whiskey in my coffee goes a long way. Have some?"

"Why not?" she said. "What do we do when it's empty?"

"There's more in the chopper. I'll make a whiskey run if we get low."

Colley grinned when Mama asked, "Why were Belinda and Sam staring at me as if I were an alien from another planet."

"Hell, Mama, this is Oklahoma. Segregation is still pretty much the order of the day, at least among certain portions of the population. You okay?"

Mama grinned. "I grew up in the south and I've been black all my life. I'm used to it."

Colley toasted her with the flask. "I didn't think it would bother you."

"You're not prejudiced, are you?"

"All of us are prejudiced against something or other," he said. "I try to keep mine in check."

"What about Jake?"

"Hell, half his employees are something other than white. You met Angie. She makes more money and has more power than I do, and I've been with Jake since he started Cryptid Hunter."

"Just wondering," she said.

"I'm just an ol' country boy. What you see is what you get. Jake's a sophisticated person and a different story. I don't believe he has a prejudiced bone in his body, but you need to ask him directly."

"Will he tell me?"

"Jake's the most honest person I ever met. He'll tell you."

Every time a nurse appeared to check the medical devices, Jake would awaken long enough to quiz them.

"Dr. Blake will be doing his rounds shortly," one of the nurses told him. "He'll fill you in."

The older woman smiled when Jake said, "I'd like to hear your opinion."

"He has some recovering to do. He'll be fine."

As the nurse had said, Dr. Blake arrived shortly. He was thirty-something, his hair already thinning in front.

"Your son sustained a near-fatal blow to the head. It was touch and go for awhile but his chances of recovery are high."

"Full recovery?" Jake asked.

"The end result of head trauma is difficult to predict," Dr. Blake said. "We may not know the full extent of the injury for months, perhaps even years."

"Not the answer I wanted to hear," Jake said.

Dr. Blake patted Jake's shoulder. "Jeff's alive. This time yesterday I wasn't so sure he was going to make it."

It was late afternoon when Colley's phone rang. After a short conversation he returned it to his pocket.

"Sam and Belinda are down the hall. They'll take over for us when we hit the elevator."

"I'm staying with Jeff," Jake said.

"No, you're not," Colley said. "We're doing this in shifts. Right now, you're off duty."

"What am I supposed to do?" Jake asked.

"Take your ass downtown, check the office and then get something to eat. Now move it. I'm not taking no for an answer."

Jake didn't argue as they exited the room and headed to the helicopter. The hospital wasn't far from downtown Tulsa, the chopper landing at a pad atop a multistoried office building. As they stepped out of the craft onto the roof of the building, Mama noticed a smile had replaced Jake's morose hospital demeanor.

"This is Huntington Tower," he said. "Even though I own the whole building, Huntington International Studios only occupies the top two floors."

"Impressive," Mama said.

Once Mama and Jake had cleared the props, the helicopter rose into the air, banked and disappeared over the tops of Tulsa's skyscrapers.

"Where's he going?" Mama asked.

"We have a hangar at the airport. Colley's putting the chopper away. I told him to go home and get some sleep."

Mama and Jake took a service elevator to the ninth floor. Everyone had gone home, the office complex only dimly lit. Jake took the stack of phone messages on the receptionist's desk. There were many windows, the work environment mostly open with lots of hanging plants.

Jake's office wasn't what Mama expected. There wasn't even a desk, at least a normal desk. Posters of cryptids covered the walls. For the next half hour, Jake returned phone calls as Mama stared out a big picture window at the skyline and sidewalks of Tulsa.

"Hungry?" he asked.

"Starving," she said. "I can't believe I didn't pack an overnight bag. I've had this dress on for more hours than I can count."

"I can remedy that," he said.

Jake punched the up button on the elevator, the door opening into his personal penthouse suite. The large room featured wood floors, Oriental rugs and expensive art.

"Oh, my!" Mama said.

"My little piece of paradise right here in the heart of downtown Tulsa."

"Is this all yours?" she asked.

"All 15,000 square feet of it. Come see my bedroom."

Mama stared out the large picture window. "The view is magnificent," she said.

"The bedroom faces west. Wait till sundown. You're in for something spectacular."

"Can't wait," Mama said.

"That's the bathroom," Jake said, pointing. "There's a walk-in closet with more clothes than you can imagine. Enjoy a hot shower, and then take all the time you want choosing whatever outfit makes you happy."

Jake was on his laptop when Mama exited the bathroom dressed in a white, frilly dress. Jake applauded when she pirouetted to show him what she was wearing.

"Fits perfectly," she said.

"Hope you don't mind wearing Belinda's clothes. She's about your size and she never wears the same outfit twice."

"Must be nice," Mama said. "I couldn't afford a single designer dress in that entire huge closet. Sure she won't mind?"

"Belinda hasn't spent a night here in years and will never miss the clothes she left here. It didn't stop her from filling the closets when she was. Feeling better?"

"Wonderful," Mama said.

"Allow me to shower and clean up a bit and then I'll show you around downtown Tulsa."

Jake exited the bathroom looking refreshed, and dressed in shorts, tee-shirt and running shoes. They spent the next hour walking the sidewalks of downtown Tulsa, visiting eclectic shops, gazing at window displays and mingling with the summer crowd.

"I love it," Mama said. "It's so. . ."

"Art deco?" Jake said, finishing her sentence.

"Yes."

"Tulsa was once the oil capitol of the world. There are more millionaires per capita here than almost any place on earth."

"Love it," Mama said. "Let's find someplace to eat. I'm starving."

"Like Italian?"

"Love Italian," she said.

"There's a cafe right around the corner. It's my favorite place to eat in downtown Tulsa."

They were soon sitting in a dimly-lit Italian bistro. The owner and all the wait staff knew Jake. Without asking, they tossed an elaborate Caesar salad at their table.

"Like chicken livers and cream gravy?" Jake asked.

"One of my all time favorites," Mama said. "If they're prepared correctly."

"Then let's find out," Jake said.

They were soon sipping Chianti, dipping their chicken livers in cream gravy and enjoying each other's company. Mama's demeanor turned graver when she ordered a martini.

"I have questions," she said.

"Ask me," he said.

"Belinda and Sam seemed shocked when they saw me. Colley suggested it's because I'm black."

Jake smiled. "They could care less what color you are. It just gave them a reason to throw more hate my way."

"Did you bring me here to elicit that particular reaction?"

Jake took Mama's hand. "I don't give a damn what Sam, Belinda, or anyone else in Tulsa thinks. I have feelings for you and everyone can go straight to hell if they don't like it."

Mama took a bite of her fettuccini. "You mean it?"

"Politics and friendship make strange bedfellows. Tulsa is the location of the worst race riot in American history. There are people in this city whose values are still locked in the Jim Crow era. I'm not one of those people and luckily most Tulsan's aren't that way. I can't speak for Belinda and Sam."

"Colley said you're an honest man."

"I'm not a saint. I have my faults. Racism isn't one of them."

"I thought so," Mama said. "You're not just attracted to me because I'm black?" Mama asked.

"I'm a sucker for great legs," he said. "Belinda's are world class. You have her's beat by miles."

Mama squeezed Jake's hand. "You're intelligent, good looking, and rich beyond imagination. You're penthouse suite is gorgeous and I love your bedroom, but. . ."

"But what?"

"We only just met. I can't sleep with you. I think you need to find me a hotel room."

## Chapter 12

Jake's reaction to Mama's comment was an unexpected question.

"Are you up for a friendly wager?"

"Like what?"

"It's still daylight. Tulsa has some of the most beautiful parks, jogging and biking trails in the country down by the river. We'll race. You win I'll put you up in the fanciest hotel in Tulsa. If I win, you spend the night with me."

"Though I'd like nothing better than to take you up on that bet, I didn't bring any shoes or running shorts," Mama said. "And besides, we both already know you're not as fast as I am."

"Afraid to race me?"

"That's not what I said."

"Equipment is no problem. Tulsa has thousands of joggers. My favorite running shop is just around the corner. Come on, I'll buy you what you need."

Mama followed Jake to a running store that reminded her of one visited the last time she'd run the Boston Marathon. That store was owned by a local legend who had won the Boston Marathon more than once. Though Tulsa

Runners wasn't a national chain, the owner was a local legend. Mama thought he was a bit too friendly with Jake and she wondered about their connection.

"Mama, this is Billy Tillman, the most famous runner in this entire city. Don't know if you've heard of Mama, Billy but she ran for the University of South Carolina."

Tillman was fiftyish, past his prime as a runner but still sleek and trim.

"One of the best finishers in the sport," he said. "Mama had the best women's 10,000 meters in the country her senior year. Mind telling me why you didn't go pro?"

"Personal reasons," she said.

"Ever regret your decision?" Billy asked.

"Every now and then," she said. "I try not to dwell on it because I have my hands full teaching English lit at Tulane University in New Orleans."

"My customers are students of the sport of track and field. Mind if I take a few pics of you to display on my walls?"

Mama didn't mind though she wondered why Billy included Jake in all the pictures.

When Billy finished, he invited Mama to browse the shop. Unlike a major chain store, Billy had stamped his own personality on his. Mama examined a pair of the most expensive running shoes she'd ever held in her hands.

"You can't be serious," she said. "No one pays two-hundred-fifty dollars for a pair of running shoes."

"Worth every penny," Jake said. "Try them on. I promise, you'll never buy anything else once you've experienced how they feel."

Mama was in awe as she walked around the shop in the expensive shoes.

"I can't believe how light and responsive they are," she said. "It's like having nothing at all on my feet. At any rate, I can't afford them."

"I can," Jake said. She also needs a racing outfit."

"Lord," Mama said. "I wish someone made a bra as comfortable as these shoes."

"Those shoes will subtract a minute off your 10-K time, guaranteed. Jake told me you two are about to race. You're going to need every second you can muster."

"Pardon me?" Mama said.

"Jake holds the record for the fastest 10-K ever run in the ACC. Didn't he tell you?"

Billy shook his head when Mama said, "He only told me he likes to jog."

"I know you're fast, but you're gonna need every second of advantage those shoes will give you. Wish it was on camera because I know it's going to be a classic."

"You're scaring me," Mama said.

"I doubt you've ever been scared. Still, I hope you don't have a bet on this race," Billy said.

"You're a son-of-a-bitch," Mama said as they exited Billy's running store.

"You can still back out of the race," Jake said.

"Not on your life. I'm going to kick your scrawny ass," Mama said.

"Good luck on that," he said.

After returning to Jake's penthouse to change into their running attire, they took a doorless yellow Jeep to a parking lot by the river. Unlike the Mississippi, the Arkansas River was in a different way just as scenic. Someone had spent millions of dollars developing a system of trails and parks melding perfectly with the scenic waterway and rolling terrain.

"Oh my God, it's beautiful," Mama said.

"Waterfalls, rapids, expensive art, statues,

and worldclass scenery, all funded privately by one of the richest men in Oklahoma.

"I'm impressed," Mama said. "We need something like this in New Orleans."

"It only takes money," Jake said.

"Lots of money," Mama said. "What are the rules?"

"There's another park exactly 10,000 meters from here," Jake said. "When you pass the statue of a giant blue heron, you'll know you've reached the finish line. It won't matter, because I'll already be there."

Mama gave him a look, "I'm going to relish kicking your ass," she said.

As Jake began to stretch and loosen up, Mama noticed the muscle tone of his legs and wondered if she would be able to carry through with her boast. Because she actually relished the idea of spending the night with Jake, it made her wonder if she even wanted to win. It was something she decided to worry about later.

"You ready?" Jake asked.

He nodded when she said. "I stay ready."

"Then go," he said, sprinting forward at a fast clip.

Mama had half expected Jake would give her a headstart. He was off, running well in front of her before she had a chance to adequately process her mental error. She started away at a fast clip before realizing it was madness to try and close the distance between them too quickly. It was probably what he planned for her to do: exhaust her strength early to gain back an unfair advantage. She'd run too many races to fall for that old trick.

The flagstone pathway had two lanes, one for cycling and one for jogging. Even at this late evening hour, Mama and Jake were far from the only runners and cyclists on the trails. It didn't matter. Jake was flying, Mama running faster than was comfortable for her just to keep up with him. Realizing something special was occurring, cyclists and other runners slowed to let them pass.

The landscape was visually amazing, Mama in awe as they raced ahead on the scenic path by the river. At one point in her life, she'd been a world-class athlete. She was still pretty damned good though she was having trouble maintaining Jake's breakneck pace. She still maintained enough sense of speed to realize their first mile was probably sub-five minutes. Jake didn't seem to notice as he increased the pace.

Unlike most of the past 10-K's in which Mama had run, this race had no mile markers. She had a sense they were closing on two miles though had no way of knowing. One thing she did know, if Jake didn't slow drastically or she didn't start closing the gap, she was destined to lose. Mama didn't intend for that to happen.

As they continued along the path at a breakneck speed, it became evident to Mama there were interested spectators lining both sides of the trail. Billy Tillman had apparently gotten the word out that two world-class runners were racing. Tulsa, a Mecca for running enthusiasts, had begun showing up in droves to witness the event.

As they neared the halfway mark, Mama realized if Jake were still in his prime she'd have no chance of beating him in a 10,000 meter race. She also knew he was probably ten years older than her and had lost a step or two along the way. By now, blacks, whites, males and females had lined both sides of the running path. Some were yelling for Jake and some yelling for her. Somehow, she found another gear and began closing the distance separating her and Jake.

As the beautiful river scenery and screaming spectators began melding into her subconscious, Mama had reached a sacred mental state known by athletes all over the world as the "zone." All pain was gone, replaced by the feeling she was suddenly moving in a higher plane of consciousness. Her mind drifted to a time in her distant path when she was barely eighteen. Mama's mother was crying as she wiped the blood oozing from her daughter's broken nose.

"God damn it, baby! You need to leave that mother fucker before he kills you."

"He loves me," Mama said.

"He's a beater and a cheater. He don't care for nothing except himself."

"I'm pregnant. What do you expect me to do?"

"Leave his sorry ass."

"I have no place to go. He wants me to abort the baby."

"He's gonna bring you nothing but sorrow and heartache. I won't let him kill my granddaughter."

"I have no choice," Mama had said.

"Fuck that motherfucker," Mama's mother had said. "We all have choices; none more important than our own."

Her mother's words rang in her ears as she increased her pace, realizing at that moment it was her responsibility to finish the race a winner or drop exhausted trying.

Mama's thoughts returned to the moment when she stepped on a rock and lost her footing. Reeling for a second, she regained her traction and accelerated ahead as the ever-growing crowd howled their excitement.

"Four-fifty-nine," someone with a stopwatch called as she passed.

Half the crowd was chanting "Ma-ma, Ma-ma," the other half "Jake, Jake."

The only thing that mattered to Mama was that she was pumped, and running as fast as she could ever remember running. Jake wasn't slowing. It didn't matter because she was closing on him. In the distance, she saw the statue of a giant blue heron. If she were going to win the race, she had to make her move.

As the blue heron grew ever closer, she began gradually closing the distance to Jake. It was then that something unexpected happened. Inexplicably, he slowed and let her race past him. The crowd went absolutely wild as she crossed the finish line just ahead of him.

Billy Tillman had done more than alert some of his runner friends. There were at least two camera crews and several reporters waiting to interview them. The raucous crowd was so noisy Jake had to put his mouth next to Mama's ear for her to hear his remark.

"Must be a slow news day," he said.

"You let me win," she said. "Why did you do that?"

"I jumped the gun at the start and I had 10,000 kilometers to consider my action," he said. "I don't know where our relationship is going from here. The time I had to think about the situation made me realize I didn't want to start out by cheating. Hell, you were coming up on me so fast you'd have probably beaten me anyway."

"I don't believe that, and neither do you," Mama said.

"Doesn't matter. I still want you to spend the night with me but you won the race. When we finish here, I'll get you checked in to the best hotel in Tulsa."

Mama kissed him. "No, you won't. I have less of a clue than you do about where our relationship is going. Doesn't matter because I'm staying with you tonight. If you still want me."

Jake took her hand. "The only thing in the world I want right now more than that is for Jeff to be okay and out of the hospital."

The crowd, and cameras were starting to close in around them. One smiling reporter holding a microphone began asking questions. Feeling better than she had all day, Mama returned the woman's smile and answered them.

## Chapter 13

Two alleyways border each side of the St. Louis Cathedral. The alley on the Uptown side, between the cathedral and the Cabildo, is known as Pirate's Alley. Legend maintains it was a haven for pirates, Jean and Pierre Lafitte's gang of privateers in particular.

It's true William Faulkner wrote his first book in 1925 at a space he rented in the alley. Pirate's Alley is still one of the most mysterious and colorful places in the Vieux Carre and the location of the absinthe bar La Fée Verte where I was headed.

Old flagstones, damp from the rain paved the narrow alleyway. Mostly shaded from the sun, the colorful green and red doors to the shops and bars were open. A blast of cold air chilled my neck when I entered La Fée Verte.

The little bar was much smaller than Bertram's, though probably still quite profitable because of the extra tourist traffic. It seemed a student of history had decorated the interior as everything about it shouted antiquity. Only the slowly revolving ceiling fans seemed out of place to a bar that might have looked exactly the same more than two hundred years ago.

Posters of absinthe labels lined the walls. When I saw one I recognized I knew I'd come to the right place. The bar was mostly empty and I grabbed a stool in front of the attractive female bartender.

The woman's raven hair draped to her shoulders and matched the color of her dark eyes. The hem of her long green dress touched the floor though it was low-cut and did little to hide her ample breasts. Realizing the sight had fixated me, she smiled and leaned on the bar to give me a closer view.

"Up all night or just getting an early start?" she asked.

"Little bit of both," I said,

"I'm Yvonne. What's your name?"

"Wyatt."

"You're cute, Wyatt. Want something to drink?"

I laid a twenty on the table. "I don't drink. I'm only here for information though I don't expect you to work for nothing."

Yvonne stashed the twenty between her ample cleavage.

"You like my tits?" she asked.

A smile crossed my face. "Was I staring?"

"If you weren't, I'd be worried about you. Besides, they're supposed to be looked at."

"I'm a fan," I said. "They definitely caught my attention."

"You from out of town?" Yvonne asked.

"Actually, just right down the street."

"Married?"

"Nope."

"Girlfriend?"

"Don't have one," I said.

"You're gay, dammit!"

"Wrong again."

"Between women?" Yvonne asked.

She giggled when I said, "Way between."

"I just came on shift. Stay with me awhile?"

"Why not? I said. "I have no place else to go."

"Let me make you an absinthe cocktail," Yvonne said.

"I'm an alcoholic," I said. "I'd take a glass of tea or lemonade, though."

"Damn," she said. "I was going to get you drunk and take advantage of you."

"You don't have to get me drunk to do that," I said.

"Why are you here, Wyatt? Are you a cop?"

I showed her the card Calpurnia had dropped.

"Private detective," I said. "I'm looking for the green fairy."

"You need a muse?"

"Don't know," I said. "Do I?"

"I'll be your muse," she said, again bending over the bar.

Before I had a chance to reflect on Yvonne's remark, two people entered from the alley and sat beside me.

The couple were both dressed in matching shorts and purple Polo shirts. The attractive middleaged woman carried an expensive handbag and had a diamond on her finger the size of Dallas. Sensing a big tip, Yvonne turned her full attention to them.

"I'm Yvonne. What's your names?"

"I'm Ben. This is Doris," the man said.

"Hi, Ben and Doris. Are you from out of town?"

Because of the man's accent, both Yvonne and I already knew they were from someplace other than the Big Easy. Ben's expensive watch, short-cropped gray hair and precisely manicured nails hinted he was a corporate lawyer, or maybe even a CEO.

"New York," Ben said. "Is it always this hot here?"

"August is our hottest month," Yvonne said.

"I think our travel advisor let us down," Doris said. "Ben and I couldn't help but notice there aren't many tourists here in the French Quarter."

Despite the heat and humidity, Doris's peroxided hair was perfectly coiffed. She'd noticed Ben was ogling Yvonne's breasts, and wasn't happy about it. Not wishing to lose a fat tip, Yvonne backed away from the counter.

"August is the best time to visit New Orleans," she said.

"Why is that?" Ben asked.

"Because you can spend time in the refrigerated air of our wonderful drinking establishments, enjoy ice-cold cocktails in the middle of the day and not feel guilty about it," Yvonne said. "Let me prove it to you. Absinthe cocktails are our specialty. First one's on me."

"It's not real absinthe," Doris said. "I read that it's illegal in the states."

"Not anymore," Yvonne said. "It's perfectly legal. What we sell is the real deal, just like Edgar Allan Poe and Ernest Hemingway used to drink."

Yvonne smiled when Doris asked, "It won't cause hallucinations, will it?"

Grabbing a green bottle, Yvonne showed it to the couple.

"This brand is distilled right here in New Orleans. The only ingredients are all botanicals: the holy trinity, fennel, anise, and wormwood. The alcohol content is high and will fuck you up if you drink too many or too fast. Hallucinations, not so much. Want to try one? I'm buying?"

Doris shot her husband a dirty look when he said, "You're one hell of a salesman. I need to take you back to New York to work for my company."

"Pay me enough and I'm on board," Yvonne said.

As if just realizing I was sitting beside him, Ben glanced at me.

"I'm Ben and this is Doris. What's your name and claim to fame?"

"Wyatt," I said. "Pleased to meet you. No fame here."

"He's a private dick," Yvonne said. "Isn't he cute?"

It was Ben's turn to frown when Doris gave me an assessing look and nodded. It didn't take a rocket scientist to realize they were both jealous types. Yvonne had apparently reached the same conclusion and turned her head away, grinning when I winked at her. Ben pulled a roll of bills from his pocket, counted out five crisp hundreds and laid them on the bar.

"Like you said, not much to do on a hot August day in the Big Easy except stay in the air conditioning and get drunk. Make Doris and I an absinthe cocktail, and one for Wyatt."

"I'm a recovering alcoholic," I said. "I'm working on a case and can't afford to get shitfaced."

"Nonsense," Ben said. "You're in a French Quarter bar, not at a job."

"I'm an alcoholic," I said.

Ben glanced at Yvonne, shook his head and held up three fingers. Having just stashed the hundreds in her cleavage, Yvonne was in no position to argue.

She leaned over the bar, shielding her mouth with her hand and whispered to me, "I'll drink it if you don't."

Being a teetotaler in New Orleans isn't easy. I'd resisted more drinks than I could count from friends and associates insisting they buy me one or two. I'd make a pretense of taking a sip and then dump it in a potted plant when no one was looking. None of my friends or associates had ever been the wiser.

Not wanting to rain on Yvonne's parade, I motioned her to prepare a cocktail for me. I watched with interest as she moved an ornate cutglass vessel with four spigots to a spot on the bar in front of us.

"What is it?" Doris asked.

"An icewater tap," Yvonne said. "Creating an absinthe cocktail is a ceremony, the tap a needed implement."

After pouring absinthe into three chilled glasses, she positioned them beneath the taps. A metal device that looked like a slotted spatula rested atop each glass. She placed sugar cubes on the spatulas, adjusted the taps such that icewater dripped on the sugar, through the slot and into the glass of absinthe.

"Interesting," Doris said.

Yvonne kept up an informative banter as the water began dissolving the sugar cubes one drop at a time.

"Notice how the clear liquid in the glass is becoming milky and beginning to swirl."

We watched, mesmerized by the performance as the liquid in the glass began to turn green, although slowly at first.

"What causes the absinthe to turn green?" Ben asked.

"The three main ingredients are infused with herbs such as hyssop and melissa. The herbs contain chlorophyll which gives the spirit its green color," Yvonne said. "Connoisseurs say it is the green fairy making her appearance."

"Green fairy?" Doris said.

"La Fée Verte. Absinthe has been the alcoholic drink of choice for authors, artists and poets the world over. Degas, Picasso, Edgar Allan Poe and Van Gogh. They all thought La Fée Verte was their muse and never created without it."

"Get out of here," Ben said.

When the cubes of sugar had all dissolved, Yvonne swirled the glasses. We watched as the beautiful cocktails became emerald green. She handed each of us one of her creations.

"Drink it slow," she said. "It may not make you hallucinate though I guarantee it's potent enough to fuck you up."

Ben and Doris both smiled and sipped their cocktail, unmindful of Yvonne's easily dropped four letter word. As if to take a sip, I put the drink to my lips. What happened was an unexplained force that tilted the glass and caused me to dribble some into my mouth.

"Ugh!" Ben said. "It's horrible."

"Anise is the culprit," Yvonne said. "It's what licorice is made from. The sugar helps cut the taste though lots of people just hate licorice."

Ben made a face and pushed the drink across the bar. "Think I'd rather have a scotch and soda," he said.

"Don't give up too quickly," Doris said. "The taste grows on you. Please, try some more."

Ben took a sip, and then another.

"The buzz I'm getting is unlike any alcoholic reaction I've ever had. It makes the awful taste of the cocktail almost bearable."

"Slow down," Yvonne said as she raised her palm. "I'm warning you, before you know it it'll kick your ass."

Yvonne wasn't lying. My brain was abuzz with an alcoholic rush I'd never felt. I knew I needed to set the drink on the bar. I was powerless to do so. My cocktail was all but gone when Ben returned his attention to me.

"See," he said. "Now, that didn't hurt you."

"I'll tell you after my eyes uncross," I said.

"So, you're a private investigator," Ben said. "Are you working on a case now?"

"I am. I'm trying to return this piece of jewelry to its original owner."

Removing the moonstone pendant from my pocket, I showed it to him. Doris was suddenly all eyes and ears.

"May I see it?"

Ben handed her the pendant and she examined it closely.

"Doris is a rare jewelry buyer for the largest jeweler in New York City," Ben said.

"This piece is extremely valuable. I'll give you fifty thousand dollars for it."

The alcohol had loosened my libido. Though I remembered Madam Toulouse and Armand warning me not to show the pendant to anyone for any reason, Doris's words only caused me to snicker.

"You're not close. That piece is priceless. A cool million is closer to its value."

Ben and Yvonne stared at me as if I were out of my mind.

"I can do a million," Doris said.

"It's not for sale," I said, reaching for the pendant.

"You can't be serious," Ben said. "You're walking around the French Quarter with a piece of jewelry worth more than a million dollars?"

"See the poster of the green fairy behind Yvonne?"

"What about it?" Ben asked.

"Look at the necklace around her neck."

"It does look like the one you have," Ben said.

"Not just look like it; it's the same necklace," I said.

"Let me see?" he said.

With the necklace in hand, Ben went behind

the bar and held it up to the poster.

"Impossible," he said. "This must be a fake."

"No fake," Doris said.

"There's a stone missing," he said. "That lowers its value."

"It's the missing moonstone I'm looking for," I said.

"What do you intend to do with it even if you find the missing moonstone?" Ben asked as he handed it back to me.

"Like I said; return it to its rightful owner.

## Chapter 14

Addiction is a curse. Try as I might, my alcoholism always seemed to bubble to the surface during inopportune times. Though it didn't seem to matter as I finished the last sip of my absinthe cocktail, it hadn't made Yvonne happy.

"I told you not to drink it so fast," she said.

My only answer was a happy smirk. "No problem," I said. "I can't remember ever feeling this good. Make me another?"

Yvonne wasn't smiling. "You've already had enough."

"What are you talking about?" Ben said. "Wyatt's happy face tells me he needs another."

"Not everyone can handle their alcohol," Yvonne said. "I don't want to kill him."

"Nonsense," Ben said. "He couldn't be happier and in no danger of dying."

"There's a fine line between being a happy drunk and a raving lunatic," she said.

"Wyatt's a long way from being a raving lunatic," Ben said. "Maybe you need an incentive."

Yvonne's arms uncrossed, her frown

disappearing when Ben shelled out five more hundreds.

"Listen to him, baby," Doris said. "Money talks, bullshit walks."

"Okay," Yvonne said. "One more."

After giving Yvonne a thumbs up, Ben and Doris began a whispered discussion. Yvonne looked anything but happy as she leaned over the bar.

"Give me the pendant," she said.

"For what reason?" I asked with slurred words.

"I don't trust those two," she said. "I think they're trying to steal it."

"They're not thieves."

"You're wrong about that," she said, holding out her hand. "I work here every day. I recognize a thief when I see one."

Neither Ben nor Doris saw me drop the pendant into Yvonne's hand, my reality fading as I closed my eyes. When I reopened them, the bar had changed.

The ceiling fans above the bar had disappeared. It was dark, lighting dim, and the air warm and humid. Gone were the electric lights replaced by gas lamps that flickered and popped. The ghost I'd seen in the brown suit at the Old François Place was sitting at a table playing solitaire and drinking an absinthe cocktail. He looked very much alive. I had to believe it was Felix François.

The doors to the establishment were open, the patter of rain on the alleyway cobblestones drumming a backdrop to the solitude of the bar. Felix François, if that's who it was, didn't seem to notice me. Something about the situation wasn't real. I was floating three feet off the floor and I wasn't wearing a stitch of clothes. My persona changed rapidly as I descended to the floor. Seeing no one behind the bar, I ran behind it, looking for something to wear.

A door behind the bar led to a cloakroom where I found clothes just my size. Not knowing if I was just lucky, or the recipient of Madam Aja's planning, I glanced around to see if anyone was looking before putting them on. Properly dressed in an outfit of another era, I exited the cloakroom. Felix spoke to me without looking up.

"I was beginning to think you weren't coming," he said. "Join me."

"It's pouring out. I started to stay home," I said. "Looks like everyone else did."

"Yvonne," he called. "Bring Wyatt a cocktail."

Yvonne must have worked at the bar for centuries as she appeared at our table dressed in the same outfit as when I'd last seen her. She didn't bother saying hello or acknowledge she knew me as she slid the absinthe cocktail across the table. Felix broke out a backgammon board and handed me the dice.

"You want to just skip the game and give me your money?" he asked.

Felix's words made me laugh. "Screw you," I said as I rolled the dice.

Though I didn't play Monopoly and Clue when I was young, my dad had me playing backgammon and pinochle before I was ten.

"Let Wyatt be a child," my mom would say.

"If a man can win at backgammon and pinochle, he can succeed in life," my dad had said. I want Wyatt to be somebody."

I'd never quite known what my dad had in mind, and I didn't endear myself to him by my lack of prowess at backgammon, or pinochle. I hated both games. Felix François soon bested me and held out his hand.

"I'm momentarily bereft," I said. "You'll have

to put it on my tab."

François grinned and shook his head. "Lucky you are my friend," he said. "Yvonne, get your lazy butt to work and bring me another cocktail."

"The place is dead tonight," I said.

"Not for long. Maurelle will be joining us soon."

"In this rain?" I asked.

"Maurelle is a creature of the forest. She isn't human and revels in the elements."

François's words proved prophetic when a giant Luna moth flittered through the front door. I watched as the wondrous creature transformed into a beautiful woman. It was then I realized I was either dreaming or hallucinating, or maybe both.

Maurelle was tiny, less than five feet tall though anything but a little girl. Instead, she was a fully developed woman, apparent by her diaphanous garb that did little to hide her voluptuous body. She had long black hair that framed, even if ever-so-wildly, her handsome face and hypnotic eyes. Her lustrous skin was tinted a light shade of green. The moonstone pendant around her neck radiated a mesmerizing glow, all three moonstones present.

The wedding ring she wore looked exactly like the one Jake had given me. I fished in my pocket, momentarily forgetting I'd given my pendant to Yvonne. As I was pondering the ring, she dropped the strap of her sheer garment off her shoulders, oblivious to the fact she was exposing her upper body. When Maurelle rotated her neck and shoulders, butterfly wings unfurled, a prism of colors pulsating through the flickering gas lights.

"Wyatt," she said. "I was hoping you would be here."

"Seems like I'm always here," I said. "Now, I'm glad you are."

I felt Felix's burning stare on the back of my neck. Maurelle gave him a sly glance and said, "You are Felix's only friend."

Felix's frown deepened when a black man appeared from behind the bar. He was tall, his regal outfit, and braided ringlets framing his handsome face. His starched white frilly shirt, open to the waist revealed tribal tattoos on his barrel chest. In another life, he'd been a warrior and a chief, his presence and bearing an indicator he thought he still was.

I noticed the momentary glance the man and Maurelle exchanged. From their uneasy expressions, I could see both Felix and Yvonne had also noticed. Felix confirmed my suspicion when he spoke.

"Joffrey, quit staring goggle-eyed at Maurelle's tits and get your black ass over here."

"Yes, Master," Joffrey said, his dark eyes flashing a moment of anger quickly becoming a smile. "You must be Master Wyatt. It is not a fit night out for man nor beast."

"No it isn't." I said."

Felix interrupted our conversation. "There is not enough business to keep the lights on. Maurelle and I are returning to the townhouse. Get the carriage and wait for us out front."

"Yes, Master," Joffrey said.

Joffrey donned a long coat and top hat from behind the bar and then disappeared out the front door. Felix put away his cards and backgammon board before donning his own long coat and top hat. From a clothes rack, he found a dark cloak for Maurelle. After wrapping it around her shoulders, he handed her a rain bonnet.

Sometime later, a horn sounded outside the door. Felix and Maurelle disappeared into the rainy night without so much as saying goodbye. I'd learned two important things during my visit to antebellum La Fée Verte: The theft of the moonstone from the pendant had yet to occur, and Maurelle was still wearing her wedding ring.

Thoughts of Maurelle disappeared when Yvonne gave me a wink. She was polishing a glass behind the bar and I grabbed a stool. She pushed another absinthe cocktail toward me.

"What's the story on Joffrey?" I asked.

"Felix won him in a backgammon game. From the way he was looking at Maurelle, I'm sure he wishes he had lost."

"He has such a regal demeanor and speaks with a distinct accent."

"A down-on-his-luck English lord owned him. Joffrey was not getting enough to eat and was glad to have changed masters."

Yvonne grinned when I asked, "How do you know so much about him."

"You saw how handsome he is."

Her smile disappeared when I said, "Maurelle did."

"And Felix noticed," Yvonne said. "If she didn't possess the magic pendant, he would surely punish her."

"Her pendant is magic?" I said.

"You know well how powerful it is," Yvonne said. "Felix is afraid of the power she possesses."

"If it wasn't for the magical pendant," how would Felix punish Maurelle?"

"God only knows. I have seen him do horrible things."

"Such as?"

Yvonne turned away, lowering her blouse to her waist such that I could see her back. Angry red whelps glared at me in the flickering light of the gas lamps.

"What did you do to deserve such a beating?"

"Real or perceived?" she said.

"Either."

"Working the bar is not my only job. I have other duties.

"Such as?"

"Servicing the master," she said.

"You're not a slave."

Yvonne pinched my cheek between her thumb and index finger. "We are all slaves to someone, sweetie. You just do not know it yet. Are you hungry?"

"Starved," I said.

Yvonne brought me a bowl of lentil soup from a kettle heating on a spit in the kitchen oven. I winced when I touched my fingers to the pewter bowl.

"It's hot, silly boy. I just pulled it from the fire." Grabbing my hand, she put my fingers in her mouth. "Does that make it better?"

"It's made me forget the soup and start thinking about other things."

"Plenty of time for other things," she said. "You'll need your strength. Eat the soup."

Yvonne's moist lips and knowing smile were like a healing salve for my fingers. There were bits of bacon in the soup and I used a big wooden spoon to eat it with. Yvonne watched until I'd licked the last tasty morsel off of the spoon.

"I love to watch a man eat," she said.

"Then you'd be happy around me. Where do you live?"

"A room in back. Felix lets me use it as part of my wages."

She smiled again when I said, "I'll bet."

"I would leave if I had another job, a husband, or a place to go. Are you available?"

"I'd love to oblige but I have trouble taking care of myself," I said.

"Then we will have to make do on a rainy French Quarter night in my dark little bedroom."

"I can hardly wait," I said.

"I can't," Yvonne said, leaning across the bar. Clutching my head in her arms, she kissed me.

"Your absinthe cocktail has gone to my head. I may have trouble living up to your expectations."

"I do not think so," she said. "My bed is cold when I sleep alone. I think you are going to warm it up quite nicely. I'll lock the front door and douse the lights."

"I'm not going anywhere," I said.

I was wrong. Joffrey reentered the bar before Yvonne had a chance to lock the door and douse the lights. She wasn't smiling when he placed his big hand on my shoulder.

"Sorry to disturb you. Master Felix wishes you to accompany me to the townhouse."

"It's not what I had planned," I said, glancing at Yvonne.

Joffrey smiled. "Don't worry about Yvonne. I will warm her bed. Right now, the carriage is waiting outside in the alleyway. If we hurry, we can reach the townhouse before the rain resumes.

## Chapter 15

My clothes were of the era to which I'd found myself transported. Grabbing the top hat and long coat, I followed Joffrey out the door. When I turned to say goodbye to Yvonne, she blew me a kiss.

Dark clouds, the weather wet and humid dimmed the moon and stars. The chill in the air did more than suggest it wasn't August. I didn't ask Joffrey what month it was as I climbed aboard the one-horse carriage. The big roan started away with a jerk the moment I was seated.

The Old François Place wasn't far from the little bar on Pirate's Alley. A short, bald black man was waiting, holding open the carriage door to allow us entry into the courtyard.

"How are you, Abel?"

"Can't complain, Mister Joffrey."

Abel walked behind us as Joffrey drove the carriage to the stable. Taking the reins, he led the horse to shelter. Abel had a crooked nose and smiled when Joffrey winked and tossed him a coin. I followed Joffrey around the townhouse to the frontdoor.

"The master awaits your presence," he said. "I am returning to the stable to help Abel."

"You won't be driving me home after my meeting with Monsieur Françoise?"

"Master Felix intends for you to stay the night."

"The reason?" I asked

"He will tell you himself," Joffrey said.

I heard Felix's booming voice the moment I walked through the door. "Is it you, Wyatt?"

"Yes."

"Then join me," he said.

Unlike the times I'd visited the Old François Place, I found no holes in the ceiling or cracks in the floor. The woven rugs on polished wood were clean and not mildewed. Like La Fée Verte, the large room was lit by flickering gas lamps and quite magnificent. Just as I had imagined it might have been when visiting during another lifetime.

"Sit with me," Felix said.

Felix reclined in an overstuffed chair looking comfortable enough to sleep in, a red velvet robe covering his silk pajamas. The chair in which I sat was as comfortable as it looked. Light from one of the lamps cast a greenish hue through the glass Felix held in his hand. The green muse of absinthe gripped his neck, his eyes half-closed and a silly grin dancing on his lips.

"Cain," he called. "Bring Monsieur Thomas a cocktail."

A short black man with a bald pate quickly appeared with an absinthe cocktail for me. He was dressed in a dark uniform and looked exactly like Abel the gateman.

"Twins," Felix said, "right down to their crooked noses which I personally had to break to cure their insolence."

Felix was in his cups. I didn't comment even though I had the urge to break his nose. Instead,

I closed my eyes and sipped the absinthe.

"What's so urgent you felt compelled for me to come to your house on such a stormy night?" I asked.

"Problems," he said.

"What problems?"

"I am sure you have heard of the slave troubles we planters are experiencing all along River Road."

"I've heard," I said.

"Five years have passed since the last slave rebellion. We managed to quell the insurrection without the need to execute anyone. Not so this time. The LaFleurs who own the plantation south of Moonmont had to execute one of their slaves last week. Instead of helping the situation, it exacerbated it. Tomorrow, I return to Moonmont. My desire is for you to accompany me."

"May I ask why?"

"You are my advocat. I want you to keep me from running afoul of Code Noir."

"Louisiana is now owned by the Americans. Code Noir no longer applies."

"We French still consider it the law of the land and abuse of slaves is not tolerated," Felix said.

Felix's words caused me to realize I wasn't simply a casual visitor to another century. I was his advocat and perhaps even his best friend, and reoccupying a body I had once possessed.

Code Noir defined how slave owners like Felix treated their slaves. There was hell to pay if they crossed the line. In Felix's mind, breaking the obsolete law continued to have consequences he didn't want to shoulder.

"Do you intend to execute one of your slaves?"

"Nothing that drastic."

"Then what."

"Disciplinary precautions."

"Disciplinary precautions that might result in a violation of Code Noir?"

Felix must have sensed something by the concerned tone of my voice because he smiled and shook his head.

"Absolutely not. Slaves, especially strong field hands are too valuable to kill."

"Then I ask you again, why do you need an advocat?"

"Only for the sake of appearances. Besides, you owe me lots of money. I will forgive your debts and pay you well for your work."

"You don't have to pay me," I said.

"Yes, I do. There must be no question of friendship entering the equation. You will be present to vouch for my behavior."

Felix frowned when I said, "You're confusing me."

"You ask too many questions. Will you accompany me?"

"Of course," I said.

"Then enjoy your absinthe. We will leave for Moonmont at dawn."

"Will Maurelle be accompanying us?"

"She will remain in New Orleans."

"You once told me how much she loves Moonmont."

"Too much," Felix said. "I have not told her about our impending journey. I pray you will say nothing about it to her."

Rain drumming the roof, a relaxing chair and the intoxication of absinthe plunged my thoughts into a state of nirvana. It forced me to focus on Madam Aja's mission which had propelled me to an exotic place in my distant path. Felix was having a similar problem with his eyes. He smiled and opened them a crack when I posed a question he hadn't anticipated.

"You never told me how you and Maurelle met," I said.

"At Moonmont, many years ago. She was a timeless creature who lived in the forest behind the swamp. When I was a boy, I often explored far beyond the cane fields, sometimes not returning to Moonmont until well after dark. I met Maurelle quite by accident."

"Tell me," I said.

"Moonmont is situated near a sweeping bend in the river. Because of this natural bend, the current lessens considerably. It has resulted in the river dropping massive amounts of sand and forming a substantial sand bank on the Moonmont side of the river."

"A natural levee?" I asked.

"Exactly," he said. "The extra deposits of rich soil is what makes Moonmont Plantation so valuable."

He nodded when I said, "A gift of the gods."

"A pristine lake formed behind the dunes; a body of water supporting all manner of exotic vegetation and wildlife. I was exploring the live oak forest near the lake when I first cast eyes on Maurelle."

"You sound awestruck. It must have been quite a sight."

"She was in a shallow rock-bottomed pool near the grassy bank and was quite naked. It was the first time I had seen the perfect body of a woman since reaching puberty. To say it was life changing is to downplay its importance in shaping my life."

"Maurelle never seems to age," I said.

"Because she is a fairy, a supernatural being with magical powers. She looks exactly the same now as she did the day I first saw her. It was also the first time I had seen a beautiful woman with gossamer wings the colors of the earth, the morning, and the sky."

"You were in awe," I said.

"In awe, lust, and love. My mind and body were saturated with emotions I did not know I possessed."

"How old were you?"

"All of eighteen, no longer a boy though not quite a man. It did not matter because I was instantly smitten."

"Was Maurelle frightened when she saw you?"

"Not in the least. She continued bathing as if she were alone, though we both knew she was not. It was the first of our meetings. We were inseparable that summer. When fall arrived, I became terribly unhappy when I learned my father was intent upon sending me to France for a university education. In the end, he won out."

"What happened?" I asked.

"I remained in France for a year before leaving university and buying passage on a ship back to New Orleans. My return trip to Moonmont was eventful."

"I can only imagine. My father wouldn't have tolerated such insolence," I said.

"Nor did mine. A horrible argument ensued. He would have beaten me, though by this time I was bigger and stronger than he was."

"And."

"In a snit of anger, my father rode away from Moonmont, his horse rearing when it stepped on a snake. He was dislodged from the saddle, breaking his neck in the fall. That night, I lost my father and became head master of Moonmont. I was barely twenty years old."

"A story I've never heard. I'm so sorry," I said.

"My father was a cruel bastard who loved tormenting the slaves, and torturing my mother. I was more than happy to see him dead, and after all these years my mind has not changed.

Maurelle moved into Moonmont shortly after my father's death."

"How did that work out?"

"My mother was an heiress, her marriage to my father welcomed by both families as a means to cement their wealth and power."

"She didn't love your father?"

"Hah! Detest is the word, and not love. Her scorn turned to hate when he began to abuse her."

"He beat her?"

"Worse. He forced her to perform debasing sex acts with slaves, both male and female, while he watched."

"Why didn't she leave him?" I asked.

"Family politics. She never had a choice in the matter," Felix said.

"How do you know all of this?"

"A black handmaiden told me the story. I am quite sure all the slaves knew firsthand."

"I'm so sorry," I said. "At least you know your mother loved you."

"I was conceived after a night of forcible rape. My mother never felt any love toward me. She coped with the situation by burying her anger and resentment in endless bottles of sherry."

"What happened after your father died?"

"Mother hated me and Maurelle. In a drunken rage, she finally told me her true feelings."

"I understand how that must have upset you," I said.

"More than upset me," he said. "I had Henri, a slave I owned take her in a boat to the middle of the river where he cut her throat and tossed her overboard."

"You had your own mother killed?"

"I made sure she was drunk."

Felix was also drunk and didn't react when I said, "Small favor."

"When Henri returned to the plantation after killing my mother, I confronted him and had him arrested. I beat him senseless, reviving him many times until he confessed to everyone watching he had killed my mother."

"My God!" I said.

"After he had confessed, I blew his brains out with my pistol." Felix's features darkened. "It was at that moment, I became master of Moonmont."

Felix's smile gone, he called Cain to bring us more absinthe.

"Matilde, my mother, rarely left her room the last ten years of her life. The plantation was doing extremely well, my financial fortunes rosy. Maurelle and I hosted many lavish parties. She was the toast of River Road and New Orleans. All the while, she held tremendous power over me because of her magic. There were other things."

"Such as?" I asked.

"Her beast."

"Please explain"

"A monster with crooked teeth accompanied Maurelle from the forest. He is dangerous and deadly. At this very moment, he is not far away."

"What the hell are you talking about?" I asked.

"A large creature with the face of a dog, leathery skin and a reptilian fin that runs from the nape of its neck to the tip of its tail."

"You can't be serious. Have you seen this creature?"

"Many times. It watches over Maurelle. She protects it with her magic. If I tried to hurt her, the beast would kill me."

"Why would you hurt Maurelle?" I asked.

"There are times when everyone needs punishment," Felix said.

"Even your own wife?"

"If my father taught me anything, it was

sometimes the only way to control a woman is with carefully measured doses of pain."

"You have never hit Maurelle, have you, Felix?"

There have been times when I have wanted to kill her."

"I thought you were very much in love," I said.

"Maurelle does not approve of the way I handle the slaves. In public, she is my wife; in private, she scorns me."

"You abuse your slaves?" I said.

Felix's smile returned briefly. "I only have feelings for human beings. Slaves are little more than animals; a chicken whose head you wring to provide the meat for Sunday dinner. No more, no less."

"I disagree with you, Felix. Slaves are as human as we are. Even the Mother Church believes as much. It's wrong to treat them like animals."

Felix's face flushed. He had to breathe deeply before he could speak.

"Have you ever owned slaves?"

"Never," I said.

"Why not?"

"It's not something I could ever bring myself to do."

As my advocat, you are bound to defend me no matter how you feel about me personally."

He had closed his eyes and was snoring softly when I said, "It might not keep me from killing you."

## Chapter 16

Mama awoke the following morning when Jake stumbled into the bedroom. Not immediately remembering where she was, she covered herself with the blue satin sheet on the bed.

"Didn't mean to startle you," he said.

Mama threw back the covers and opened her arms for Jake to give her a hug.

"Sorry for my reaction," she said. "It took me a moment to remember why I was lying naked in a strange bed."

"I'm not complaining. Hungry?"

"You kidding? After last night how could either of us be anything but famished?"

"I know I am." After another kiss, he walked to the bedroom door. "I'm cooking breakfast for us. Take your time. I'll be in the kitchen."

After a shower, Mama found a terrycloth bathrobe and joined Jake in a kitchen she would kill for. In addition to the wonderful view, there was an eight-burner professional stove, a huge refrigerator, and a pantry with almost anything a working chef could wish for.

"Whatever you're cooking smells wonderful"

she said.

"Eggs Benedict and hash browns," Jake said. "My specialty." Mama grinned when he added, "Also, the only thing I've ever successfully cooked."

"If it tastes as good as it smells, it'll be wonderful."

They were soon sitting at a table gazing out at the Tulsa skyline as they drank coffee, ate eggs Benedict and hash browns.

"I got up early and went to the hospital to check on Jeff," Jake said.

"How is he doing?" she said.

"He's young and did lots of recovering since we saw him yesterday. The hospital is releasing him."

"Oh, how wonderful," Mama said.

"I still think of him as my little boy but he's twenty-seven and very much an adult. He also has very specific grievances about Belinda and me."

"Such as?"

"How we treat each other; our indifference which he says is impacting our lives and his."

"He wants you to get back together?"

"He's more mature than I gave him credit for. He wants Belinda, Sam and I to work out our differences and quit treating each other like shit; his words."

"He wants you to begin counseling?"

"He has more of Granddad Hunt in him than I realized," Jake said.

"Explain."

"Sam and I grew up together. When he wasn't at my house, I was at his. We were like brothers. Brothers don't always get along. Mom and Dad once left me with Hunt while they visited Europe. Sam stayed with us most of the time. One summer day, we had a serious altercation."

"How serious?"

Jake chuckled. "It doesn't seem like much now though I don't ever remember being as mad as I was at Sam. The feeling was mutual."

"And?"

"Hunt had one of the butlers go into town to purchase boxing gloves. They constructed a ring in the backyard. He told us we had to settle our differences in the ring. Why are you laughing?"

"I've never known anyone who actually had a butler. What happened?"

"Hunt and the entire staff watched as Sam and I duked it out in the makeshift ring."

"Did it rid you of your aggression."

"We both ended up in the emergency room, me with a busted nose and Sam with an ear half torn off. It strengthened the friendship of Sam and I. We never had another disagreement, at least until he started sleeping with Belinda."

"What did your parents think about your grandfather's little experiment?"

"Lucky for him we were healed up by the time they returned home."

"So what's this story have to do with Jeff?" Mama asked.

"He wants me to do something I find abhorrent."

"Like what?"

"Meet with him, Belinda, and Sam at Huntington Manor. He wants us to come prepared to spend the night."

"Sounds like a plan," Mama said.

"Sam and Belinda agreed only if you won't be there."

"That's okay. This place is lovely. I'll stay here."

"I informed them the only way this crazy experiment was going to happen was if you are with me."

"You didn't, did you?" Mama said.

"Yes I did. Once Jeff saw how Belinda and Sam reacted to my pronouncement, he made your presence part of the rules."

"Rules?"

"Hunt's boxing gloves," Jake said.

"What rules?"

"Jeff's going to explain everything tonight at Huntington Manor. The accommodations will be stark."

"Stark?" Mama asked.

"I retired all the servants several years ago."

Jake grinned when Mama said, "That sounds cruel after years of service."

"Trust me, they were all at least in their sixties and I gave them substantial pensions. They have nothing to worry about the rest of their lives. Meanwhile, except for grandpa's ghost the place has been vacant."

"We'll make do," Mama said.

"Colley told me Jeff is taking care of the food and alcohol. At least we'll have plenty to eat and drink."

Mama glanced at the dirty pots and pans. "I'll take care of the dishes," she said.

"Not alone, you won't. I dirtied them; I'll clean them."

"What time are we expected at Huntington Manor?" Mama asked.

"Fivish," Jake said. "Why?"

"I'm up for more exercise until then."

"Then I'll change into my running gear after helping you with the dishes."

"No need putting on anything," Mama said with a sly grin. "The sweat I'm thinking about working up doesn't require clothes."

Mama and Jake drove his yellow Jeep along a

road winding up a scenic bluff overlooking the Arkansas River. The old mansion they found at the end of the road was magnificent, reminding Mama of some of the houses in the Garden District of New Orleans. This brown stucco had a red tile roof and was three-stories tall. A Jeep that looked exactly like Jake's, except it was blue, was parked near the front door.

"Colley and Jeff are already here," Jake said. "I don't see Sam's Escalade. Maybe I'll have a chance to speak with Jeff alone before he and Belinda get here."

The inside of the Huntington Manor was even more magnificent than Mama had expected. The windows were freshly washed. There was no dust in the air, and the furniture and floors were uncovered and immaculate.

"I can't believe it," Jake said. "Who cleaned up the place?"

"Jeff called a custodial service when we got here," Colley said. "They weren't gone thirty minutes before you arrived."

"Good work, son," Jake said.

"Hunt wouldn't have wanted us to spend the weekend in a dirty house."

Jake gave Mama a glance. "We're staying for the weekend?" he asked.

"You aren't chickening out, are you?" Jeff said.

Mama nodded when Jake gave her another glance. "At least I thought about the food and drink," he said.

Colley was drinking a tall can of Coors. "At least you're good for something," he said.

"Thanks, pal," Jake said. "Since we arrived before Sam and Belinda, do we get to hear about your plan?"

"No way," Jeff said. "Everyone needs to be here. I'll explain everything after dark."

Jeff's bandages were gone, the bruises on his face and forehead already beginning to fade.

"You're looking good," Jake said. "This time yesterday, I wasn't sure what we would find when we got to Tulsa."

"I'm sore all over, my back hurts and it's even difficult to smile. Doesn't matter because I'm pumped about what we might accomplish this weekend."

"And you won't even give us a clue?" Jake said.

"Nope. You'll learn soon enough."

A car drove up outside, the brakes groaning when it pulled to a stop. It was Sam and Belinda. Belinda's frilly dress, deep blue the same color as her eyes, barely reached her knees. Mama glanced at her athletic legs, the product of walking, running, cycling, or a combination of all three, and understood why Jake had been attracted to her. She couldn't run very fast in the expensive high heels she was wearing, Mama thought.

Sam's monogrammed shirt was the same color as Belinda's dress. Mama looked at the pointed toes of his cowboy boots and wondered how in the world they could be comfortable.

"Anyone hungry?" Colley asked.

"Starved," Belinda said, as if seeing Colley for the first time.

She gave him a friendly kiss and then another for her son.

"Jeff laid out quite a spread in the kitchen," Colley said. "It's like an old-time oil industry Christmas party. There's no one here but us, so you'll have to serve yourselves."

"We can handle it," Sam said. "Lead the way."

The spread in the kitchen turned out to be less than advertised, much less like an old-time oil industry Christmas party. The choices were various luncheon meats and white bread. Mama made do with a turkey sandwich and a few carrot sticks. Still working on the drink he'd brought from the penthouse, Jake didn't eat anything.

"Want to see the garden?" he asked.

"Love too," Mama said.

Jake led her outside to a large cement deck surrounding the back of the mansion. A sculptured ledge enclosed the deck and it overlooked a beautifully maintained garden complete with fountains, arbors, and a gazebo with a red-tiled roof.

"I still employ a gardener and he's here at least once a week," Jake said when he saw Mama's disbelieving stare.

"It's beautiful," she said. "It reminds me of a Venetian garden."

"Exactly how it's meant to look," Jake said. "Hunt designed it following a trip to Venice back in the fifties."

"I love it," Mama said.

Jake sat his drink on the ledge overlooking the garden.

"It's warm," he said. "Think I'll grab a beer. Wait for me?" he asked.

"I'll go with you," she said.

"I won't be long," he said. "There's all manner of birds and ground squirrels living in the garden to keep you occupied."

Entranced by the beautiful garden, Mama made friends with a rambunctious chipmunk, feeding it a carrot stick when Jake returned with their drinks.

"You're wonderful," he said. "I've lived here most of my life and I've never had a chipmunk eat out of my hands."

"You didn't try hard enough," she said.

Mama had finished eating and she and Jake were holding hands, when Colley opened the patio door a crack and peered out.

"Jeff wants us all to gather in the Great Hall," he said.

"You must know what's about to go down," Jake said. "Give us a clue what Jeff has on his mind."

"Sorry, Boss Man. I'm taking orders from another boss tonight. Better grab another drink before joining us. I recommend a tall one," he said before shutting the patio door and disappearing back into the house.

Mama found the Great Hall magnificent. Huntington Manor was situated on a bluff overlooking the Arkansas River. Jeff had opened the curtains covering the gigantic picture window offering a spectacular west view of the river. Sam and Belinda were sitting on a leather couch providing them a great view. Mama and Jeff found a place on another couch.

Colley was seated in a big chair, an opened bottle of whiskey and can of Coors on a wooden stand beside him. Jeff was standing, pacing the floor near the picture window.

"We're more than curious," Belinda said. "When are you going to tell us why we're here?"

"Relax, Mom," Jeff said. "Nothing's going to happen until after sundown."

"Why not just tell us now?" she asked.

"I don't remember much about Great Grandpa Hunt. I do remember sitting on his knee, right here in this room, watching the sun set over the river. I believe he's here with us now and I intend to wait until after sundown to make my intentions known."

Mama whispered in Jake's ear. "He's trying to summon your grandfather."

"For what reason?" Jake asked.

"Guidance," she said.

As the sun set behind the horizon, the light in

the Great Hall began to wane. It was almost like watching a panoramic movie through the large window. The view was perfect, the fiery red orb pulsating and radiating dying rays of yellows and orange. It was like a giant, natural fireworks show. The sunset was the most spectacular Mama had ever seen.

"I've watched sunsets all over the world. "Never one that compares to this. It's breathtaking."

"Reflections off dust in the air," Jake said. "Oklahoma sunsets are hard to beat."

Once the sun had disappeared, Jeff lit several candles and sat in a chair in front of the two couches.

"What I have to say might take awhile," he said.

Candles lighted the room with a dim glow. There was no traffic noise, the patio door to the garden ajar, the hooting of an owl not far away.

"What now?" Sam asked,

"I've kept you waiting long enough," Jeff said. "It's time I told you why you're here."

## Chapter 17

Everyone waited for Jeff to tell them why he'd insisted they spend the weekend at Huntington Manor. Jeff made them wait a while longer, the whistle of a distant train breaking their uneasy silence.

Belinda finally spoke up. "Please don't keep us in suspense any longer. Sam and I are dying to know why we're here."

"I'll tell you soon enough. For now, thanks for coming," Jeff said. "I was worried that none of you cared enough about me to follow through."

Belinda, Jake, and Sam all began protesting. In deference, Jeff held his comments until they had all spoken.

"How can you say that?" Belinda asked. "I love you more than life itself."

"You know there's nothing in the world I wouldn't do for you," Jake said.

"You're as much my son as you are Jake's," Sam said. "There's no one more important to your mother and me than you are."

"The three of you are the most important people in my life," Jeff said. "When the paramedics were struggling to free me from the car wreck, one thing kept running through my mind."

Jeff choked up a moment and Belinda rushed to his side.

"My poor baby," she said.

"I'm neither poor nor a baby," Jeff said. His grave expression disappeared when he glanced at Colley and saw him grinning. "I have a big problem in my life. What I need is for something to change."

"A drug problem you haven't told us about?" Sam asked.

"Nope," Jeff said. "More serious than that."

"You haven't killed someone, have you?" Jake asked.

"Not that serious," Jeff said, his smile returning.

"Then please tell us," Belinda said.

"I have a big problem with how you, Dad and Sam treat each other. It's ruining my life and yours. I'm sick of it. I have a plan to change things."

"Then tell us," Belinda said.

"First, I want to apologize to Professor Mulate. You're now, through no fault of your own, an integral part of this experiment. I only hope you don't hate me when it's over."

"Tell them what's on your damn mind," Colley said. "You're even starting to piss me off."

"Sorry," Jeff said. "My plan goes like this: Colley and I are leaving shortly. The four of you will remain, agreeing to stay for the entire weekend and not leaving the grounds."

"No problem," Jake said. "There's plenty of food and drink. Mama and I will relax and enjoy the vacation."

"Not so simple and it won't be a vacation," Jeff said. "I've devised a contest and the four of you will be the participants. Two teams. You'll be competing against each other."

"What kind of a contest?" Sam asked.

"We called them scavenger hunts when I was a kid. They were popular around Halloween," Jeff said.

Jeff ignored Jake's levity when he said, "Sounds exciting."

"Each team will have a single written clue. If you solve the clue, it will lead you to the next clue, and so on. The first team to solve the puzzle and reach the final destination will be the winner."

"That should be easy enough," Belinda said.

Sam and Belinda bristled when Jake said, "Mama and I will have their asses on a platter."

"Mama's not your partner," Jeff said. "Sam is."

"Sam?" Jake said.

"That's right," Jeff said. "You are Team 2, and Mom and Mama are Team 1."

"Now wait just a minute," Belinda said.

"Are you crying uncle?" Jeff asked.

"I't's just that. . ."

Belinda didn't finish her sentence.

"In or out?" Jeff asked.

"In," Belinda said.

Jeff acknowledged his mother's answer with a nod.

"No matter what happens, there will be no communication between teams. You are not to speak to each other until the contest is over."

Belinda gave Mama a quick glance. "Is that all?"

"Team members must remain within thirty feet of each other at all times. You'll stay in the same bedroom and not, under any circumstance, consort with a member of the other team. Agreed?"

"Do we have a choice?" Belinda asked.

"If you're afraid to accept the challenge, you can leave now. I won't hold it against you," Jeff said.

"I'm in," Sam said.

"Me too," Mama said.

Amidst the dying sunset and flickering candle light, Belinda and Jake exchanged a look.

"I can handle it," Belinda said. "Count me in."

"What's the prize?" Jake asked.

"No questions," Jeff said. "In or out?"

"Seems I have no choice," Jake said. "You have a choice," Jeff said. "There's the door. Don't let it hit you in the ass."

Everyone, even Belinda, smiled when he said, "Then I'm in it to win it."

Twenty minutes later, Jeff and Colley stood at the front door, preparing to leave.

"One more thing," Jeff said. "While I was talking, Colley took the food out of the refrigerator and put it in ice chests. The electricity is switched off. You'll have to make do with candles."

"What about air conditioning?" Jake asked. "August in Tulsa isn't exactly frosty."

"Grandpa Hunt had no electricity when he built this place. All the windows can be opened. Deal with it. Oh," Jeff said before walking out the door. "Give me your cell phones and car keys."

"What if there's an emergency?" Sam asked.

"Your problem, not mine. Your instructions are in these envelopes. You can open them after Colley and I leave. And remember, the two teams aren't allowed to communicate, or assist each other in any way."

With the electricity turned off, it didn't take long for the temperature, along with the humidity, in the old mansion to start rising. Belinda and Jake opened their envelopes and extracted the directions.

"We have the master bedroom here on the first floor," Jake said.

"Fine," Sam said. "How do you suggest we find our way there in the dark?"

Jake took the candle Jeff had left and broke it in two. After lighting the second candle he'd created, he handed one to Belinda.

Jake pointed to the door. "You want to lead the way, or shall I?"

"Right behind you," Sam said.

Belinda and Mama followed them into the hallway.

"Guest suite, second floor," she said. "Mine and Jake's bedroom when we lived here with Grandpa Hunt."

Belinda grew silent, ignoring Mama as they ascended the stairs. A gasp of humid air engulfed them when they opened the bedroom door. It didn't take long for Mama to start opening windows, a welcome breeze wafting the room's sheer curtains.

"What the hell!" Belinda said. "There are bats and spiders, and God only knows what else out there. Are you crazy?"

"I can deal with bats and spiders. If we don't open the windows, we'll suffocate. Your choice."

Belinda sat in a chair and kicked her high heels across the floor.

"Don't talk to me," she said.

"Fine," Mama said, "though I doubt we'll have much luck winning a scavenger hunt without talking to each other."

"I don't need your help," Belinda said.

Mama shook her head and turned away. There were candles and matches in the room. She lit them and patted the mattress as Belinda read through the instructions.

"At least the bed's soft," she said.

"My bed," Belinda said. "I'll be sleeping in it alone."

"Not unless you want to fight me for it."

"I'm not a fighter."

"Nor am I," Mama said. "The bed is big enough for both of us."

"I'll sleep in the chair."

"Suit yourself. Doesn't look very comfortable to me," Mama said.

Belinda wadded the instructions she was reading, tossing the paper across the room. Drawing her legs up to her chest, she crossed her arms tightly. Mama picked up the wadded sheet of paper off the floor and unfolded it.

"What the hell is that gobbledygook supposed to mean?" Belinda asked.

Mama read the passage aloud. "There are places beneath Polaris where only dead men live."

"Like I said, gobbledygook," Belinda said.

"It leads us to where to find the next clue," Mama said.

"I'm blond, though not stupid," Belinda said. "Stop treating me like I am."

"Then stop acting as if you are. Where do dead men live?"

"In graves," Belinda said.

"Exactly. Is there a graveyard on the premises?"

"Grandpa Hunt's," Belinda said.

"Can you find it?"

"I can't remember. Beneath Polaris, whatever that means."

"Maybe you aren't as blond as you let on," Mama said. "Polaris is the North Star. Which way is north?"

"The picture window where we watched the sunset is the west side of the house," Belinda said, heading for the door.

"Stop right there," Mama said. "You aren't going anywhere without me. Remember the rules?"

"Screw the rules," Belinda said. "How's Jeff going to know?"

"Infrared cameras. I saw one in the hallway. My guess is he's had them mounted all over the house and yard. Besides, you can't go in the yard without your shoes."

"Dammit!" Belinda said, returning to the room and picking up the high heels she'd kicked across the floor.

When she tried to put them on, she found her feet were swollen. She kicked them back across the floor.

"Dammit, dammit, dammit!" she said.

Mama began rummaging through the closet, returning with running shoes, socks and a jogging outfit.

"You left all sorts of clothes in the closet when you moved away. Put these on," she said. "You won't get very far in stocking feet, and that frilly little dress of yours," Mama said.

Belinda wasn't happy taking orders from Mama, her face red in the dim light of the candle as she stripped off her dress and stockings, replacing them with pink jogging shorts, athletic bra and running shoes. She also wasn't happy when Mama donned a similar running outfit from the closet.

"I didn't give you permission to wear my clothes," she said.

Mama's dark mane radiated in the candle light as she disregarded Belinda's words and continued lacing the new pair of running shoes she'd found in a box in the closet.

"Chill out, sister," Mama said. "You didn't even remember you'd left them here."

"I'm not your sister."

"Thank God for small favors. Now quit acting like a nitwit," Mama said. "We have work to do and we're in this together. Get used to it."

"I hate pink," Belinda said. "You could at least have given me the blue outfit you're wearing."

Mama immediately began stripping off her shorts and matching sports bra.

"Quit your bitching and trade with me," she said.

Belinda seemed happier, though not much, as they traded outfits. Mama stopped when she opened the door to the hallway.

"I forgot we have no electricity. It's dark as a tomb in the hall. Grab a couple of candles."

Belinda handed Mama a lighted candle. "Let's get this straight. I'm the boss here, so stop trying to order me around."

"Whatever rings your bell," Mama said.

"Slow down."

"Then try to keep up." Mama stopped when they reached the stairs. "Hold on to the banister on the way down. We don't need any broken bones."

"Jake and I lived here for years. I've walked down these stairs more times than I can count."

"Not in the dark. Grab the banister, please," Mama said.

"Whatever!" Belinda said as she clutched the railing with her free hand.

After descending the stairs with no mishaps, Belinda led them to the Great Hall.

"Which way is north?" she asked.

After glancing at the picture window through which they'd viewed the sunset, Mama turned ninety degrees to her right.

"This way, she said.

A side door led them to a covered deck on the north side of the house. A sky fraught with clouds cloaked the moon and stars, the only light emanating from Mama and Belinda's flickering candles. They could see the tops of trees, twenty feet above the ground. The distant owl they'd heard in the Great Hall hooted in the trees somewhere below them.

Ornate railing enclosed the deck. Except for the door through which they'd come, there was no way to go anywhere else except back the way they came.

"No way to get to the ground from here," Mama said. "Let's go outside through the front door."

Belinda had other ideas. "You do what you want. It can't be that far to the ground."

"Unless the tops of those trees we see below us are dwarfs," Mama said.

"Ten feet at the most," Belinda said. "Can't be much more than that."

Before Mama could protest, Belinda vaulted the railing and jumped. She heard a crash and a groan as Belinda fell into something below.

"Belinda, are you okay?"

When she got no answer, Mama hung over the railing, kicking out with her legs until she connected with a brace bar securing the wooden deck. Though she was no mountain climber, she had spent time in a New Orleans' gym that featured a climbing wall. A few minutes later, she was safely on the ground. She couldn't see anything as the burning candles were still on the deck above her.

"Belinda, where are you?"

Although Belinda didn't answer, Mama could hear her low moans coming from somewhere nearby. The same shrubs Mama found herself struggling to extract herself from had broken Belinda's fall. After Mama pulled her free of the vegetation, Belinda stood up, coughing and trying to catch her breath.

"You okay?" Mama asked.

"How did you get down here so fast?" Belinda asked.

"By doing what you should have done. I climbed down."

## Chapter 18

Sam and Jake stopped at the kitchen on their way to the main bedroom. They found two large ice chests filled with cold beer, sliced meat, mayonnaise, etc. There was also a bar stocked with mixers and various bottles of liquor. There was no Bombay Gin.

"I can't find my favorite gin," Jake said.

"You're probably looking in the wrong place," Sam said. "It's so damn hot, all we really need is cold beer."

"Maybe so," Jake said. "Give me a hand. Let's take one of these ice chests to the room. It'll save us return trips to the kitchen."

"What about the whiskey and gin?" Sam asked.

"Not enough hands here. We'll come back for them once we're situated."

They each grabbed a handle of the ice chest and started for their assigned bedroom. Carrying the candles in their free hands, they made it through the darkness with no mishaps. After shutting the door behind them, they began unbuttoning their shirts. It wasn't long before they opened all the bedroom windows. The marauding owl was hooting from a tall tree outside.

Sam grabbed a cold beer from the chest, tossed one to Jake and then sprawled on the bed. By this time, he'd removed his shirt as he lay bare-chested on the mattress.

"Say, Jake, I've never had the chance to talk to you alone since Belinda and I became a number. Do you hate me?"

"What the hell are you talking about?" Jake asked.

"You know damn well what I'm talking about. Belinda was your wife and I stole her from you."

"Kiss my ass," Jake said. "Belinda's a wonderful woman but I never loved her and I know damn well she never loved me. Our marriage was a sham. I'm glad she ended up with you."

"Still, I stole her from you," Sam said. "Sure there's no animosity there?"

"You think you stole her from me? You're hallucinating. Like I said, kiss my ass. Hell, buddy, you and Belinda were a number all through high school. It was the other way around. I stole her from you."

Sam popped the top of his beer. Jake joined him on the bed and opened his own ice cold can.

"Come to think of it, you're right about that," Sam said. "I've been worried about having hurt your feelings after all these years and all along it was you that's the sorry asshole."

Jake reached across the bed, tapping beer cans with Sam.

"Amen, brother, you're right about that."

"You mean I've spent some of the best years of my life worrying about destroying our friendship and all along it should have been you doing the worrying?"

"Suck it up," Jake said. "You know when it comes to women I've always been the best man. Remember the cheerleader you were so hot and heavy for?"

"Rhonda?"

"I slept with her," Jake said.

"You did not," Sam said.

"It was your own fault."

"How is that?"

"Every night when you'd come in from a date you'd tell me how good she was in bed. I finally decided to find out for myself."

"You didn't?"

"Oh, yes I did," Jake said.

Sam chugged his beer, tossed the empty can on the floor, and then rolled off the bed. After rummaging in the ice, he fished out two more cans and tossed one to Jake. Jake chugged the beer in his hand and tossed the can at a trashcan across the floor. Sam grinned when he missed miserably.

"Good thing you were such a great runner. You could never hit shit on the basketball court or football field."

"Shut the hell up. You're just going to let me tell you I screwed your best girlfriend and do nothing about it? What the hell are you smiling about?"

"I'm laughing about you, dating the prettiest girl in Oklahoma. You thought you were big man on campus. The homecoming queen, for God's sake. Remember the night she stood you up?"

"You didn't?" Jake said.

"Yes I did," Sam said.

Jake chugged the second beer, this time dropping the can to the side of the bed.

"Damn you!" he said.

Sam chugged his beer, tossing it at the trashcan and making it.

"Your turn," he said.

Jake climbed off the bed and fetched them two more beers.

"Good thing you were such a stud at throwing footballs and dunking basketballs. You couldn't run a lick with those size fourteen clodhoppers of yours."

"Jealous?" Sam asked.

"Hell no, I'm still man enough to kick your ass."

Jake soon had Sam in a neck lock, beer spilling all over the bedspread as they wrestled. They were both laughing when they tumbled off the bed onto the floor.

When their levity abated, Sam tossed Jake another beer.

"I'm so happy you aren't my enemy," he said. "You can't imagine how long I've worried about it."

"Hell, Sam, you're my best friend. Always were, always will be. You've taken better care of Belinda and Jeff than I ever did."

"I saved your skinny ass from drowning when you got a cramp in the middle of the White River during that camping trip we took to Arkansas," Sam said.

"I could out swim you any day of the week," Jake said.

"Not that day."

"The river stays fifty-two degrees year round," Jake said. "You have more muscle and body fat than me. My body fat at the time was non-existent."

"Hypothermia has no friends," Sam said.

"It's true; you saved my butt and you'll never let me forget it."

"No, I won't," Sam said. "Come to think of it, this is sort of like a camping trip. I'm enjoying the hell out of it."

"Yeah, well we'll have hell to pay if we let the girls beat us in Jeff's little game."

"They're no match for us," Sam said.

"Don't be too sure. Mama's a PhD. That stands for pretty damn smart."

"She's beautiful and has a body to match. How's she look naked?"

"Gorgeous personified," Jake said. "Her legs are as good as Belinda's, her ass even better. I haven't even told you about her tits yet. Whatever you do, keep your hands off of her."

"I don't play around anymore. I'm a family man now and I wasn't kidding when I said Jeff and Belinda mean the world to me. I would never do anything to abuse their trust."

"I have eyes," Jake said. "I worry Jeff thinks more of you as his father than me."

"No way. To Jeff, you're the best pop in the world. He never stops talking about you."

"He doesn't like cryptids," Jake said.

"Shit, bro, who does?"

"Everyone in America except apparently you and Belinda."

"I watched your show once when Belinda got drunk and fell asleep early. Pretty good stuff for a Tulsa homeboy."

"Thanks, I think," Jake said. "Doesn't make me stop wishing Jeff would join my production company and help me out instead of toiling in an industry I detest."

"Jeff's turning into one hell of an oilman. He would have made Granddaddy Hunt proud, I can tell you that."

"The old man made quite an impression on you," Jake said.

"He's the reason I became a geologist and have spent my life exploring for oil and gas."

"Better you than me," Jake said.

"When did you start dating black women?" Sam asked.

"When did you start being a racist prick?" Jake said.

"I'm not a racist."

"How many black friends do you have?"

"Not many," Sam said.

"More like not any," Jake said.

"My tax lawyer and his wife are black. Fred and I have lunch once or twice a week. He's a few years younger than me but played football at OU. He's one of my closest friends. We've been fishing together a dozen times. I've wanted to ask Fred and his wife to the house, but. . ."

"Belinda?"

"You know how she is," Sam said.

"I know," Jake said. "If you look up racist in the dictionary, her picture comes up."

Sam sipped his beer. "Not quite but pretty much. I can't swear to it but I think her dad was a Klan member."

"He was pretty far out there," Jake said. "He never liked me and the feeling was mutual. Guess he passed along his racial biases to Belinda."

"Maybe that's why Jeff devised this game we're playing. I can almost promise you Belinda and Mama aren't getting along well."

"Jake said, "Mama can handle herself. What say we go back to the kitchen and bring a couple of bottles of the real stuff back with us?"

"Good idea," Sam said. "After that, let's open the letter and read it before we get too drunk to stand up."

Mama patted Belinda's back until she stopped gasping. She backed away when Belinda caught her breath and shoved her away.

"Take your hands off me," she said.

Tall trees surrounding the north side of the house blocked any light from the moon and stars. Though lack of vision mattered, Mama had possessed unexplainable sensory perception she'd first discovered as a little girl. When she asked her grandmother about it, she'd gotten an answer that took her many years to learn the meaning of.

"Baby," her grandmother had said. "You got the touch. Don't ever misuse it."

Mama remembered her grandmother's words as she took Belinda's hand and started away through the darkness. Their eyes had dilated and they could see when they emerged from the trees amid a full moon and starry sky.

"How did you do that?" Belinda said.

"Don't ask. Does anything look familiar?"

Belinda yanked her hand out of Mama's. "I told you not to touch me," she said.

"My black doesn't rub off," Mama said. "Where are we?"

"I remember a path that leads to the gravesite," she said. "I don't see it."

Astral bodies weren't the only objects emitting light. The luminescent glow of fireflies pulsated around them as the chirp of crickets melded with a chorus of tree frogs.

A nearby rose garden filled the humid air with sugary fragrance. The odor further heightened Mama's sense of awareness. The softening of Belinda's rough edges signaled she was also feeling something.

"I smell roses," Mama said.

"Hunt's grave is beside the rose garden. I'm not sure which direction," Belinda said.

"I do," Mama said. "This way."

Belinda followed without asking her how she knew where she was going. Mama's sense of smell proved true. The scent of rose perfume grew ever stronger as they reached the flagstone walkway leading into the rose garden. Belinda clutched Mama's hand when she saw a blue light casting an unearthly glow into the sky.

"Don't be afraid," Mama said. "Whatever you see or think you see from this point on won't be real."

Mama gave Belinda's hand a yank, pulling her forward along the flagstone path.

Belinda had little conviction when she said, "There's no such things as ghosts."

"Yes, there are. Most are benevolent and wouldn't hurt a soul," Mama said.

The heavens turned suddenly dark, clouds covering the moon. Lightning began flashing across the darkened sky. Belinda held her ears to block the thunderous tumult erupting all around them. The wind had begun blowing their clothes when Mama grabbed Belinda's shoulders and shook her.

"What's happening?" Belinda said.

"Withdraw into your mind," Mama said. "None of this is real. Something is trying to frighten us. Don't let it."

Mama's words didn't matter as Belinda wrenched free from her grasp.

"We have to get out of here. Get back to the room."

A dark pit opened up in front of Belinda. She took a step, losing her footing and screamed as she slid into the pit.

"Oh my God! Leeches! Get them off of me."

Belinda was lying on the ground. In her mind, she was in a pit of leeches sucking her blood. Screaming hysterically, she grabbed at her arms, neck and face, trying to extricate herself from the bloodsuckers invading her eyes, nostrils and mouth. Mama took her hand and yanked her off the ground.

They had failed to find the second clue because they never reached Hunt's grave. Belinda was a head case, sobbing and speaking gibberish as Mama pulled her toward the house. Once the bedroom door was shut, Belinda collapsed in a fit of angst onto the floor as Mama began filling the antique brass bathtub with tepid water.

Not waiting for it to fill, Mama stripped off Belinda's clothes, and then her own, and dragged the distraught woman into the bathroom and under the shower. Belinda continued to weep as Mama scrubbed her with a washcloth.

"I'm washing away the leeches," Mama said. "They're going down the drain."

When the old brass bathtub was almost full, Mama fished in her backpack and found some essential oils: lavender, bergamot, frankincense, geranium, chamomile, and the woodsy scent of vetiver. Belinda was still crying, though softly now, when Mama led her to the tub and helped her into it. Mama followed her into the brass vessel, holding Belinda tightly until tepid water and the fragrant, earthy odor of therapeutic oils began working their magic.

# Chapter 19

Felix was asleep in his chair when Cain came for me. He didn't bother awakening his master, leading me upstairs instead to a guest bedroom. I wasn't prepared for the room's regal accommodations.

"I will return to awaken you tomorrow," he said before shutting the door behind him.

A priceless oriental rug covered much of the polished wood floor. The four-poster bed was made of teak, as were the various cabinets and tables. Even the wash basin was trimmed in gold and silver. I had undressed for the night and put out the candles when I heard someone running up the stairs outside my room. Opening the door a crack, I peeked out to see who it was.

Cain must have extinguished the gas lights after exiting my room because the hallway was dark. Only dispersed light from the floor below provided any illumination of a woman peering over the banister.

The young woman's body wracked with sobs as she stared at something or someone below her. She was naked beneath the translucent negligee gathering light from below. Sensing someone was behind her, she wheeled around, catching my gaze. Her stare lasted but a brief moment before she turned and hurried away down the darkened hallway. Though I had barely a glimpse of the young woman's face, I realized I knew her.

Except for the woman I'd seen in the hall, Cain was the last person I saw that night and the first person to greet me the following morning. It was still dark outside as he helped me gather my belongings.

As the sun arose on the other side of the mighty Mississippi River, we were already on our way to Moonmont plantation. Felix continued to sleep in the carriage. I sat up front with Joffrey. Having passed the outskirts of New Orleans, the carriage preceded along River Road, the bucolic thoroughfare bordering the edge of the giant river.

We passed many regal plantations, shirtless slaves already at work in the fields. The melancholy chants of a work gang echoed across the river as they pulled a barge with thick ropes. Joffrey spoke when he saw my look of concern.

"Even strong men die early on the river."

"Because?"

"Heat, humidity, dysentery, malaria and yellow jack. Many of those men will never see thirty."

"Do any ever escape?"

"Most do not even attempt it."

"What happens if they do?" I asked.

"If they are caught, their ears are cut off and they are branded. If they try and fail a second time, they are crippled by the severing of their Achilles tendon. They are branded again. If they try and fail a third time, they are executed."

"I see why few attempt to escape," I said.

"You don't sound like a slave. What's your story?"

"My British master saw to it I was educated."

"To what end?" I asked.

"He trusted no one except me."

"Not even his family and British cohorts?"

"He knew I had no bias and would always tell him the truth. I am sure it devastated him when Felix won me in a board game." Joffrey smiled for the first time. "He was born into wealth and not good at making decisions."

"You don't sound too displeased," I said.

"If it were not for his ill fortune, I would have never met Maurelle."

I rose a foot in the air when the carriage hit an unexpected pothole. Joffrey was grinning. It took me a moment to remember what we were discussing.

"Joffrey, I saw a young woman in the hallway outside my room last night. She was in her nightgown and appeared upset. Who is she?"

Joffrey seemed taken aback by my question. "The daughter of Felix and Maurelle."

"You just told me Felix and Maurelle have never consummated their marriage."

"She was born out of wedlock, years before the marriage occurred."

"If Maurelle is a fairy, how did she conceive a human daughter?"

"As I told you, Maurelle has all the feelings and emotions of a human woman. She is quite capable of making love and becoming impregnated."

"Please tell me about this daughter of Felix and Maurelle," I said.

"What you saw last night was a ghost. The daughter of Felix and Maurelle died when she fell over the banister."

"You think the person I saw was a ghost?"

"She would have to be," Joffrey said. "Aura Lea is dead."

"Aura Lea?"

"You seem surprised," Joffrey said.

"I know a woman named Aura. The woman I saw last night could have been her."

"There are many ghosts in New Orleans. Aura Lea is one of them."

We passed a paddle wheeler steaming toward New Orleans. It was so laden with bales of cotton its hull was barely above the waterline. Saving the tidbit of information about Aura for later, I asked another question.

"I thought sugar cane was the main crop around here," I said.

Joffrey's teeth gleamed in the sunlight when he smiled.

"I was born in Africa and I love African cooking, though nothing is better on earth than a plate of syrup and biscuits. Moonmont makes its own syrup and it's like sugary heaven."

"Syrup and biscuits was the only thing my father and I ever agreed on. Few things cure depression like syrup and biscuits. If you're having a bad day, or just need your soul uplifted, a plate of ambrosia of the gods is the answer."

When I reached to give Joffrey a high five, he stared at me as if I were crazy.

"You are not going to hit me, are you?" he asked.

"I was trying to give you a high five."

"What is a high five?" he asked.

"Stick your hand in the air," I said. When he did, I gave it a slap and grinned. "That, my friend is a high five."

Something sparkled on Joffrey's hand when we exchanged the high five. It was Maurelle's wedding ring. She was wearing it when I saw her at La Fée Verte.

"I thought you were warming Yvonne's bed last night."

"Yvonne slept alone. The rainstorm kept me at the Old François Place."

"I noticed Maurelle's reaction when you entered the bar. Felix also noticed. Are you and Maurelle romantically involved?"

Joffrey showed me the ring on his little finger. "We are married."

"Maurelle is married to Felix," I said.

"Their marriage was never consummated. Felix is a drunk, addicted to absinthe. He is jealous beyond belief though he remains unable or unwilling to complete his marital duties."

"Felix told me he was only twenty when they met. Surely. . ."

"To Maurelle's great dismay, they have had no sex since Felix became master of Moonmont. It is as if Felix's father returned from the dead and imparted his wishes and desires on his son."

"Is such a thing possible?" I asked.

"Maurelle believes it is."

"According to Felix, Maurelle practices powerful magic. If she believes Felix's father has invaded his body, why doesn't she use her magic to send the old bastard straight to hell?"

"Maurelle practices fairy magic. She would need a voodoo woman to accomplish what you suggest," Joffrey said.

He smiled when I said, "There are plenty of mambos and houngans in New Orleans. Why not pick one?"

"She still has feelings for Felix. If she thought she could rid him of his father's demon without killing him, she would surely do so."

"Did your marriage take place last night?" I asked.

"How did you know that?"

"Your ring was on Maurelle's hand last night at La Fée Verte. Is that the reason you didn't return to Yvonne's bed?"

"You ask too many questions? Joffrey said.

"May I ask one more?"

"Ask it," he said.

"What's Moonmont like?"

"Words cannot begin to describe it," Joffrey said. "The furniture, the rugs, the art are the finest money can buy. Because of sugar cane, Felix's father became rich beyond imagination. Felix's mother made many trips to France to purchase the trappings of their wealth. You will soon see."

"How did Felix's father treat his slaves?" I asked.

"He abused a few and bedded even more," Joffrey said. "He had no evil streak such as the one the master possesses."

"Am I going to rue my decision about visiting Moonmont?"

"Not if you are a typical white man, though I do not believe you are."

"Maybe I can arrange to put some arsenic in Felix's syrup and biscuits."

"Maybe," he said.

"How do the slaves feel about having such a cruel master?" When Joffrey looked away without answering, I said, "Something going on you want to tell me about?"

"Nothing is going on," he finally said.

"Who does Felix intend to punish?"

"I do not believe he knows as yet."

"You have to be kidding. We've come all this way to punish someone who hasn't done anything?"

"To make an example of," Joffrey said.

"And you have no idea who the person will be?"

"Slaves are valuable. It will be someone the master sees as expendable; an old man or woman. Someone the other slaves look up to. He will concoct some transgression which he will characterize as grave."

"Does this happen often?"

"Only when the master begins to believe the slaves are becoming too uppity," Joffrey said. "Perhaps we should talk about something else."

"Sorry," I said. "This is painful for me. I can only imagine how it makes you feel. What's this beast Felix was telling me about? The one that protects Maurelle."

"His name is Grishorn. He is immortal. Maurelle says he has been on earth since the beginning of time."

"Have you seen him?" I asked.

Joffrey nodded. "He stays close to Maurelle. He can read people's minds, and their hearts."

"What does he look like?"

"Like a big hairless dog with crooked teeth and a fin that runs down his back to the tip of his tail."

Joffrey shook his head when I asked, "You think this beast is a dog?"

"He is a supernatural creature who can walk on his back legs, leap twenty feet into the air, and climb up a vertical wall like a spider. He is no dog."

"How do you know he is dangerous?" I asked.

"Once, when Maurelle was walking near a pond, an alligator attacked her. Grishorn came screaming from nowhere and took the giant alligator in his mouth. He literally bit him into two pieces."

"How big is he?" I asked.

"Grishorn is a creature indigenous people call a shapeshifter. He can grow wings and fly, and change his body from the size of a mouse to a monster-sized beast."

"No wonder Felix is afraid of him. Seems he would never do Maurelle any harm as long as Grishorn is around."

"All of her powers lie in the magic pendant she wears around her neck," Joffrey said.

"I've never heard that. What would happen if she lost her pendant?"

"Grishorn would be powerless to protect her and Felix would likely kill her."

"You can't be serious," I said.

"Felix likes to dominate, and not be dominated."

"He has no power to steal the pendant, does he?" I asked.

"I am the only one that Maurelle trusts enough to even touch the pendant."

"Would you steal it from her?"

Joffrey's grave expression indicated my unexpected question was a worry to him.

"Of course not. Why would you even ask?" he said.

"Just wondering," I said.

"I would never violate Maurelle's trust."

"Not even for a greater good?" I said.

"I have no idea to what you are referring," Joffrey said.

"Just jabbering," I said. Felix looks at least twenty years older than Maurelle."

"Maurelle does not age."

"Is she immortal like Grishorn?"

"Except for her wings, she is a normal woman in every way."

"Sure about that?"

Joffrey didn't answer my question and his stilted explanation caused me to wonder what he knew to be true. Seeing my questions were causing him to withdraw, I decided to pursue the subject another time.

"How far are we from Moonmont?" I asked.

"We'll be there within the hour," he said.

Joffrey turned away, refusing to engage me further in conversation. We passed more steamboats on the river, more chain gangs monitored by whip-brandishing bosses. A flock of seagulls, engaged in an insect feeding frenzy, flew overhead. Another hour passed before we reached the plantation.

Moonmont proved more magnificent than I could have imagined. Columns reminiscent of a Greek portico surrounded the epic three-storied structure centered in the middle of a live oak forest. Fully a dozen tuxedoed and regally dressed slaves awaited our arrival as Joffrey pulled the carriage to a halt.

Finally awake, Felix exited the carriage, walked up the steps and disappeared into the magnificent cut glass and cypress front door without so much as a smile. He greeted no one from any of those awaiting his arrival. The people in the reception party seemed to expect as much and quickly dispersed.

"Hope that's not a sign of things to come," I said.

"Everyone knows why the master is here. Someone has hell to pay. The staff is nervous, none of them knowing who is destined to take the brunt of his punishment," Joffrey said.

"How can that be?" I said. "Surely, he has someone in mind that has committed an act of insubordination."

"You do not know the master very well," he said.

Before I could answer, a regal black man with snowy white hair covering his head helped me down from the carriage.

"I'm Samuel," he said. "You must be Monsieur Thomas."

"Yes, I am. Pleased to meet you, Samuel."

He quickly pulled his hand loose from my grasp when I attempted to shake it.

"Sorry, sir," he said. "It is not allowed for slaves to shake hands with white people."

When I glanced up at the dispersing crowd on the porch, I realized Felix, his arms tightly folded around his chest, was watching us. The stern expression on his face quickly informed me he didn't like what he was seeing.

Samuel also saw Felix and the look on his face was nothing less than abject fear. He grabbed my bag and hustled up the steps leading to the cypress porch surrounding Moonmont.

"Hope I didn't get him into trouble," I said.

Joffrey didn't answer as he drove away in the carriage.

## Chapter 20

When I opened my eyes, I was in the little bar on Pirate's Alley. Though it seemed I'd been away for days, La Fée Verte was exactly the same as if I had only closed my eyes for a brief moment. One noticeable thing was different. Aura was standing behind me and looking very much concerned.

"What are you doing here?" I said.

"I followed you. Everything okay?"

"Don't know. I can't seem to keep my eyes open."

"Maybe you've had too much to drink."

"I'm an alcoholic. I don't drink. Remember?"

"Uh huh," she said. "Then why is there an empty drink glass on the bar in front of you?"

"Someone else's maybe?"

Aura's head moved in a slow motion denouncement of my excuse.

"I don't think so," she said.

How long have you been here?"

"Long enough to meet Yvonne, Ben and Doris. Excuse me a moment. I have to visit the ladies room."

As Aura walked away, I noticed the dirty look

Yvonne was giving me. "Thought you said you were unattached."

"I am," I said.

"Not according to Miss Big Tits."

"She's not my girlfriend, and I never noticed her tits being that big."

Yvonne's answer dripped with sarcasm. "I'll bet you haven't."

"We're just friends."

"Not what she said."

"What did she say?"

"Nothing, at least in so many words. Doesn't matter. Women can always tell."

"You're wrong. We've never even held hands."

Ben and Doris were involved in a whispered conversation of their own and ignoring our bantering. Their absinthe glasses were also empty though neither seemed impaired by the alcohol they had consumed. When Aura returned, I got off the stool and let her sit.

"Have one of Yvonne's absinthe cocktails. I'll be right back."

The cocktail I'd drank was strong, my legs weak and head woozy as I walked to the men's room to pat cold water on my face. When I returned, Aura and Yvonne were talking. Standing behind Aura, I rubbed my hands up and down her back.

"What the hell are you doing?" she asked.

Pulling back my hands, I said, "Nothing."

"Well, stop it, you creep."

"Sorry."

The brief feel I'd copped of Aura's back and shoulder blades answered the question the ghost in the hallway had raised in my mind. Though I still didn't know if I'd been dreaming, or imagining my visit to the past, the vestigial bumps near Aura's shoulder blades confirmed it was possible she was part fairy. I pulled up the empty stool beside her.

"You were zoned out when I arrived," Aura said. "I started to call 9-1-1."

"I'm fine," I said.

Yvonne shoved another absinthe cocktail in front of me.

"Compliments of Ben and Doris," she said.

"How many have I had?"

"This one's your second."

"Sure about that?" I asked.

"I keep tabs."

She grinned when I said, "I'll bet you do."

After Yvonne had disappeared into the back, I slid the absinthe cocktail toward Aura.

"You drink it," I said.

"Maybe a sip," she said, touching the glass to her lips. The sip caused her to have an instant reaction. "Whoa! That's strong."

"What are those two bony bumps on your back?" I said.

"It's not nice to bring up someone's deformities."

"No deformity. They could be anscestral wings," I said.

"You're drunk."

She stared at me as if I were a complete idiot when I said, "I'm not drunk."

"That's not what it looks like to me," Aura said.

"I wasn't passed out. I was time traveling."

Aura pushed the drink farther away from me. "You really don't need this," she said.

"Something triggered my journey into the past. I think it was the absinthe."

"What sort of fantasy are you having?"

"No fantasy. I was born with a special talent."

"Such as?"

"The ability to travel through time, though I've yet to figure out how to trigger it. It must have been the absinthe cocktail."

A boisterous couple carrying on in the alley outside the bistro door interrupted Aura's cocked-head stare.

"You're talking nonsense," she said.

"I spent last night in the guest bedroom of the Old François Place. Only thing is it was two hundred years in the past. I heard a commotion outside my room. When I peeked out I saw a woman in a transparent negligee."

Aura smirked. "You were having a wet dream."

"I only got a glimpse of the woman's face. It was you."

"You're crazy," Aura said.

"When I quizzed Joffrey the following morning, he told me it was the daughter of Felix and Maurelle."

"I have no idea who those people are," she said.

"Felix François was the rich sugar planter who owned the Old François Place, Moonmont Plantation, and this bar. Maurelle was his wife, the fairy in the portrait at the top of the stairs, and just maybe the woman in refrigerated storage at UNO."

"And Joffrey?"

"A slave Felix won in a backgammon game. He speaks with a British accent, is quite intelligent, and is Felix's personal assistant."

"Assuming I believed any of your time travel BS, what's it have to do with the Cryptid Hunter reality show?"

"The pendant Madam Aja gave me has a missing moonstone. The pendant's magic only works if the missing moonstone is found and restored to the pendant."

"What does any of that have to do with time travel?" Aura asked.

"The clues I need to find the moonstone lie in the past. Someone took the pendant from Maurelle. I believe that person was Joffrey, her lover. Someone she trusted."

"For what reason?"

"Don't know yet." I said. "Bottom line is it makes you, or your long dead ancestor, the daughter of Maurelle, your DNA half-fairy, half-human."

"I'm not a fairy. You can see how tall I am," she said.

"Part fairy."

"You are so full of shit!"

"Am I? You have ancestral wings."

"They're just bony bumps. A defect of birth."

"I don't think so," I said. "We had just arrived at Moonmont, Felix's sugar cane plantation when I awoke back here in the bar. I was geting a handle on an important slice of unwritten history when the absinthe wore off. I have to return to Moonmont Plantation."

"You're either still drunk or else bat shit crazy," Aura said.

"Neither. Please, trust me."

"I find your story full of holes and impossible to believe. There's no such thing as time travel."

"I could have been dreaming while I was passed out. I don't think so. If I wasn't really there then how did I know about the bumps on your back?"

"I have no clue. Doesn't matter because I'm a scientist and don't believe in the paranormal."

"This little adventure began with a paranormal experience. Madam Aja visited me after she'd died. She gave me Maurelle's pendant. Now, like it or not, you're part of it."

"Impossible," Aura said.

"Suspend your disbelief. Science can't explain everything."

Aura pushed the absinthe cocktail toward me.

"Then chug it and see what happens," she said.

Light from a crack in the curtains awakened me. I was beneath the covers of a four-poster bed in a darkened room I didn't recognize. I wasn't alone. Aura was beside me. We both sat up in bed.

"Where are we?" she asked.

"Moonmont Plantation, I think. What are you doing here?"

"You drank half of the absinthe cocktail. I slugged the rest and grabbed your arm. You're naked!"

She covered her breasts when I said, "I'm not the only one."

"Why are we naked?"

"Clothes can't pass through time portals," I said. "This has happened to me before."

"Why didn't you tell me?"

"I didn't know you were coming with me. Now that you're here, we have a problem."

"What problem?"

"Felix thinks you're dead. Hell, it may have even been him that killed you."

"I'm not dead. Stop talking about me in the past tense," she said.

"Sorry. Turn around."

She turned her back to me, sensing what it was I wanted to see.

"I've always been self-conscious about the bumps," Aura said. "I haven't had sex with that many men. Most of them never noticed. That prick Seth Daniels noticed."

"Did he say something insensitive?"

"He thought the bumps were kinky and was caressing them the entire time we made love. I should have known then what a pervert he is."

"Stop talking about it," I said. "Your body's on fire and radiating enough heat to raise my own ten degrees. I'm horny enough without erotic commentary about one of your sexual escapades."

"You're an asshole but I feel it too," she said. "Doesn't matter. Now isn't the time or place for hot, sweaty sex."

"Maybe not but it's the only thing on my mind right now."

"Mine too," she said. "Let's find some clothes before we start acting out our thoughts."

Early morning sunlight filtered through the edges of the room's curtains. The room became flooded with light when I opened them, Aura primping in front of the mirror on an antique dresser. Her nudity highlighted a yellow butterfly tattoo just below her belly button. Grabbing her shoulders, I ran my hands down her back.

"I can see why Seth was so horny," I said.

"Hurry up and find us some clothes to wear. And keep your hands to yourself," she said.

"Spoil sport."

Aura opened an armoire and began rummaging through the clothes inside it.

"There's probably underwear in that chest of drawers," she said. "Find us some, and hurry."

We were both soon outfitted in regal clothing fit for French royalty some two hundred years ago.

"Now what?" Aura asked.

"Do you have a middle name?"

"What's that have to do with anything?"

"Just tell me," I said.

"Lea. My full name is Aura Lea Hartel. Why?"

"Aura Lea is the name of Felix and Maurelle's daughter."

"My dad is a college history professor, his specialty the Civil War. Aura Lea was a popular song for both the Union and Confederate soldiers."

"I'm guessing we have a good fifty years or so before the Civil War begins."

"Doesn't matter. Aura Lea was a common name for a lengthy period of time. It's just a coincidence I have the same name as Felix's daughter."

"Not when you consider your wing bumps."

"You're annoying," she said.

"Coincidence or not, it's going to raise more questions than we can answer if Felix finds you here with me."

"You have a plan?"

"I don't. Until we do, you need to make yourself scarce."

"How do you suggest I do that?" she asked.

"It's still early. Let's see if we can find an empty room where you can hang out unnoticed for awhile."

"Sooner or later, people will know I'm here."

"We have to do something."

"I need to stay with you until we return to where we came from. If I don't, I'll be stuck in the past."

"My last dose of absinthe lasted less than two days. Since we just arrived, we should have until at least noon tomorrow to do our business."

"What if you're wrong?" she asked.

"This is a working experiment. It's the best I can do."

"I'm hungry," Aura said. "I can't go until noon tomorrow without food and water."

"Let's find you a place to hide. I'll bring you something to eat and drink."

After finding a locked bedroom down the hall, I used my burglary skills to open the door. The interior of the bedroom was musty, sheets covering the furniture and the four-poster bed.

"It's creepy in here," Aura said.

"No one has been in this room for years," I said.

"Except maybe a few dozen ghosts."

"I didn't think you believed in ghosts."

"Doesn't stop me from having a vivid imagination."

"Ghosts or not, it's perfect. I'll bring you a pitcher of fresh water, and food. You'll be fine."

"And what if I'm not?" she asked.

"I'll check in with you every few hours. What could go wrong?"

"You're leaving me with plenty of doubt as to why I should trust you."

"You have a better plan?" I said.

"Get the hell out of here before I claw your eyes out," she said.

Aura had removed the dropcloth from the bed and was lying on the royal blue comforter when I returned with the pitcher of water from our room.

"Don't forget me," she said as I shut the door behind me.

The sound of a crowd resounded from outside when I returned to my bedroom. Something was about to happen in the liveoaks beneath my window. I stared out to see what the uproar was.

A crowd of mostly slaves encircled a spectacle waiting to happen. A shirtless black man was on his knees, his wrists shackled around a stump, his back exposed to the bull whip in the hands of Felix François. The old man moaned when wet leather slashed a long red welt across his back. Every slave in the circle moaned and began crying along with him.

Shrieks of pain continued until Felix had delivered twenty lashes. I watched from the window, sick at my stomach and unable to speak.

Felix stopped the beating, glancing upward as lightning flashed across a darkened sky. The lightning was close because a clap of thunder quickly shook the house. As rain began to fall, Felix tossed the bullwhip to an aide and hurried to the covered porch of Moonmont Plantation.

The room and my conscience, consumed with guilt for witnessing such a brutal act and doing nothing to stop it grew dark. To make matters worse, the old man still shackled to the stump, bleeding and gravely injured was Samuel, the man whose hand I had shook the previous evening.

## Chapter 21

Joffrey barged into the bedroom, his angry glare a visual signal he thought I was responsible for the beating I had just witnessed.

"Will Samuel be okay?" I asked.

"The sudden thunderstorm saved him, or the master would surely have beaten him to death. It will take him weeks to recover, if he ever does."

"I'm so sorry."

Joffrey's glare softened. "You could not have known," he said.

"Doesn't make me feel any less guilty. Is there anything I can do?"

"The master had salt water thrown on his back. It didn't kill him and will probably stop infection. The women are salving his wounds. Only God knows if he will survive."

"I'm so sorry," I repeated.

"Slaves have short memories, or else they would not survive for long. Grief is reserved for freemen. Right now, the master wishes to see you," Joffrey said. "Come with me."

Priceless rugs covered the hardwood floor, original art painted by French masters, fit for a

Paris museum, hung from the walls. I had no idea Felix's family possessed such enormous wealth and was blown away by the trappings of affluence gracing a lonely hallway most people would never see. Felix's office was no less spectacular.

The Old François Place, Felix's Creole townhouse in the French Quarter was impressive. Compared to Moonmont Plantation with its spiral staircases, marble, alabaster, and ebony details, the Old François Place was a pauper's hovel. Felix's study amazed me even more when Joffrey opened the door and beckoned me to enter.

Felix sat behind a intricately carved French country desk, not bothering to rise or even look up when I entered the room. Flocked-red wallpaper, complete with original art, covered the walls. A large window behind the desk allowed Felix to keep an eye on the plantation.

"You wished to see me?" I said.

Without glancing up from the paper on which he was writing, he said, "Please, sit. I am all but finished."

Though I tried to recline in the high-top chair situated in front of his desk, its forward cant made it seem as if I were about to slide off on the floor. I had little doubt Felix had designed it that way. He finally finished the letter and put away his fountain pen. As a lawyer, a profession that prizes beautiful pens, I wondered what Felix's instrument would be worth in modern-day New Orleans. Felix must have noticed my gaze.

"You like the pen?"

"It's beautiful," I said.

"From England. One of the first of its kind ever made. It cost me a small fortune." I flinched, almost dropping the valuable pen when he tossed it to me. "Take it. It is yours."

"I can't," I said.

"Of course, you can. Every successful advocat

must possess a valuable pen to prove to the world how potent they are. There may soon be an occasion for you to use it on my behalf."

Felix smiled when I said, "Does it have anything to do with your expertise with a bullwhip?"

"You read my mind," he said. "I am hosting a meeting of all the plantation owners tomorrow, Jean Albard Trintignant, a government official from New Orleans will be the guest of honor."

"An unexpected guest?" I asked.

"An official visit designed for maximum intimidation of planter's on River Road.."

"The Americans own Louisiana now. How is Trintignant involved with their regime?"

Felix made a face and spit into a trashcan beside his desk.

"There are always those who are willing to forsake their heritage in order to advance their personal fortunes," he said. "The Americans own Trintignant. He is no friend of the French planters along River Road."

"The Americans may think they control Louisiana but French planters still own all the sugar cane plantations on the river. What are you afraid of?" I asked.

"Trintignant has been appointed by the Americans to impart their will upon us."

"To what purpose?" I said.

"To wrest control of our plantations," Felix said.

"That's an unfounded conspiracy theory," I said. "There's no proof of that."

"Proof depends on the provider of the evidence," he said.

"Even if the conspiracy is true, what part does Trintignant play?"

Felix leaned back in his well-stuffed chair. Outside the open window, a woman shouted at a group of children playing in the rain. When thunder struck, and a gust of wind sent the chandeliers rattling, Felix got out of his chair and shut the open window.

"The slave revolt in Haiti changed everything on River Road," he said. "Slaves who have made their way here from Haiti have fomented rebellion and ideas of independence. The planters have already had to quell several minor attempted insurrections. We are here today because the pot is beginning to boil."

"Is that the reason you chose to discipline Samuel?" I asked.

"Slaves outnumber planters many times over. Though they have no firearms, they could wreak havoc if they had a leader and joined forces against us."

"You suspect something?" I asked.

"More than suspect. We have informants among the slaves who are loyal to their masters. There have always been rumblings of dissent. Things are different now."

"How so?"

"As yet, all we have are rumors."

"Rumors?" I said.

"Clandestine meetings taking place between slave emissaries from various plantations."

"Sounds more serious than rumor."

"We sugar cane planters are having our own meetings to try and assuage the situation. Samuel's beating was not one of a kind."

"And Trintignant is here to try to intimidate the planters?"

"To convince us, by brute force if necessary, to proceed along a path that will ultimately result in the Americans annexing our property."

"What do you need me to do?" I asked.

"Cover my ass," he said.

"You were within your rights to discipline

Samuel."

"The Americans are more corrupt than the Spanish. If they can manipulate reality, they may concoct a way to seize our property."

"I await your instructions," I said.

"When the time arrives, use your expensive pen to sign an important document with which you will be provided."

He smiled when I said, "Will I get to read it first?"

"Of course you will," he said.

I'd had little time to process Felix's words when a large hand clasped my shoulder. It was Joffrey. I realized he had been in the room throughout the entire conversation.

"The meeting is concluded. Please come with me."

Felix didn't bother acknowledging the end of our meeting as I followed Joffrey into the hall.

We were halfway down the corridor when I said, "You're a spy."

Joffrey grinned, not bothering to deny my allegation. He was apparently an important person, not just with Felix but also with the house servants, many of whom we passed on the way to the kitchen.

"Are you hungry?" he asked.

"I can't remember the last time I had something to eat."

"Then it is time you did."

Three women in long dresses, aprons and with tignons covering their hair greeted Joffrey when we entered the kitchen. One of the women was stirring something in a large black kettle over a fire in the hearth. An entire pig was roasting and a savory aroma filled the large room. I joined Joffrey at a plank table.

"These ladies are the finest cooks in all of Louisiana," he said. "Monsieur Wyatt cannot remember the last time he ate and we need to feed him."

"You know there is always food in the Moonmont Plantation kitchen," the woman wearing a flowered dress and yellow tignon said.

"That is an absolute truth," Joffrey said.

"Only the finest for you, Joffrey."

"I think you are lying," Joffrey said, "but a beautiful liar who is also a wonderful cook."

"Sugar would not melt in this one's mouth," she said.

Joffrey was grinning when he said, "Wyatt, this is Esther, the queen bee of Moonmont Plantation.

Esther was more than attractive; she had the regal nose, eyes and facial features of a black Cleopatra. Her dark eyes and hint of a smile revealed she had deep feelings for Joffrey. It was apparent he also knew it.

"You know you love me, Esther."

"Not as much as you love yourself," she said. "I cannot speak for Shug and Miss Peach."

Esther's comment resulted in titters of laughter from the two young women cutting vegetables on a plank table. Both were dressed alike. When they turned to face us, I saw they were identical twins.

"Those two are the most beautiful girls on this plantation," Joffrey said. "Come hug my neck."

All smiles, Shug and Miss Peach did just that. Shug giggled when Joffrey patted her behind. Not done, he pulled both young women into his lap. The three were quickly laughing, tickling each other and getting out of control when Esther began tapping her foot.

"You girls get back to work before I lift those pretty purple skirts you got on and paddle your behinds."

Shug and Miss Peach unraveled themselves from Joffrey's grasp and returned to cutting vegetables, both giggling at his parting remark.

"You are so right, Esther. Shug and Miss Peach need a good spanking though instead of your paddle I would use the palm of my hand on their bare bottoms."

"Do it," Esther said. "They both need it. Just let me be there to watch."

"Good thing this isn't the twenty-first century," I said.

"I beg your pardon," Joffrey said.

"Nothing," I said.

We were soon eating a succulent pork and vegetable stew. After Joffrey had downed a second heaping bowl, he kissed Esther's cheek and pinched her bottom.

Shug and Miss Peach giggled when he said, "Bring those two girls to my room later tonight, Esther and I will show you the proper way to discipline kitchen help."

Esther was smiling as we exited the kitchen and headed up the stairs. Joffrey had a big surprise when we entered the bedroom. Not liking the room where I'd left her, Aura had returned to mine. When Joffrey saw her, he grabbed his heart and took a step backward.

"Is that you, Aura Lea?" he asked.

"I'm Aura. Who are you?"

"Are you a ghost?"

"I don't think so," she said. "How did you know my name?"

Joffrey touched Aura's shoulder. "You are alive," he said. "I was staring into a pine box last time I saw you."

"Very much alive," Aura said. "I have no idea who you are, or what the hell you're yammering about."

Joffrey glanced at me for an explanation.

"A voodoo woman zombied her," I said. "Except for her name, she doesn't remember anything about her past life."

Joffrey touched Aura's face with the back of his hand.

"You do not look like a zombie," he said.

Aura glared at me when I said, "Trust me, she is."

"Where did you come from?" Joffrey asked.

"She's here with me," I said, "She needs something to eat."

"Zombies need neither food nor drink."

"To hell with that," Aura said. "I haven't eaten for hours and I'm starving."

"I will get her something," Joffrey said.

I grabbed his arm, stopping him when he started for the door.

"You mustn't tell anyone Aura is here."

"And why is that?"

"Aura and I are here to help with the insurrection."

Joffrey locked my gaze for a long moment. "You are lying. You are the master's advocat," he finally said. "Here to stop an insurrection not to abet in one."

"Have you heard of Madam Aja?"

"Everyone knows Madam Aja," Joffrey said. "She is dead."

"No more than Aura is dead. Madam Aja zombied Aura and sent her here to help you. Esther knows. Ask her if you don't believe me."

"I will consider your claim," Joffrey said before disappearing down the hallway.

"Who is Esther and what was that all about?" Aura asked.

"According to Joffrey, Esther is Moonmont's queen bee."

"How does she know Madam Aja?" Aura asked.

"I don't know that she does."

"Then what makes you think she'll corroborate your story?"

"I have a feeling," I said. "Maybe Madam Aja will intercede."

"You're a trusting bastard," Aura said. "What's all the malarkey about zombies?"

"You're the student of history. When did the largest slave revolt in Louisiana occur?"

"1811," she said. "What about it?"

"I think we've reverted in time to 1811, Joffrey a primary player in the revolt yet to occur. The skeletal finger with the wedding ring we found at the Old François Place is Joffrey's finger. The wedding ring belonged to Maurelle."

"We found a gold Napoleon dated 1811 at the dig," Aura said.

"I don't have a clue where to look for the missing moonstone but I'm convinced it was Joffrey who took the pendant from Maurelle. I believe the pendant has something to do with the slave insurrection."

"What made you think Joffrey would know about Madam Aja and believe I'm a zombie?"

"Madam Aja is a famous voodoo woman, and she is a Traveler. She's the person who gave me the magic pendant. She knew Maurelle so it makes sense she also knew Joffrey."

"Most people don't believe in zombies," she said.

"Joffrey spent much of his life in Haiti. Hell, he's probably seen more zombies than we can imagine."

"Tell me again about Joffrey and Maurelle"

"Joffrey is Maurelle's husband," I said.

"Felix is her husband."

"Their marriage was never consummated. Joffry told me so."

"Then why didn't she just divorce him?" Aura

asked.

"Divorce him so she could marry a slave? I don't think so. Their marriage was symbolic even if very real in their own minds."

"So what's your plan?" Aura asked.

"The revolt turned out badly for all the slaves involved. Joffrey lost his head and a hand. Someone chopped off Maurelle's wings. Felix disappeared and his body never found."

"Who told you that?" Aura asked.

"Armand and Madam Toulouse Joubert, two authenticators I spoke with before going to La Fée Verte."

"You trust them?"

"They know more about New Orleans than anyone alive."

"What else did they tell you?"

"The moonstone pendant Madam Aja entrusted me with is quite famous. It's known by collectors as the Moon of Erato. The moonstone's brilliance, according to Armand and Madam Toulouse, is caused by microscopic flaws in the surface of the stone. The flaws produce the stone's brilliant colors. They are rare, and some believe to be magical. Collectors call the cyclical bands of fiery light Cycles of the Moon. Somehow, Maurelle lost the pendant."

"Felix didn't take it from her?" Aura asked.

"Seems to me only one person had the opportunity," I said.

"Who?" Aura asked.

I waited for thunder to stop rocking the walls of Moonmont when I said, "Joffrey."

# Chapter 22

Jake and Sam returned to the kitchen for scotch and Bombay Gin, Sam fingering Jeff's envelope as he mixed himself a tall scotch and water. Jake was searching the cabinets for a bottle of Fentiman's Tonic Water.

"Damn it," he finally said. "There's no Bombay Gin and no Fentiman's."

"Suck it up," Sam said. "Have some scotch instead."

"Gin is my favorite."

"Then drink what you have."

"I refuse to drink this cheap swill," Jake said. "Throw me that bottle and a glass."

Jake poured three fingers of scotch into the glass and then added a splash of water, not bothering with ice. He didn't make a face when he took a drink. Sam was smirking and shaking his head.

"I didn't think you liked scotch," he said.

"Once, Colley and I were lost in a dark chamber of an Egyptian pyramid."

"Sounds serious."

"All we had to drink was a bottle of cheap scotch Colley had managed to buy in Cairo. The bottle was empty when our rescuers found us. I was about to panic."

"Then you do like scotch."

"Colley likes Kentucky whiskey. It didn't stop him from drinking scotch."

Sam laughed as he touched glasses with Jake. "Let's open this envelope before our candles go out," he said.

"Do it and tell me what it says," Jake said.

Sam read the letter, made a face and said, "Hell, it's some sort of riddle."

"Then read it to me."

"There's a hole in the earth where spirits abound, the color purple 1892 the spot where you'll find your clue."

"What the hell's that supposed to mean?" Jake asked.

"Damned if I know. I'm not good at riddles even when I'm sober," Sam said. "Maybe we should find something to eat and tail off the alcohol."

"To hell with that," Jake said. "Jeff's messing with our minds. The clue we are looking for has to be someplace in the house."

"No, it doesn't. Jeff said it could be anywhere on the grounds of the estate."

"You and I have explored every foot of this place," Jake said. "If there were holes in the ground, we'd know where they were."

"Swimming pool, maybe? Doesn't really matter," Sam said. "I'm too drunk to swim to the bottom of the pool."

"The water in the pool is blue, not purple," Jake said.

"Where, then?" Sam asked.

"There's one place we never went. Hunt wouldn't let us."

"You're right," Sam said. "Hunt's wine cellar. He kept it padlocked. Have you been down there?"

"I cut the lock after he died. When Belinda and I lived here, I'd go down occasionally and fetch us a bottle of prize wine."

"That's gotta be it," Sam said. "Our clue is in Hunt's wine cellar beneath a bottle of 1892 red."

"Has to be," Jake said. "Let's have another drink and then go check out the cellar."

Jake and Sam's candles were little more than stubs when they left the kitchen and started down the dark hallway to the entrance of Hunt's wine cellar. The temperature in the old house steamy, both men's shirts were soaked in perspiration by the time they found the door. It was so dark, they couldn't see to the bottom of the steep staircase.

"Good thing we're not drunk," Jake said.

"Speak for yourself," Sam said. "Where's the rail on these damn stairs?"

"Hunt didn't make it easy."

Sam took a cautious step. "An understatement," he said.

"Better let me go first," Jake said. "The stairs aren't even. I almost broke my neck first time I came down here."

"Hunt again?"

"He booby trapped them," Jake said.

"My candle's gone," Sam said. "I can't see a thing. Maybe we should go back upstairs and find more candles."

"This won't take long," Jake said. "Hunt was anal retentive, all the bottles arranged by year and color. Let's find the clue and get the hell out of here."

"You scared?"

"You want to go first, big boy? If not, then let go of my shoulder before you crush it."

"Sorry," Sam said.

Jake's candle went out when they reached the bottom of the stairs. The temperature was no longer stifling, their sweat-soaked shirts becoming cloyingly cold to the touch.

"Doesn't matter how anal Hunt was," Sam said. "It's dark as pitch down here. We'll never find anything. Let's go back upstairs."

"Amen to that. I'm right behind you," Jake said.

Jake clutched Sam's shirttails as he slowly ascended the stairs. When they reached the door, Sam grabbed the handle.

"Holy hell!" he said. "It's locked."

"Impossible," Jake said. "The door doesn't have a lock."

"Then you try it," Sam said.

He waited as Jake grabbed the door handle and began yanking on it.

"Son of a bitch," he said. "Now what?"

"Turn around and look," Sam said.

Mama tossed a fluffy towel to Belinda and used another to dry herself. After wrapping the damp towel around her hair, she rifled through a chest of drawers until she found two baby doll nighties, one blue and one pink. She tossed the blue one to Belinda. Mama adjusted the skimpy straps on her shoulder.

"Kind of like erotic lingerie, don't you?" Mama asked.

"Shut the hell up," Belinda said.

"Our candles are all but gone," Mama said. "There's nothing more we can do tonight. I'm going to bed."

The hour had grown late, a cool breeze blowing in through the open windows. The temperature had finally lowered enough to where Mama thought she could get some sleep. She tossed an orange Afghan to Belinda who was sitting in the chair. She was barely asleep when the temperature in the room turned icy.

An ephemeral glow had suddenly lighted the room. Belinda's eyes were opened wide as she stared at the shadowy wraith standing before her. The owl outside the window flew away in a flurry of beating wings.

Belinda didn't hear the owl, and was unable to scream. Barely the peep of a word rasped from her mouth.

"Help!"

Mama was instantly awake. Jumping out of bed, she rushed to Belinda's chair and grabbed her shoulders.

"I'm here," she said. "It's Grandpa Hunt."

Whoever the ghost was, they wanted to make themselves known. Bathed in green light, it finally appeared.

"Who are you?" Mama demanded.

"Your arch enemy," the ghost replied.

"Are you Hunt?" Mama asked.

"It matters not who I am," the wraith replied.

"If you have no right here," Mama said, "then get ye hence."

"This is my house," the wraith answered.

"Then you are Hunt," Mama said. "Answer me. Who are you?"

"Hudson Huntington," the ghost replied. "This is my house."

"Not any longer."

"My son doesn't want it. He has forsaken his heritage."

"Not so," Mama said. "He's living the dream you instilled in him as a youth. He's doing what you secretly wanted to do yourself."

"Then who will take care of this house?"

"It is your grandson's house. You helped pull him through the car accident, didn't you?"

"He needed me," the ghost said.

"And he survived. This is his house now. Relinquish it to him."

"There is no place for me to go," the ghost said.

"Yes, there is," Mama said. "You answered the call. You are free to cross over. Do it now."

A glowing light appeared behind the ghost of Grandpa Hunt. It seemed to call to him because he turned and stared. Finally, he started toward the beckoning glow. When he passed through it, the opening closed as he disappeared. Mama was holding Belinda and she was crying.

"Hunt is gone," Mama said. "He'll never haunt Huntington Manor again."

Belinda put her arms around Mama, her tears wetting her shoulder.

"Was that really Grandpa Huntington's ghost?"

"Yes. I gave him a reason and permission to cross over. He's gone."

"Cross over?"

"Move on to a different astral plane." Mama led Belinda to the bed and covered her with a sheet. "You're safe here. I'll sleep in the chair."

Belinda grabbed Mama's hand. "No, come to bed with me."

"You sure?" Mama asked.

"Please," Belinda said. "I don't want to tell you what to do. This bed's big enough for both of us."

Mama climbed into the other side of the bed, covered herself with the sheet and closed her eyes. Belinda started to giggle.

"What are you laughing at?" Mama said.

"My parents were both the worst racists. We had black servants and my mom treated them like shit."

"Blacks aren't exempt from racial intolerance," Mama said. "My grandmother thought all whites were liars and cheats."

"My dad had a black girlfriend," Belinda said.

"No way!"

"Diane was the lead singer of a Motown trio I know you would recognize. Back then, their affair was the talk of Tulsa."

"You're kidding," Mama said.

"Mom used to search for him when he didn't come home. He had his favorite bars. Mom would find his car and let the air out of his tires."

"No way," Mama said.

"Things got worse when his affair with Diane began and Mom got worried he was going to leave her. She went looking for him one night and couldn't find his car anywhere."

"And?"

"She caught Dad and Diane in flagrante in his office downtown. He told Mom she was a cleaning lady."

"She believed him?" Mama asked.

Belinda grinned again. "Probably not, but she forgave him."

"How do you know about Diane?" Mama asked.

"Dad had a red Ferrari convertible. He and Diane went everywhere in that car. They used to take me for ice cream."

Belinda smiled when Mama asked, "You never told your mom?"

"I was an only child, Dad my hero. I would never have done anything to hurt him."

"And Diane?"

"She still sends me birthday cards. When I was in college, she'd always include a hundred dollars inside the flap. She was the nicest person I ever met. I know she loved me."

"When was the last time you spoke to her?"

Belinda started to cry. "I'm such a piece of shit," she said.

"No, you aren't," Mama said, daubing her tears with a corner of the sheet.

"When she performed in Tulsa," Belinda said, "she sent me front row tickets."

"You went to the concert?"

"I did. She was wonderful. What a voice."

"You spoke to her afterward?" Mama asked.

Belinda began to sob. "I bought my own ticket because I didn't want her to know I was in the audience. I'm such a piece of shit!"

"No you aren't," Mama said. "I'm giving you permission to call her tomorrow."

Belinda's tears dried up. Light from the moon was shining in through the open window and Mama could see she was grinning."

"Now, what are you grinning about?" Mama asked.

"Diane used to hug me, tell me how smart and pretty I was. My mama was so straitlaced, she never hugged me and I don't remember her ever kissing me."

"What's so funny about that?" Mama asked.

"She wanted to. She just didn't have it in her to actually show emotion." She grinned again. "I can only imagine her and Dad making love. I bet she just lay there with her arms to her sides, stiff as a board, never making a sound."

"Belinda, that's not a nice thing to say about your mom."

"But true."

"I'm positive your mother loved you," Mama said.

A tear appeared in the corner of Belinda's eye. "She did. She just couldn't bring herself to show it. Until."

"Until when?"

"When Mom was on her death bed, I cried and hugged her. At first, she was stiff, and then she put her arms around my neck and drew me to her. I didn't think she was ever going to let me go."

"Your mom loved you, even if she didn't always show it."

'That's what Diane told me," Belinda said.

"It's hell losing your mom," Mama said. "Mine has been gone ten years and I still miss my talks with her."

"I'm calling Diane tomorrow," Belinda said. "Tell her I love and miss her."

"You go, girl," Mama said.

They lay in bed without speaking until a distant sound outside the bedroom door disrupted the silence.

## Chapter 23

Jake turned away from the door and stared at the ephemeral light illuminating the wine cellar below them.

"What the hell is it?" Sam asked.

"It's gotta be Hunt's ghost," Jake said.

"You don't believe in that shit, do you?" Sam asked.

"You think I'm a charlatan?" Jake asked.

"What the hell are you talking about?"

Jake's arms were crossed and he glared at Sam. "I've spent my life looking for ghosts, cryptids, and the paranormal. Do you think my whole life is a lie?"

"I'm your best fucking friend," Sam said. "I've never had a bad thought about you. Stop being so damn paranoid."

Jake's anger began to cool. "Then believe me when I tell you Hunt's ghost is lighting the wine cellar."

"Don't mind me, bro. I'm drunk enough I almost believe you. What do we do?"

"Go down the stairs," Jake said.

"After you, buddy," Sam said.

Jake moved past him and started down the

steps. Sam followed. Though the ephemeral light continued to illuminate the room, they found no ghost when they reached the wine cellar.

Racks of wine filled the cellar. Sam grabbed one from the rack and read the label,

"Châteauneuf-du-Pape, 1907. Is that a good year?"

"Do I look like a wine connoisseur?" Jake asked.

"I'm damn sure not," Sam said. "Let's find the 1892 bottles."

As Jake had said, Hudson Huntington had been anal retentive and they soon found the red 1892s. Though search as they might, they didn't find Jeff's hidden clue.

"What now?" Sam asked.

"I'm thirsty," Jake said. "Let's open one of these bottles."

"Which bottle?" Sam asked.

"Hell, I don't know," Jake said. "They're all good. Just pick one."

Sam still had the bottle of Châteauneuf-du-Pape in his hand.

"How about this one?" he said.

"Great," Jake said. "How do you intend to open it? With your teeth?"

"There has to be a corkscrew down here someplace," Sam said.

"Oh yeah? Where would it be?" Jake asked.

"I have no clue," Sam said. "Get off your fat ass and help me look."

Despite scouring every inch of the wine cellar, they could find no corkscrew.

"Now what?" Sam asked.

"My pocket knife," Jake said. "We can cut up the cork and push it down into the bottle."

"Hud would kill us if he were alive," Sam said.

"Well, he's not. Give me the damn bottle."

Sam watched as Jake dug at the cork on the

old bottle with his pocket knife.

"I don't have a good feeling about this," he said.

"It's just one bottle," Jake said. "Not like we're destroying Hunt's entire cache of wine."

"Tell it to Hunt," Sam said.

"If he were here, he'd understand."

"I've never seen a ghost. From the weird blue light, maybe Hunt really is here with us."

"And maybe he'll help us drink some of this wine," Jake said.

Giving up on removing the cork, Jake pushed it down into the wine, tipped the bottle up and took a swig.

"Can't believe you desecrated a thousand-dollar bottle of wine with a pocket knife and are drinking it straight from the bottle."

Jake handed it to Sam. "Believe it," he said. 'You'll have to strain the bits of cork through your teeth."

Sam and Jake had finished the bottle and were laughing when Sam said, "Oh, shit!"

"What?" Jake asked.

"Hunt is here. We pissed him off opening one of his prized bottles of wine with a dirty pocket knife."

"What the hell are you mumbling about?" Jake asked.

"Down by your foot."

On the stone floor by Jake's foot was a corkscrew.

"Where the hell did that come from?" Jake asked.

"Out of Grandpa Hunt's ethereal pocket is my guess," Sam said.

A big grin spread across Jake's face. "Hi, Gramps. Me and Sam are drinking your liquor. Better join us." The cellar suddenly went dark, the gloom only lasting a moment. "We want to drink the best wine you have in the cellar before we're too drunk to enjoy it. Can you help us?"

The light dimmed again, only a diffused beam spotlighting a bottle high up on the rack. Sam stood on his tiptoes and retrieved the bottle. When the lights returned, Jake and Sam stared at the label.

"Chateau Lafite, 1869," Sam said. "Wonder how much this is worth?"

Jake had already stripped the wax and was removing the cork with the corkscrew.

"Don't ask," he said. "Hunt obviously wants us to enjoy ourselves."

Sam took a drink and made a face. "A bit sour."

"Give it to me," Jake said.

After sipping from the bottle, he said, "You're right. Doesn't matter. We opened it and can't just pour it down the drain."

He took a drink, made a face and then handed it to Sam. Sam held his nose, closed his eyes and took another drink. Hud's cellar had a drain in case of flooding. Sam poured the remaining wine down it.

"Oh, yes we can," he said. "Sorry, Hunt."

"Hunt doesn't give a shit," Jake said. "You can't take it with you. It's just as well we're keeping it in the family, so to speak."

"From your lips to God's ears," Sam said.

A sound outside the door of the bedroom interrupted Mama and Belinda's conversation. It was so far away neither of them could make out what was making the sound. Mama got out of bed and opened the door.

"What is it?" Belinda asked.

"Can't tell," Mama said.

"I'm worried about Jake and Sam," Belinda said.

"Why is that?" Mama asked.

"They've probably killed each other by now."

Mama smiled. "How old are you, girl?" she asked.

"What difference does that make."

"You don't know men very well."

"What do you mean by that?" Belinda asked.

"They aren't tearing each other apart," Mama said. "Hell, my guess is they're comparing our tits and legs."

"No way," Belinda said.

"You're so naïve," Mama said.

Belinda ignored Mama's words. "I hear something again."

She joined Mama in the open doorway. "Sounds human," she said. "Maybe we better check."

Belinda found her running shoes, sat in the chair and began lacing them."

"You can't go out there like that," Mama said.

"Like what?"

"In your nightie. You're half-naked."

"Who cares? There's no one to see us."

"Good point," Mama said.

Mama began lacing her own shoes and they were soon in the dark hallway. The light from the moon shining in through the open bedroom windows had provided enough illumination that they could see. There was no such lighting in the hall.

"We won't get far without candles," Belinda said. "Jeff could have at least provided us with flashlights."

"There are more candles in the kitchen. The box of matches on the nightstand should be enough to help us get downstairs."

The sound they'd heard had ceased. It didn't matter because the glow of the matches provided scant lighting, and made the descent of the stairway precarious at best. The only candles they found when they reached the kitchen were a couple of stubs. Mama lit one and placed it on the cabinet.

"This is a hell of a mess," Belinda said. "Now what?"

"Let's mix a drink and then worry about it. I'm having vodka. What about you?"

"Make it two," Belinda said. "I'm starving. Is there anything to eat in the ice chest?"

"Bologna, cheese, mayonnaise and mustard. There's a loaf of white bread and a knife on top."

Sarcasm flavored Belinda's words when she said, "Jeff went out of his way with our food choices."

"And he's not a connoisseur of vodka," Mama said. "I haven't drunk any of this brand he bought us since I was a freshman in college. We'll both have splitting headaches if we drink too much of it."

"I'll have a heart-to-heart with that little brat if we ever get out of here," Belinda said. "We'll have to make do with bologna and cheap vodka until then. I'll make the sandwiches."

"I'll find some glasses," Mama said.

Belinda began digging in the ice chest. She made two sandwiches, handing one to Mama as she took a sip of the vodka.

"Ugh! What else is there to drink?"

"Nothing but cheap swill," Mama said.

"Never knew my son was such a cheapskate," Belinda said.

"We'll live," Mama said.

"You like wine?" Belinda asked.

"Why?" Mama asked. "Did Jeff leave us a bottle of Mad Dog 20-20?"

Belinda grinned. "Wouldn't surprise me if there's a bottle around here someplace. I was thinking of something a bit more expensive."

"I'm all in for that," Mama said. "You know where there's a secret cache?"

"Hunt's wine cellar. God only knows what treasure we might find."

"Can we get there from here with only the stub of our last candle?"

"Let's have another bologna sandwich and then find out," Belinda said.

When they finished their sandwiches, Mama left her half-empty glass of vodka on the kitchen counter.

"I'm banking on us finding Hunt's wine cellar. I can't drink another sip of that swill," she said.

Belinda sat her glass beside Mama's. "You're right, it sucks. Ready?"

"Right behind you," Mama said.

With the candle stub in her left hand, Belinda kept her other hand on the wall as she advanced down the darkened hallway.

"Not much farther," she said. "I'm sweating so badly, this nightie is sticking to my tits."

"Mine too," Mama said. "Good thing there are no lechers around."

When Belinda tittered, the sound echoed down the empty hallway.

"We should be so lucky," she said.

The candle went out as they turned a corner in the hall. It didn't matter. A strange light emanated from an open doorway at the end of the long hallway. That wasn't all. The sound that had started their search had begun again: the discordant voices of men singing. Belinda froze in place.

"You said the ghosts were gone."

"They are."

"Who, then?" Belinda asked.

"I've never heard Sam sing, but one of those out-of-tune voices is Jake's."

"You're right," Belinda said. "If he'd had to

make his living cutting records, he'd have been belly up years ago. What are they doing down there?"

"From the songs coming up the stairs, I'd guess they're enjoying a few bottles of Hunt's wine."

"More than a few, if you ask me," Belinda said.

"What now?" Mama said.

"Join them," Belinda said.

"That'll lose us the contest."

"Screw the contest," Belinda said. "I'm thirsty."

They found Sam and Jake sitting on the stone floor of the cellar, having stripped down to their undershirts and boxer shorts. They were singing out of key as they shared a bottle of wine. Hearing something behind him, Sam glanced around and stopped singing.

"Oh my!" he said. "We are in luck, big boy. Our song attracted two half-naked goddesses."

Jake struggled to stand though somehow managed to stumble to the stairs. Sam fell on his face when he tried to follow him. Belinda was laughing too hard to speak.

Mama said, "What in holy hell are you two into?" She had to grab Jake's arm to keep him from falling on his face. "I've never even seen you tipsy. How did you get so drunk?"

Jake almost drug Mama to the stone floor when he put his arms around her neck and leaned on her,

"Hunt's wine," he said.

"Did you leave any for us?" Belinda asked.

"You kidding? We've barely made a dent. How about a taste of one of Hunt's two-hundred-eighty-year-old wines?"

"Hunt will kill us," Belinda said, grinning.

"No he won't. He left the light on for us."

The cellar was alit with an unearthly glow. Gone was the basement's normally chilly temperature.

"Help me get him back over there," Mama said.

Belinda put Jake's arm around her shoulder and she and Mama managed to return him to the spot where Sam was staring at them with a silly grin on his face.

"You two are gorgeous," he said. "Where have you been all my life?"

"Back up the stairs unless you share your wine with us," Belinda said.

"You two are talking?" he asked.

"You kidding?" Belinda said. "Mama's my best friend. First person that says something bad about her in my presence is gonna taste a knuckle sandwich."

Sam showed her his palms. "Not me," he said.

Three opened bottles were lined up beside them, four empties in a heap not far away. Sam struggled to hand a bottle to Belinda. Her facial features melted after taking a sip.

"Oh my God!" she said. "This is the best wine I've ever had the pleasure to drink. Mama, You gotta try this."

Mama put the bottle to her lips and drank until wine gushed out of her mouth in rivulets down her bare neck to form a deep purple wet spot on her pink nightie. Sam didn't try to look away, and it was apparent no one cared.

Mama and Belinda laughed when he said, "Good thing I have no control over my body or you two gorgeous women would be in trouble."

Mama and Belinda had lots of catching up to do and succeeded in drinking the majority of the next two bottles. The overhead lights had come back on and they were singing bawdy sea ditties and didn't' notice when someone descended the stairs behind them. It was Jeff and Colley. Colley extended his arm, blocking Jeff from passing him.

"Better stop right there, partner, unless you want to see your mother lying half-naked on the floor."

## Chapter 24

Late afternoon sunshine filtered through a layer of thin August clouds as Jake's jet helicopter waited on the roof of Huntington Tower. Jake, Mama, and Colley were saying goodbye, Mama and Belinda exchanging hugs.

"I'm going to miss you," Belinda said.

"Mardi Gras is just around the corner. I'll show you places you never knew existed," Mama said.

"Can't wait. I called Diane today."

"Good for you," Mama said. "What did she say?"

"She was so happy to hear from me. We talked for over an hour. We were both crying. She promised to spend Christmas with Sam and me."

"Wonderful," Mama said

"Jake's a rolling stone," Belinda said. "I hope you're still together when we're down for Mardi Gras, but . . ."

Mama held Belinda at arm's length, staring directly into her limpid blue eyes.

"Jake doesn't define me," she said. "He's his own person. So am I. Whatever happens between Jake and me will have nothing to do with us.

When I make a friend, it's forever."

When I make a friend, it's forever."

"You're more than just my friend, you're the sister I never had," Belinda said.

Colley shook hands with Sam and Jeff and kissed Belinda's forehead.

"We'll be back in a week or so," he said.

Colley laughed when Jeff said, "Bring Mama with you."

"That's up to her and Boss Man," Colley said.

Colley climbed into the chopper and cranked the engine as he waited for Jake and Mama to say their goodbyes. Sam's grin grew when he bumped Jake's fist.

"I'm holding you to that golf trip at your resort in Scotland," he said.

"No one on earth I'd rather golf with than my best friend," Jake said.

"Am I included?" Jeff asked.

"You bet," Jake said. "You'll have to close your ears when we start talking about our old girlfriends."

"Old girlfriends I don't mind," Belinda said. "I know how you two can get into trouble."

"Us?" Sam said. "No way."

Jeff, Belinda, and Sam waved as Mama and Jake climbed into the helicopter. As they disappeared over the Tulsa skyline, Jake began mixing a martini for Mama.

"I can't believe my son's a teetotaler," he said.

Mama grinned. "The Old Shoe Sole he left for us at Huntington Manor was bad."

"Tell me about it," Jake said. "I'd forgotten how awful cheap gin tastes."

"At least he's fiscally responsible," Mama said.

"My ass!" Jake said. "If he wasn't bigger than me, I'd have given him a good whack on the butt."

"Not allowed," Mama said.

"You must be a democrat," he said.

"I confess," she said.

"How are we going to make it together?" he asked. "I'm the most conservative republican you'll ever meet."

He smiled when she said, "You have your good qualities, and your bad. No one's perfect."

"Let's agree not to talk politics," he said.

"Not even pillow talk?"

"Especially not pillow talk. That's when I'm most vulnerable."

"Why are we even talking about politics?" she asked. "We only met a few days ago. I'm not even sure I like you."

"I'm sure I like you," he said.

It was hours before sundown, the visibility endless. Boats pulling skiers were visible on the lake below them.

"I'm worried," she said.

"That I'm lying about how much I like you?"

Mama gave Jake a peck on the cheek. "Your fidelity isn't what I'm worried about," she said. "Wyatt hasn't answered his cell phone since we left New Orleans."

"I'll call Angie," Jake said.

Jake made it impossible for Mama to follow his conversation when he turned his back on her. Trying not to seem too interested, she mixed them another drink.

Jake almost spilled his gin when she asked, "Are you and Angie a number?"

"Hardly," he said.

"Sure about that?"

"I don't fraternize with my employees. They play me like a worn drum."

"I find that hard to believe," Mama said.

"Angie and the crew accomplished absolutely nothing while we were gone. She was still in bed just now and hadn't even thought about calling

Wyatt. What gave you the idea Angie and I have something going?"

"The way she was looking at you in the UNO parking garage," Mama said.

"I think I detect a hint of jealousy."

"Do I have reason to be jealous?" Mama asked.

"Angie and Bradley are shacking up. Have been for over a year. You're the only girl in my life."

"Happy to hear it" Mama said. "What about Wyatt?"

"We'll be in New Orleans in a few hours. I instructed Angie to have the crew begin filming at the Old François Place, and to look for Wyatt. I could almost hear her kicking Bradley out of bed. She'll find Wyatt."

"There are things I haven't told you about him."

"Such as?"

"He's a Traveler."

"What's that?"

"A person with the ability to travel through time."

Mama laughed when Jake said, "What a talent. I'll have to do an episode on it."

"Problem is, he's an accidental traveler and has no clue how to invoke his talent. The times he's traveled, he's had assistance," she said.

"We haven't even talked about the project the past two days. I was so relieved Jeff was okay, and having such a great time, I totally forgot about it."

"Wyatt's obsessed with the story," Mama said.

"Because of Madam Aja?"

"It's such a coincidence you and your crew became involved."

"I don't believe in coincidences," Jake said.

"What, then?"

"Madam Aja has something to do with the Cryptid Hunter arriving in New Orleans."

"Maybe we should talk with Senora."

"Tell me again who Senora is."

"Madam Aja's daughter," Mama said. "She lives in Fauborg Marigny. She's also one of the persons who have enabled Wyatt's time travels."

"How so?"

"She was with Madam Aja when the old woman explained to Wyatt where a time portal would be. Seems likely she knows a bunch about time travel.

Colley gave Jake a thumbs up when he spoke on the microphone and said, "Have Bradley pick us up at the airport."

The sun was low on the horizon when they reached New Orleans Lakefront Airport on the banks of Lake Pontchartrain.

"Seth is coming with us," Jake informed Mama. "He's waiting in the limo with Bradley."

Mama turned away from the chopper's window, the look she gave Jake a bit disturbed.

"You trust him?" she asked.

"Of course I do. He's the reason we're here. He called me when they recovered the body at the Old François Place."

"Wyatt and I thought there might be a connection," Mama said.

"I've known Seth for years," Jake said. "He's a bit of a bounder, though an honest bounder. Seth will help us understand what's going on here. I'm also bringing a cameraman."

"Senora will be dumbstruck," Mama said. "Let's don't blow this opportunity."

"Trust me," he said. "My instincts are good. This will work out."

"Last time a man asked me to trust him, I got pregnant," Mama said.

Jake grinned. "No worries there," he said.

"I've had a vasectomy."

Bradley, Seth and a single cameraman were waiting in the lobby of the airport when they landed.

"Mama, you know Seth and Bradley. This is Carlos Sanchez, the best cameraman in the world."

Carlos was forty-something, his black hair turning gray at the edges. He was short, his handlebar mustache barely reaching Mama's chin. The expensive-looking camera he cradled in his arms marked him as a professional.

"Hi, Carlos," she said. "I'm Mama."

Seth rested his hand on Jake's shoulder. "My assistant Aura has gone missing. I can't tell you how worried I am."

"We can't locate Wyatt either," Mama said. "Maybe they're together."

"That's why we're here," Jake said. "When did you last see Aura?"

"I gave her a ride back to her hotel after visiting UNO. She left in a huff."

"Because?" Jake asked.

"No idea," Seth said.

Jake halted his questions when Mama elbowed him. She winked when he gave her a quizzical look.

They had a drink at the little airport bar as they waited for Colley to batten down the chopper and join them. They had to wait for him to order a whiskey and beer chaser before exiting to the waiting limousine. Jake was already mixing drinks when she joined him.

"You should consider moving to New Orleans," she said. "Few people have your tolerance for alcohol. You would be perfect here."

"Maybe it's something we should discuss," he said.

"I'm putting it on my list of things to

remember," she said.

Daylight was waning as Bradley headed the limo toward Fauborg Marigny.

"Are you going to ring Senora to advise her we're on our way?" Jake asked.

"She's so shy, I'm afraid she might leave the house if she knew we were coming."

"Your call," Jake said.

"There's a liquor store up ahead. Can you have Bradley stop and get us something?"

"This is the best-stocked limo in America," Jake said. "What do you need?"

"Bottle of Old Crow."

"We're not that well stocked," he said. "Bradley, stop at a liquor store and get us a large bottle of Old Crow."

They waited in the parking lot for the tall chauffeur to return with the cheap bottle of bourbon. Bradley let them out in front of Senora's house.

"I'll find a place to park," he said. "Call me when you're ready to leave."

Mama and Senora hugged when Madam Aja's daughter opened the front door.

"I've brought some people with me," Mama said. "Hope you don't mind."

"You're the Cryptid Hunter," Senora said before Mama had a chance to introduce them. "Madam Aja and I never missed your program. It was Madam Aja's favorite. It's still mine."

"I would loved to have met her," Jake said. "This is Carlos, Seth, and Colley. Mind if we come in?"

"Of course," Senora said, throwing open the door. "To what do I have this pleasure?"

"A few questions about Madam Aja," Jake said.

"What questions?"

"Nothing you'll be afraid to answer," Jake said

with a grin.

"Please find a place to sit," Senora said. "I'll get us something to drink."

They took seats in the cozy little house. Mama helped Senora fill everyone's drink order. Everyone except Carlos, who was busy filming. Senora was smiling when she presented Jake with his beverage.

"Bombay Gin and Fentiman's," he said. "How did you know?"

"I told you, Cryptid Hunter was our favorite show. Madam Aja always wanted to meet you and had me buy a bottle of Bombay Gin and Fentiman's just in case she ever did."

"I'm honored, and also impressed." Jake said.

"Please tell me why you are here," Senora said.

"Is it possible Madam Aja knew I was coming to New Orleans?"

"Madam Aja knew things beyond a normal woman," Senora said.

"She was anything but a normal woman," Mama said.

When Senora joined Colley on the couch, he said, "What are you drinking, Miss Senora?"

"Vodka, Mr. Colley, the drink of the gods."

"Boss Man here doesn't give me much time off. I'd love to spend some time with you while I'm in New Orleans."

"There's a jazz joint in Bywater," Mama said, "The place will be hopping right about now."

"I can't," Senora said. "I'm still grieving over Madam Aja's passing. Maybe in a month or so."

"That's okay," Colley said. "Boss Man and me will be back in town for Mardi Gras. I'll give you a call."

"Even better," Jake said. "How would you like to be in an episode of Cryptid Hunter?"

"Oh my!" Senora said. "I'd love it. Madam Aja

would have been absolutely blissful. Too bad she can't participate."

"Maybe she can," Jake said.

## Chapter 25

Aura couldn't stop talking as we waited for Joffrey to return with something for her to eat. She finally calmed down enough to sit quietly on the side of the bed. At least for a moment.

"This is so surreal," she said.

"I'm with you on that one," I said. "Odd, weird, strange, or any other adjective you care to use."

The rain hadn't let up all day and continued peppering the windows. Dirt plowed up from the cane fields ran in rivulets down the glass. Clasping her arms across her chest, Aura shivered.

"Doesn't it ever stop raining?"

"Rain like this is unusual for August. It seems more like spring or fall to me."

"Except for the temperature. It's nippy outside," Aura said.

"I'll ask Joffrey what month it is."

"What difference does it make?" Aura asked.

"You don't always land in the same month when you're traveling through time."

"I don't think Joffrey trusts you."

"Probably not, but he's the only lead I have."

Aura had grown silent as Joffrey returned with a covered pot laden with pork and vegetable stew. The bottle of French wine would have been worth a small fortune in modern-day New Orleans. With a large wooden spoon, Aura tore into the stew as Joffrey uncorked the bottle of wine.

"No crystal," he said. "Only the bottle from which to drink. I hope you do not mind sharing with a slave."

Aura pinched his cheek. "A cute slave," she said. "I'll try to persevere."

Joffrey drank until wine dribbled down his chin. "Wyatt?" he said.

"I'm a teetotaler," I said.

"More for us," Aura said.

"Are you sure?" Joffrey asked.

"All yours," I said.

When the bottle was empty, Joffrey said, "Why did you not tell me you are a passeblanc?"

Taken aback by the question, I said, "Who told you that?"

"Esther."

"I didn't know she knew," I said.

"What's a passeblanc?" Aura asked.

"A slave, or free person of color whose skin is sufficiently light enough that it's impossible to tell their ethnicity," I said.

Joffrey's upper lip curled into a toothy grin when Aura asked, "Why would anyone want to do that?"

"Girl," he said. "You must be incredibly naïve."

Aura glanced first at me and then gave Joffrey a look of disbelief. A tree limb crashing against the windowpane caused her shoulders to stiffen.

"Be not afraid," Joffrey said. "It is only the wind."

"How did Esther know Wyatt is a passeblanc?"

"Esther has the eyes of an eagle and the ears of a bat," Joffrey said.

"What's that supposed to mean?" Aura asked

"Just there is little she does not know," Joffrey said. "She wants me to take you to see Falala."

"Falala?" Aura said.

"An Indian witch. Maurelle will want to see you. Falala will summon her for us."

"She can do that?" Aura asked.

"Can and will," Joffrey said.

"There is something else Esther wants," Joffrey said.

"Tell us," I said.

"She wants me to take you to the meeting of slave leaders. Now that I know Wyatt is as black as I am, I will take you both."

"Slave leaders?" I said.

"Since you are the master's advocat, you could be very valuable to the movement," he said.

"Tell me more about this movement," I said.

"I will answer your questions when I return. Aura Lea cannot go out in this storm dressed in that pretty dress of hers. I will bring clothes more suitable for the occasion."

The door had barely shut behind Joffrey when Aura said, "Why would Esther tell Joffrey you are a passeblanc?"

"Don't know," I said. "Seems to me she'd think I'd be more likely as Felix's friend and advocat to help him than members of a potential slave rebellion."

"Then she must know you're not his advocat," Aura said.

"Or else she has other motives," I said.

Aura missed my insinuation and said, "No one will believe you're black."

"Joffrey does."

"Then he is the one who is incredibly naïve."

"Common thinking is if you're part black, then you're all black. The French had a different theory and classified blacks by the amount of white blood they had."

"Explain," she said.

"A quadroon was one-quarter black, an octoroon one-eighth, and a hexadecaroon one-sixteenth, and so on."

"Sounds crazy," Aura said.

"Not really. In Louisiana, there's a possibility everyone has black blood. If you're white, you have more financial opportunity than if you are black."

"That's a racist statement," Aura said.

"No, it isn't," I said. "Ask any black person what a DWB is."

"What the hell is a DWB?"

"Driving while black," I said. "Blacks are many times more likely to be pulled over by the police. It's just one of the inequities of being black."

"Maybe," Aura said. "Maurelle isn't alive. How is this Indian woman going to conjure her?" Aura asked.

"Maurelle was alive when I saw her at Le Fée Verte. It was apparent to Felix and me she had eyes for Joffrey."

"I can only see her lifeless on that gurney at UNO," Aura said. "Joffrey is so full of life. How can the skeleton we found in the courtyard be his?"

"We'll all be a pile of bones someday."

"And you think he lost his head and hand because of his involvement with the slave rebellion?"

"That and his affair with Maurelle," I said.

"What will attending this meeting of the slaves gain us?"

"Don't know," I said. "Esther wants us there for some reason. She concocted the passeblanc excuse to make it work."

Lightning flashed across the window, followed by thunder that shook the house's wooden frame. Joffrey burst through the door carrying field clothes and work shoes before Aura could comment.

"Put these on," he said.

Aura's pretty nose wrinkled when she stared at the faded shirt and ragged pants Joffrey handed to her. Without bothering to tell us to turn our heads, she unbuttoned the dress and let it drop to her feet. Joffrey waited until we were both dressed as field hands.

"How are we going to get to the swamp from here?" I asked. "We can't go walking out the front door."

"No one will see us. A secret passage leads into the forest. It will keep us out of the rain until we can get some protection from the trees."

"What about Felix?"

"Esther will cover for us."

Aura glanced at me. "Is Esther a spy?"

"She is a slave. Why wouldn't she help us?" he said.

"And Felix trusts her?" I asked.

"The Master, if you have not figured it out already, is a loner. Esther takes him his meals and he also beds her. He trusts her completely. We have planned the rebellion for months. Esther is in on it."

"Tell us about this meeting," I said.

"Though slaves have almost no firearms, we outnumber the planters many times over. We plan to march on a plantation that has a stock of pistols, rifles, and ammunition. Enough for now. You will hear everything at the meeting."

"You didn't tell us how Esther plans to prevent Felix from missing me," I said.

"She has a potion to doctor his absinthe. He will sleep through the night. Tomorrow, he will never know we were away from the plantation."

"And the rest of the house staff?" I asked.

"Esther is the real master of Moonmont. She tells everyone what to do and what not to do."

Lightning flashed across the window, followed by a crash of thunder that rocked the walls. Joffrey handed Aura a jacket when she shivered again.

"Where is this secret passage?" I asked.

"In this room."

Joffrey shifted a pastoral picture on the wall and pressed an almost invisible button. The wall groaned and began to move. An opening leading to a metal stairway appeared."

Joffrey cast Aura a confused look when she said, "Hope you have a flashlight."

Producing a candle, he lit it with a flick of his finger.

"Nice," I said. "Are you a magician?"

"A little trick I learned in Africa."

Aura and I stayed close to Joffrey as he descended the vertical stairway. The candle's dim light revealed a tunnel at the end of the stairs. Like the entrance to a mine, beams and braces reinforced it.

"Who dug this?" Aura asked.

"Slaves."

"With the approval of the Master?" I asked.

"We do many things the Master knows nothing about."

The tunnel's height and width began to diminish as soon as we'd gone ten feet into the darkness. The beams and braces soon disappeared, the roof of the tunnel growing ever lower and forcing us to walk in a crouch. Water, soaking our shoes had begun rushing in rivulets into the tunnel.

My voice echoed against the tunnel walls when I asked, "Is this normal?"

"We rarely get so much rain this time of year," Joffrey said.

"How far does this passage take us?" I asked.

"It exits in the forest about a hundred yards from the house. The tree's thick branches usually keep water out of the tunnel."

Dozens of rats scurrying past our feet caused Aura to squeal.

"Then something's wrong," I said. "The water's getting deeper, and those rats seem to be abandoning ship."

"You're scaring me," Aura said.

"Do not panic but let us hurry," Joffrey said.

"How?" I asked. "If the tunnel gets any narrower, we'll soon be crawling."

"It usually poses no problem," Joffrey said. "Keep going. We are not far from the exit."

Water was dripping on our heads, and the catch in Joffrey's voice told me he was as apprehensive about the situation as I was. Clumps of mud falling from the roof of the tunnel did little to ease my anxiety.

"There's no danger of this tunnel collapsing on us, is there?" I asked.

"Do not jinx us," Joffrey said. "We were at the deepest point of the tunnel, about ten feet below ground level when we first entered. It slants upward toward the surface, the exit little more than a hole in the ground."

By now, muddy water rushing down the tunnel was over our ankles, ever-larger clumps of mud splattering our heads and shoulders as it fell from the roof.

"This tunnel won't be here tomorrow," I said.

"Let us hope we are not still in it," Joffrey said.

Shorter than Joffrey and me, Aura had gotten ahead of us.

"You two are scaring me, and I can barely see where I'm going," she said.

Joffrey handed her the candle when we caught up to her.

"You are smaller than Wyatt and me, and we cannot move as fast as you. There is little time, so do not wait on us." When Aura hesitated, Joffrey gave her a push and said, "Go!"

More mud was falling from the ceiling, the tunnel beginning to collapse. By now, my shoes were sticking in the muddy mess the tunnel was quickly becoming.

Aura's voice sounded muffled when she called, "I'm out."

The tunnel continued falling around our shoulders. Joffrey grabbed my arm, holding on as I pushed through the mud and water. I was about to panic when I heard Aura again.

"I hear you," she said. "You're almost out."

Before we made it to the grove of trees, the tunnel roof gave way, completely covering Joffrey and me in mud. The rain had only intensified, the tunnel quickly becoming a raging stream. Joffrey was already trying to climb out. Neither of us were having any luck until Aura rushed from the shelter of the trees.

Grabbing my arm, she began trying to pull me out of the water. It didn't take her long to realize the bank of the collapsed tunnel was too slippery. Letting go of my arm, she hurried back toward the trees.

Wind from the raging storm had left broken branches on the ground. Aura found one and dragged it to the newly-formed stream of water.

Joffrey used it to leverage himself over the edge and then pulled me out of the torrent.

Adrenaline surged through my body, my heart racing as the three of us lay exhausted on the ground ten feet from the collapsed tunnel now filled with moving water. We continued to lie there until our strength began to return, and a nearby clap of thunder shook the ground around us. Joffrey was the first to get to his feet.

"We survived the tunnel. Let us find shelter beneath the trees before lightning strikes us and changes our luck."

## Chapter 26

The storm was growing even more intense, thunder rocking the nearby trees as driving rain pelted our heads and shoulders. Lightning illuminated the sky with strobe-like intensity.

I was shouting when I said, "That last lightning strike was close."

"Too close," Joffrey said.

We sloshed our way into the forest where Joffrey pulled us beneath an ancient live oak, the tree's low-hanging branches providing as much shelter as we were going to find in the blinding rainstorm. We huddled beneath the tree, only relatively safe but at least somewhat sheltered from the storm. Aura was crying softly.

"This tempest will not last forever," Joffrey said. "We will soon be safe and warm."

"The tunnel shook my nerves, though I knew we were going to survive," she said.

"How did you know?" Joffrey asked.

His eyes narrowed when Aura said, "It's not the way you die."

"You think you know how I die?" Joffrey asked.

"Just babbling," Aura said.

"That was close back there," I said.

"The rain destroyed our tunnel," Joffrey said. "I will have to get the slaves to fill the hole before the master discovers it."

"How do you intend to do that?" I asked.

"He spends most of his time in New Orleans. Esther will keep him occupied until he returns there," Joffrey said.

Though the thunder and lightning finally passed, light rain continued to fall, Aura's dripping jacket draping her shoulders. Though it wasn't cold, she continued to shiver.

"Wish I had a cup of hot tea," she said.

"Falala's cabin is close, probably no more than a mile away," Joffrey said. "Though our clothes are wet, at least the rain has washed away the mud. We will all feel better when we reach her cabin. Are you ready?"

"Lead the way," I said.

Joffrey's trek proved more than just another mile, my legs growing weary when the shadow of a cabin appeared through the trees,

"Is this it?" Aura asked.

"We're here," Joffrey said. "Falala will be waiting for us."

The little unpainted cabin hidden amid the trees seemed tiny on the outside. When a woman opened the door and bade us enter, I could see it was much more extensive. A roaring fire crackled in a brick fireplace. Aura hurried to it, warming her hands before Joffrey had introduced us to the woman. I joined Aura in front of the fire.

"Falala," Joffrey said. "This is Wyatt and Aura Lea."

I'd expected to see a squat old hag with a wart on her nose. Instead, Falala was tall, her hair jet black and her bronze skin devoid of wrinkles. Her eyes, the same color as the regal cloak she wore, were as dark as her hair.

"Pleased to meet you," I said. "Sorry that we showed up looking like drowned rats."

"I was beginning to worry," Falala said.

"We got caught out in the rain abd had to wait beneath a tree until the brunt of the storm passed," Joffrey said.

"Your fire feels wonderful," Aura said. "So sorry about dripping on your floor."

"The floor will survive. There are blankets behind that curtain," Falala said. "Get undressed and wrap one around you. It will keep you warm until your clothes dry by the fireplace."

Aura hurried behind the curtain, smiling when she exited the changing space with a blanket draped around her. Joffrey, Aura, and I were soon sitting on a fur rug in front of the fire, colorful blankets warming our bodies and our souls. The cabin glowed from the light of the flickering fire as Falala brought us steaming mugs of coffee.

"You are here to see Maurelle," she said.

"Can you summon her for us?" Joffrey asked.

"You know I can," Falala said. She touched Aura's cheek. "You do not remember me, do you?"

"I'm sure we've never met," Aura said. "You are beautiful, and I'd remember if I had."

"This forest was your home for many years," Falala said. "I am your grandmother."

"Maurelle is your daughter?" Aura said.

"I am as old as time and everyone's mother. This is the magic forest. I have lived here forever."

"Why did I live with you?" Aura asked.

"Your father Felix is mortal. Somewhere along the way, he became possessed with hate. Maurelle has continued to love him though she no longer trusts him. You moved to Moonmont on your thirteenth birthday."

"Why then?" Aura asked.

"Maurelle thought you were old enough to take care of yourself. For years you were."

As if she was afraid to hear what had happened, Aura turned away and glanced at the flames.

"What happened?" she finally asked.

"Your father killed you."

"I'm not dead."

"In this life, you are," Falala said.

Joffrey was becoming agitated with the conversation. "Is Aura Lea a zombie?" he asked.

Falala shook her head. "This Aura Lea is not of this time. She came here quite by accident on the elbow of a Traveler."

Joffrey glanced at me. "A Traveler?"

"A special being who can move through time. Wyatt is a Traveler. He has powers he barely knows he possesses. Madam Aja sent him on a quest and to correct an injustice."

"What injustice?" Joffrey asked.

"Something that involves you and Maurelle. Neither of you knows about it because it has as yet not happened."

Joffrey stared at Aura. "Is that why you knew I would not die in the tunnel?" Aura didn't answer him. "Does everyone know how I die except me? How can Wyatt travel through time?"

"Time is like a river, Wyatt, but a drop of water existing in it," Falala said.

"I do not understand," Joffrey said.

"Nor do you need to understand," Falala said.

"Then at least tell me if Wyatt is a passeblanc," Joffrey said.

"Wyatt is as black as you and as white as Aura," Falala said.

"What is that supposed to mean?" Joffrey asked.

"Whatever you want it to mean. Now, I will summon Maurelle."

"She's coming here?" Aura asked.

"Only her image," Falala said. "You will see and converse with her though you will not be able to touch her. Shall we begin?"

Falala added cream to our coffee. When I took a sip, I found it was unlike anything I'd ever tasted. Almost instantly, a marijuana-like buzz distorted my senses.

Whatever Falala had added to the coffee enhanced my perception. I suddenly felt as if I could hear every raindrop pounding the roof.

A giant owl perched on one of the cabin's beams; a real owl, not a stuffed one. The same tiger-striped cat Aura and I had seen when we explored the Old François Place lolled on a rug in front of the fire. This time, it didn't run away. The grins on Joffrey and Aura's faces indicated they were luxuriating in the same euphoria as I.

Like a drop of dye added to a glass of water, a haze of purple began saturating the room with damp moving color. I blinked. When I opened my eyes, Maurelle was floating above the floor, her green butterfly wings reflecting prisms of light from the crackling flames in the fireplace. Aura and Joffrey's eyes focused on the holographic fairy. When Maurelle spoke, her voice sounded like a tinny recording.

"Baby, is that you?" she asked.

Aura's eyes had turned red, tears beginning to roll down her cheeks.

"Mother," she said.

"I wish I could touch you," Maurelle said.

"Oh, Mother, me too," Aura said. "I have so many questions."

"And I have few answers. Your father did not mean to kill you. It was an accident."

"I'm not dead," Aura said.

"I wish it were so," Maurelle said.

Whatever Falala had put into our coffee was

doing more than enhancing our perception. Aura began recalling long-forgotten memories and had become the woman Joffrey and Maurelle once knew.

"I know how much he hurt you," Aura said. "No, baby. The only time he ever hurt me was when you fell over the upstairs railing. I am so sorry I could not save you."

"But I'm alive," Aura said.

"There is nothing in the world I would love more than to hold you in my arms like I did when you were a baby."

"I won't be here long," Aura said. I'll come to New Orleans and see you. When I'm there, I'll give you that hug."

"You do not know how much I wish it could happen."

"It will happen, Mother, I promise you."

"No promises, baby."

Maurelle's image began to flicker, the purple haze slowly dissipating. Aura reached out her hand.

"Mother. . ."

"Adieu, Aura Lea," Maurelle said before her image flickered one last time and then dissolved away into a dying crescendo of colored sparkles.

Time passed before anyone said a word. The tiger-striped cat was gone, as was the owl in the rafters. Gone also was my clarity of thought, replaced by a painful pounding in my left temple. Aura lowered her outstretched hand.

"You saw your mother," Falala said. "You achieved what you sought by coming here. Your clothes are dry. The storm has abated, and you have only limited time to reach your next destination."

A chill permeated the air when we left Falala's cabin. As she had said, the storm had ended, the rain no longer falling. In a hurry, Joffrey walked ahead of us, leading the way with a candle that didn't seem to burn down.

"Wyatt, we have to do something. I can't just let Felix kill Joffrey and then bury Maurelle alive," Aura said. "What did Falala mean when she said time is like a river?"

"I'm not sure," I said. "One other thing."

"What?"

"The moonstone pendant wasn't around Maurelle's neck. She was wearing it when I saw her at La Fée Verte. That narrows the list of people who might have taken it from her," I said.

"Who do you suspect?"

"Joffrey," I said.

"Why would he betray her?"

"Maybe we'll find out at this meeting we're about to attend," I said.

Aura's body shook with emotion. "There's something else we could do."

"Like what?"

"Kill Felix."

"How do you propose doing that?" I asked.

"Don't know," she said. "It would keep the madman from beheading Joffrey and maiming my mother."

"She's your mother now?"

Aura turned away. "At least in this life."

"Let's catch Joffrey before we get lost in the forest," I said, giving her shoulder a nudge. "Maybe we'll find out why Esther wants us to attend this meeting."

## Chapter 27

Delayed by our problems in the tunnel, our meeting with Falala had taken longer than planned. Realizing as much, Joffrey hurried through the forest, stopping when we emerged and reached the edge of a swamp.

"The remainder of our destination is through the swamp. This part of the journey could be dangerous. You must stay close and not become separated."

"Not as dangerous as the tunnel, I hope," Aura said,

Our crisis in the tunnel weighed heavily on Joffrey's mind.

"Nothing could be as bad as that was," he said. "Stay close."

The sky was cloudy, not a star visible. Joffrey's candle provided scant illumination though just enough considering our dilated eyes. We soon came to a grove of trees at the edge of the swamp.

"Be not surprised with what you see," Joffrey said.

For once, I was happy with the chilly weather, alligators and other reptiles likely huddled in a den someplace. Aura probably hadn't thought about encountering alligators, and I decided against mentioning it to her.

We soon emerged into a clearing occupied by a cabins. Because of the darkness, I couldn't tell how many. A snarling dog nipped at our pant legs when we passed one of the cabins. It ran away when Joffrey stopped in front of one of the bungalows, a warm glow beckoning from the open door.

"What is this place?" Aura asked.

"The people who pass through here call it Bolthole. It is where escaped slaves come if they are lucky enough to find it."

"I would have no idea how to find it," Aura said.

"Neither do the slave owners and their bloodhounds," Joffrey said. "It is what makes this place so special. Our meeting is in this cabin. Let us discuss a few things before entering."

Joffrey drew us closer, indicating with a finger to his lips we should talk in undertones.

"Please tell us," I said.

"The head of the revolution is Charles Deslondes. He is quite the character though his intentions are good."

"Maybe you'd better explain," Aura said.

"Deslondes fancies himself a great general. I believe he has aspirations beyond rebellion. You will have to draw your own conclusion."

"What difference does it make?" I asked.

"Many of us, myself included, doubt we have the forces necessary to win our freedom. It has not mattered as many slaves have fallen under his spell and trust every word he says."

"And you?" I asked.

"I fear the worst."

"Then why are you going along with it?" I asked.

"I have established a fair amount of power since arriving at Moonmont. I cannot afford to contradict Deslondes without losing that power."

Joffrey gave Aura a dirty look when she said, "It's better than losing your head."

"That is something I do not intend to do," he said.

"How will you make sure it doesn't?" I asked.

"I have a plan. I will reveal it in the meeting. I only wanted to apprise you of Deslondes' persona so it will not surprise you."

"We took lots of time at Falala's," Aura said. "Are we late?"

Aura's question brought a smile to Joffrey's handsome face. "Deslondes is always the last one to arrive. I am sure he has someone watching us to make sure of it."

"Anything else we need to know?" I asked.

"Deslondes is a mulatto, almost as white as the two of you. He does not trust anyone who is white, and I expect some resistance when I explain your presence."

"Resistance?" Aura said. "You didn't tell us this."

"Deslondes travels with bodyguards who carry cane knives. They tend to kill first and ask questions later. Be not afraid. They will not kill you before first hearing me out."

"Then I hope you're persuasive. I'm not looking forward to being hacked to pieces with a sharp knife."

Though Aura was joking, none of us laughed.

"They are waiting. Let us enter," Joffrey said.

Three men in cane chairs huddled near the fireplace. Only the fire and a couple of candles lighted the otherwise darkness. All three men stood straight up when they saw Aura and me.

"Who are these two?" a large man in overalls and tattered shirt asked.

Do not be alarmed," Joffrey said. "This is Aura Lea and Wyatt. Aura Lea is the daughter of Maurelle. She sides with us. Wyatt is a passeblanc and is as black as you and I."

"He does not look black," the man said.

"This is Lionel, the Chief of Bolthole."

Lionel was probably sixty-something. He stood at least six-foot-four and had the rippled muscles of someone who'd toiled in the fields his entire life. The other men, both stooped and wrinkled, looked older than Lionel.

"This is John and Paul," Joffrey said. "John is the one with snowy white hair. Paul is bald as a gourd." The two men smiled at Joffrey's description of them. "Though they have apostle's names, both have sinned enough for all of us."

None of the three offered to shake our hands. When Paul asked a question, I could barely understand him because of his dialect.

"Why should we trust you?" he asked.

Joffrey opened Aura's shirt and turned her around, showing them the bony appendages on her back. A visual wasn't good enough as all three men felt the vestigial wings with their hands and fingers.

"She too tall to be a fairy," Lionel said.

Aura tried unsuccessfully to grab Joffrey's hand when he pulled her hair back and revealed her ears.

"Fairy ears," he said.

I had never seen Aura's ears, never even given them a thought. I was as surprised as the three older men. Aura snatched the hair back over her ears.

"What about him?" John asked. "He don't look black to me."

"Esther vouches for him. Do you not trust her?"

Lionel smiled. "Everyone trusts Esther. It is

you we have a problem with."

Joffrey wasn't smiling when he pulled a piece of paper from his pocket.

"This is an explanation in Esther's own words," he said.

"You know we can't read," Paul said.

"But you recognize Esther's mark," Joffrey said. "Wyatt is not only a passeblanc. He is also François's advocat. He will be of great use to us in the future."

We were all startled when three men entered the cabin. Charles Deslondes, as Joffrey had said, was himself light enough to pass as white. He was taller than me, looking regal in a starched shirt complete with frills and black pants Felix would have been proud to wear. Mud spoiled his polished boots, and a saber hung from the red sash around his waist.

The other two men were bigger and taller than Lionel. Hours of hard labor under a hot sun had burnished their skin the color of coal. They weren't just dark brown. They were black. Both of them had their cane knives drawn.

"Good to see you again, Charles. This is Aura Lea, daughter of Maurelle, and this is Wyatt. He is a passeblanc, François's advocat. I have Esther's letter vouching for him."

Deslondes could read because he spent several minutes staring at the words. Finally, he handed the letter back to Joffrey.

"And her?" he asked.

Again, Joffrey opened Aura's shirt and turned her toward Deslonde and his two men. I could tell by Aura's eyes she was anything but pleased as Deslondes and his men mauled her, noticing more than her vestigial wings. When one of the bodyguards pawed her exposed breasts, she connected with his face in an ear-popping slap. Laughing, Deslondes pushed the man away as

Aura hurriedly buttoned her shirt.

"She also have fairy ears," John said.

Deslonde pulled up one of the cane chairs and began warming himself by the fire.

"Esther's letter is all the proof I need. Wyatt will be valuable to us as the rebellion progresses. Did you bring me something, Joffrey?"

The back pocket of Joffrey's pants was just big enough to hold the small bottle of whiskey he pulled from it. He handed it to Deslondes. The would-be general opened it and took a drink, not offering to share with anyone.

"We are ready to hear your plan," Lionel said.

"Then pull up the chairs and let us talk," Deslondes said. "We march day after tomorrow. I can speak for a hundred men. We will have more as we head down River Road and take every plantation before the planters have a chance to respond."

"What about weapons?" John said.

"We have several rifles and a few pistols, along with our cane knives and pitchforks. There are more weapons for the taking at the Andry Plantation. That is where the revolution will begin."

Lionel was shaking his head. "I do not know. There is a brigade of American soldiers in New Orleans. We do not have the men or the arms to succeed against regular soldiers."

"They are too far away to respond before we have done our damage. Our numbers will grow as we advance," Deslondes said. "Slaves freed Santo Domingo and Haiti, and they began with fewer men and weapons than we now have. When we reach the city, we will send the brigade of Americans running, and then we will occupy New Orleans. Once there, our power will only solidify."

"Then you trust this man?" Lionel asked.

Joffrey spoke up before Deslondes could

answer.

"Tomorrow, Felix François is hosting a meeting of all the planters in the region. Jean Albard Trintignant, the American ambassador from New Orleans, is scheduled to attend. Wyatt will be there for the meeting and acting as François's advocate. After the meeting, he will possess valuable information with which to assist the insurrection."

Deslondes seemed pleased by the news. "I will need to discuss the meeting with him before we start burning plantations. He will serve as my captain and march by my side. I do not know how the girl can help us."

"Joffrey, what do you think?" Lionel asked.

"Aura does not need to accompany us. I have brought something that will ensure our success."

From his sack, he pulled Maurelle's pendant. The moonstones, transfixing everyone's gaze, reflected prisms of light from the coals burning in the fireplace.

"Where did you get that?"

When Deslondes reached for the pendant, Joffrey pulled it away from his grasp.

"Maurelle didn't give you the pendant," Aura said. "You stole it from her."

Joffrey flashed the wedding ring on his finger. "We are married. She was happy to provide her magic to assist us in the rebellion."

"Give it to me," Deslondes said.

"I keep the pendant," Joffrey said. "Only I know how to invoke its power. When this is over, I will have my choice of plantations. Agreed?"

Deslondes nodded. "You are officially my Second in Command."

"I hope you are sure about the extra weapons," Lionel said.

Deslondes pulled a pistol from a sack he carried. "There are more where this came from."

"May I hold it?" Aura said.

Deslondes handed her the pistol. "Do you know how to use it?" he asked.

"Please show me," she said.

"Pull back the hammer with your thumb," he said. "The weapon is now cocked. It is loaded. All you have to do is point it and pull the trigger."

The bodyguard who had copped a feel jumped when Aura pointed the pistol at him and said, "Bang!"

Deslondes quickly snatched the pistol from Aura, released the hammer, and returned it to his sack. He was also laughing uproariously.

"This girl has the heart of a panther. Maybe I will bring her along on the campaign after all."

Joffrey stood and warmed his hands in front of the fire.

"We must go," he said.

"Hear this," Deslondes said. "When we reach Moonmont Plantation, I intend to torch the place, soon as I blow off François's head."

Deslondes was laughing, the bottle of whiskey in his hands as we exited the cabin. Lionel, John, Paul, and the two bodyguards shared a jug of local moonshine. Aura shivered as we stepped off the rickety front porch.

"That went better than expected," Joffrey said.

Aura wasn't smiling, and neither was I. Sensing the sudden dampening of our affection for him, Joffrey started away through the swamp at a fast clip. Aura and I dropped back far enough to converse without his hearing.

"Joffrey has ambition I didn't see coming," Aura said.

"Did you get a good look at the pendant?" I asked.

"Not really," Aura said. "What about it?"

"It's intact, all three moonstones present."

"So?" Aura said.

"It means someone this very night at Moonmont will remove the moonstone."

"Then Maurelle's magic won't work, and it makes Joffrey doubly stupid," Aura said.

"Joffrey doesn't yet know he'll lose his head," I said. "We do. How smart does that make us?"

# Chapter 28

Two women were walking out the door when we reached our second-story bedroom at Moonmont Plantation. They both giggled when Joffrey patted their behinds.

"Shug and Miss Peach drew you a hot bath and left a fine bottle of wine," he said. "Relax and enjoy it. Tomorrow, Wyatt has an important meeting to attend. Until then, adieu. I have my own hot bath awaiting me."

Aura peeled off her clothes and climbed into the brass tub as steam wafted up from the water. Realizing she wasn't waiting for me, I stripped down and joined her.

The scent of lavender and rose petals filled the room. The hot water was up to my neck as I reclined against antique brass. I didn't realize how sore my muscles were as I began to relax, my former tense mood quickly becoming euphoric. Aura exposed her elfin ears when she ducked her head under the water to wash out the sand.

"How long have you known you are a fairy?" I asked,

"I'm not a fairy, you asshole," she said.

"Then why do you hide your ears?"

My question made her smile. "You can't imagine how stressful it was, showering after gym class without letting my pointed ears show."

"You never told anyone?"

"My best friend, Sara. She said I had fairy blood."

"And Sara never ratted you out?"

"Who would have believed her?"

"What about your mom and dad?"

"Mom wanted me to have plastic surgery to make my ears look normal. Dad wouldn't let her. I've always had long hair. After Sara's reaction, I've kept my ears covered."

"Do you have any special powers?"

"Sometimes, I can read minds," she said.

"Can you read mine?" I asked.

"You don't have to have special powers to know what you're thinking?"

"Are you thinking the same thing?"

Aura squeezed the water out of her long hair. "Maybe. There's something I think we should discuss beforehand."

"Like what?"

"Joffrey."

"What about him."

"I'm wondering if he really loved Maurelle, or was he simply using her to achieve his ambitions."

"I was thinking the same thing," I said. "In the end, what difference does it make?"

"He stole Maurelle's magic pendant leaving her vulnerable to Felix's wrath. Maybe he deserved having his head chopped off," she said.

"He took the pendant. He's not the person who removed one of the moonstones," I said.

"Who do you suspect?"

"Shug, Miss Peach or Esther," I said. "Seems likely they're all with him right about now."

"How will you find out?" she asked.

"Don't know yet. We have to let this play out."

"You said you believe we have the capability of altering history," Aura said. "Why not do it before the rebellion begins?"

"How do you intend to do that?" I asked.

Aura pointed at her clothes beside the tub. Lying on top of the pile, I recognized a sack I hadn't noticed her carrying.

"Deslondes pistol," she said.

"You took Deslondes pistol? Who are you planning to shoot?"

"Not me, you."

"Who do you want me to kill?"

"Felix," she said. "They won't hang you. You'd leave the past first."

"What about you? You need my help returning to the future."

"It's a plan. It might work," Aura said.

"Might isn't good enough. Killing Felix won't stop the rebellion. Though Maurelle may survive, Joffrey will probably still lose his head."

"Maybe so," she said.

"The water's growing cold. Let's dry off and get in bed. We have time yet to decide what we need to do. Right now, I have other things on my mind."

Within minutes, our thoughts of the impending rebellion had morphed into glorious lust. I was moaning, Aura squealing when something grabbed my arm and yanked me forcibly off the bed. Whatever or whoever slammed me into the wall.

Some giant beast with lousy breath and long teeth had my neck in its jaws, ready to bite my head off when Aura lit a candle and yelled.

"Grishorn, no!"

When the beast stood on its hind legs, I saw the creature both Aura and Joffrey had described to me. The leathery-skinned animal with big teeth was Jake Huntington's legendary chupacabra. Aura hugged the neck of the beast.

"It's okay, Grishorn. He wasn't hurting me. We were only making love."

The beast transformed before my eyes, becoming no larger than a lap dog. Aura was smiling as she hugged it to her breast. The animal's tail was wagging as he licked her face.

"Grishorn?" I said.

Tears were dripping down Aura's reddened cheeks.

"I told you I felt I recognized Grishorn when I saw her at the Old François Place. I've had dreams of her all my life. I had blocked it from my memory."

A bruise on my chest was beginning to turn blue, and I wondered if I had a broken rib.

"I believe you," I said.

"Pet her," Aura said.

Grishorn responded with almost a purr when I stroked her head and fin.

"Good girl," I said.

"She's a shape-shifter," Aura said.

"I thought you were a scientist and didn't believe in the paranormal."

"Grishorn is real."

She carried Grishorn back to the bed with her, all the while cuddling the suddenly small creature in her arms.

"Aren't you coming?" she said. With some difficulty, I pulled myself off the hardwood floor and crawled into bed. "Well?"

"Well, what?" I said.

"We were making love, remember?"

"Maybe if you put Grishorn on the floor."

To show her displeasure with my callous comment, Aura hugged her pet even closer.

"How could you?" she said.

"My mood seems to have flown out the window," I said.

"Then let's get some sleep," Aura said, turning her back to me and snuggling Grishorn. "Now that I've finally found my baby, I don't want to ever let her go."

Grishorn was gone the next morning when Shug and Miss Peach rousted me out of bed. Shug combed my hair as Miss Peach helped me pull on my pants. As I stared into a full-length mirror, fiddling with the perfectly-fitting brown coat, I realized I looked the part of a New Orleans advocat, circa 1811. Joffrey appeared as Shug, and Miss Peach walked out the door.

"I let you sleep as long as I could. You have time for breakfast before the meeting begins."

Shug and Miss Peach were giggling as they stirred a pot hanging over the fire. Esther's smug look told me she thought she knew more than she did.

"Heard you had quite the night," she said.

"You can't imagine, I said as I forked a mouthful of bacon and eggs into my mouth.

When Joffrey and I left the kitchen, we found the front door alive with arriving plantation owners. In anticipation of meeting

Jean Albard Trintignant, they were all dressed to the nines. Joffrey opened the door for me but didn't enter the Great Room.

"This meeting is important," he said. "Do not forget a word that is said."

He disappeared back into the hallway before I could reply.

Servants had provided wine and brandy for the planters enjoying the facetime with each other. Almost an hour passed before Joffrey opened the door and entered.

"Gentlemen, please be seated."

We all found chairs as Felix strode to the front of the room, where sunlight from a big picture window backdropped him.

"Thank you for coming. We are joined today by Jean Albard Trintignant, an emissary from the Americans in New Orleans. May I introduce Jean Albard Trintignant."

An older man dressed in the finest satin and his head topped with a regal powdered wig entered the room. Once inside, Joffrey closed the door as Trintignant joined Felix.

"You all know Jean Albard," Felix said. "We are here today to hear his request."

Frowns encompassed every face in the room. No one applauded Trintignant's introduction, the meeting about to become contentious.

"Why have you betrayed us, Jean Albard?" one of the planters asked. "You are as French as we are."

"Louisiana is no longer a colony of France. Like it or not, we are all citizens of the Americas now."

"We still have rights," a planter said.

"Of course you do," Trintignant said. "That is why I am here."

"Explain yourself," a planter said.

"You are all aware of what happened in Haiti. The slaves revolted, and citizens were killed, the French regime overthrown. French and British landowners lost everything they owned. Are you prepared for that to happen here on the German Coast?"

"We have controlled our slaves for decades," a planter said.

"Yes, but our operatives tell us there are rumblings of revolt," Trintignant said.

"What do you propose to do about it?" a planter asked.

"The Americans have a plan. They have a garrison of soldiers in New Orleans that can quell any insurrection. The soldiers are ineffective unless they can respond before insurrectionists burn your plantations."

"Please explain," Felix said.

"The Americans want to build a fort in this part of the German Coast so they can respond timely to any potential threat. They seek a contribution of land upon which to build the fort. The landowners, of course, will be fully compensated."

Murmurs in the room turned quickly to an outcry of dissent.

"The Americans occupy New Orleans," Felix said. "The planters along the German Coast are not prepared to accept ceding our land to the military force of a country that none of us trusts."

Trintignant waited through ten long minutes of shouts and confusion. Everyone was talking, no one listening. When the dissonance finally abated, Trintignant raised both hands.

"The United States, not the French, owns Louisiana now. They only want to help you help yourselves. Consider my visit the opening of negotiations which will ultimately result in peace and prosperity for both the French and the Americans. I have a document the Americans wish you to consider."

"Monsieur Thomas is my advocat," Felix said. "Please give it to him."

I walked to the front of the large hall and accepted the document wrapped in a scroll from the hands of Trintignant.

With that, the American emissary strode out the door. The next few minutes grew even more contentious as planters tried to shout over each other. The discord continued until Felix pounded on his desk with a gavel.

"Gentlemen," he said. "Please, we have decisions to make."

"What does the document say?" one of the planters asked.

"It is detailed and has many clauses," I said. "It will take time for me to read and understand it fully."

"That is not good enough," a planter said. "Everyone knows the Americans are thieves and cannot be trusted."

"They only want to steal our property," a man said.

"And stick their fort up our butts," another man said.

"Let's take a vote," Felix said. "Everyone wishing to cede land to the Americans to build a fort answer by saying oui."

The room remained silent.

"To hell with the Americans," one of the planters said. "This is our land. They only want to steal it from us."

Before anyone else could speak, the hallway door opened. Aura, dressed in a ball gown and powdered wig, entered and walked down the aisle toward Felix. Recognizing Aura, Felix's eyes had the look of doubt and disbelief. He stood transfixed, the other occupants of the room silent as she walked toward him.

Not immediately knowing what Aura was doing there, I was also in horror. My trepidation turned to desperation as I noticed the image of my arm was beginning to flicker. When Aura drew Deslondes pistol and pointed it at Felix's face, I had only time enough to leave my chair, take a single step and then launch myself toward Aura's wrist.

# Chapter 29

Carlos Sanchez readied his expensive camera in Madam Aja's conjure room. Jake had converted a barstool to a makeshift director's chair. Mama was in a frantic conversation with Senora. Senora just kept shaking her head.

"I know you have extensive powers, Mama. I don't believe Madam Aja will allow us to summon her."

Senora cracked a smile when Mama said, "Not even with a bottle of Old Crow?"

"Maybe there is something," Senora said.

Senora supported herself by selling potions and magic ingredients to local voodoo practitioners. She maintained shelves in the kitchen pantry lined with jars of herbs, plants, minerals, and ground bones. Mama followed her into the pantry and watched as she began browsing the labels on the jars.

"What?" Mama said.

"Datura," Senora said.

"Dangerous," Mama said. "I've never used it."

"I've had it for years. Madam Aja and I found some moonflowers growing wild near the railroad tracks when we were searching for senna."

"I'd almost forgotten how much Madam Aja loved her laxatives," Mama said.

"Nothing better than senna if you're constipated," Senora said. "We collected the moonflowers along with the senna. Madam Aja showed me how to extract the hallucinogenic oil from it."

The baggie inside the sealed jar contained a dozen or so sugar cubes laced with datura.

"You trust it?" Mama asked.

"Madam Aja used an eyedropper to dose the cubes. Do you remember how fussy about being precise she was? I wouldn't touch one if any other person on earth other than Madam Aja made them."

"Perfect," Mama said. "She won't deny us her presence if we use her datura. I'm all in."

"The others may not be so trusting," Senora said.

"If you and I are willing, we don't need anyone else to help us," Mama said.

"Just someone to bury our bodies in case things go bad."

"Don't even think it," Mama said. "We'll be fine. Madam Aja would have never made a bad batch of anything."

"At least not knowingly."

Carlos was set up in the corner of the conjuring room and began recording when Mama and Senora returned. Seth appeared apprehensive as he sat beside Colley, propped against the wall on a kitchen chair's back legs.

"What do you have?" Jake asked.

"Datura, a hallucinogenic made from the blossoms of magic moonflowers. We're going to use it to summon Madam Aja."

"Great," Jake said. "How does it work?"

"Pop a sugar cube in your mouth and let it

dissolve," Mama said.

"Who's going to do it?"

"All of us," Mama said.

"Or none of us," Senora said.

"Hell," Colley said. "I've dropped acid."

"Not so fast," Seth said. "This isn't LSD. Datura is deadly. Kill you deader than hell deadly."

"Is that right, Mama?" Jake asked.

"Right," Mama said. "This batch was made by Madam Aja herself, and she was arguably the best herbalist on the face of the earth. That doesn't make it any less deadly."

"Are you going to take it?" Jake asked.

"Yes," Mama said.

"Then count me in," he said. "Senora?"

"There's no one on earth I trusted more than Madam Aja. I'm in."

"I can't," Carlos said. "I have a wife and children who depend on me."

"Understandable," Jake said. "Leave the camera running and wait with Bradley in the limo. Colley?"

"I once had a bad acid trip, Boss Man. I said then never again."

"No problem," Jake said. "You're the best chopper pilot I know. I don't fancy looking for another. Join Bradley and Carlos in the limo. Seth?"

"Sorry, Jake. I'm a little bit crazy but not insane."

"It's okay, old buddy." Mama, Senora, and Jake watched Seth exit the room. "Guess it's just the three of us," he said.

"What we're about to do is dangerous," Mama said. "Senora and I can do the ceremony without you. I care for you too much to have you risk it."

"No way," Jake said, moving to a spot behind the camera. "If you're in, then so am I. If you die,

I die."

Mama gave him a quick kiss. "Let's hope no one dies."

"I'm all for that," he said. "Ready to begin?"

Senora opened the bottle of Old Crow. "Not until we've all drank some of Madam Aja's favorite whiskey. A big slug."

Senora tipped up the bottle, handing it to Mama when she couldn't handle another drop. Mama made a face after chugging a mouthful. Jake's nose wrinkled when he drank all he could. Mama grinned when she handed him a sugar cube.

"Sweets for the sweet," she said.

Senora had a cloak of many colors, an article of clothing wrapped in the connection between voodoo and Christianity. She helped Mama drape it around her shoulders. It was dark outside, the room even darker when Senora extinguished the lights. Mama sat at Madam Aja's chair at the conjure table and lit three black candles.

Jake cursed to himself as he fumbled with the camera's aperture, widening it as far as it would go. He put the sugar cube in his mouth.

"Let it dissolve slowly," Mama said. "Don't swallow it whole."

Mama gave one to Senora and took one herself. There was an explosion of light when Mama began trickling white powder over the flames of the candles. Dense smoke filled the room.

Jake was trying to adjust the camera as his eyelids began to feel as though they were melting. As the smoke cleared, Mama's eyes closed. She started mouthing a secret incantation.

"Acid, cold, fire, necrotic, thunder, lightning, poison, psychic, radiant, force."

Senora's back was to the camera, and she also began to chant, "Dica, dloc, erif, citorcen, rednuht, gninthgil, nosiop, cihcysp, tnaidar, ecrof."

Mama and Senora's chants began to meld into a language Jake couldn't quite understand, though it had subliminal meaning to him. Tears began pouring from his eyes and sobs from somewhere deep in his throat.

Rapture had also seized Mama and Senora's throats. Mama opened the front of the colored cloak, ripped her blouse open to the waist, and began pouring whiskey from the bottle of Old Crow over her head. Collapsing backward in the chair, she began writhing on the floor.

Senora's head was hanging back over the chair, her mouth open and a low moan from deep in her chest sounding like a cross between a boiling teapot and the screech of a feral cat.

The floor began to shake beneath Jake's feet, and he was having a difficult time operating the camera. It didn't matter. The camera suddenly had a mind of its own as it focused first on Mama, her dress hiked up to her waist, her muscular legs in full view as she rotated uncontrollably on the floor. Senora's eyes had rolled back in her head as a flickering light began radiating up from the candles. It was the holographic image of Madam Aja.

"Senora, is it you trying to summon me?"

Senora didn't answer, her head still thrust backward over the chair and only the whites of her eyes showing. Mama didn't answer either. Jake's voice sounded strange, even to himself.

"Is that you, Madam Aja? I'm Jake Huntington," he said.

"Cryptid Hunter," Madam Aja said.

"I have questions."

Madam Aja's voice was distant and tinny when she spoke.

"What questions?"

"Our friend Wyatt Thomas is missing, as is Aura, one of the archaeologists who found the body of the fairy at the Old François Place."

"Wyatt is traveling in time."

"Is he okay?" Jake asked.

"He is in grave danger, and you must help him."

"Want me to travel back in time and save him?" Jake asked.

"You are not a Traveler. That is not possible."

"What, then?" Jake said. "I can't change time."

"We all change time, every minute of every day," Madam Aja said.

"I'm not following you," Jake said.

"Time is like a river, a force of nature comprised of tiny drops of water. When the river takes a different course, every drop is affected."

"What's your point?" Jake said.

"If the Mississippi River source is time's beginning, then the Gulf of Mexico is its end. The River of Time is continuous; hurricanes in the Gulf affect the river's flow back to its source."

"What does that have to do with Wyatt?" Jake asked.

"He's a Traveler, a raindrop falling at the source in the River of time. Can you grasp what I'm saying?"

"Maybe," he said.

"Time is continuous and has no beginning and no end. It flows in circles, like orbiting planets, or the cycles of the moon."

When Madam Aja's image began to shimmer and disappear, Jake said, "Please, wait. I have many more questions."

"Aura Lea is your answer."

"We don't know where she is," Jake said.

"You will soon find her, and she will provide your answers."

"At least give me a clue," Jake said.

"The birthing facility in the Seventh Ward."

"What does a birthing facility have to do with anything?" Jake asked.

Madam Aja shook her head and raised her hand, showing Jake her palm. "Adieu, Cryptid Hunter. Good hunting."

"Adieu, Madam Aja," he said.

The old woman's image flickered and then disappeared, flames from the three black candles dying. Jake fumbled for the lights. Senora was comatose in the chair, Mama much the same on the floor. Jake quickly dialed his cell phone.

"Angie, what's the antidote for datura?"

"No clue," Angie said.

"Call the nearest emergency room and find out, then get Bradley here."

"Where are you?"

"Bradley's outside the door. I have two soldiers down and need a Medevac, now!"

"Aye, aye, captain," she said.

Scant minutes ticked off the clock before Bradley, Colley, Carlos, and Seth burst into the room. Jake was on his hands and knees, daubing Mama's face with a wet rag.

Without asking questions, they lifted Mama and Senora and took them to the limousine. Colley had Jake by the arm as he followed them.

"Don't forget the camera," Jake said.

Carlos already had it under his arm as he hurried to the limo. Once the doors slammed shut, Bradley started the powerful vehicle away with tires squealing and rubber burning. A convoy of police cars soon joined them, sirens blasting and blue lights flashing as they headed toward the New Orleans hospital district.

White-coated emergency room workers were waiting when Bradley drove up to the entrance, Mama and Senora quickly wheeled away on gurneys as Jake, Colley, and Seth followed them through an electronic door into the ER.

"Datura poisoning," Jake said.

"Haven't had that one in a while," the nurse in a blue mask said. "No problem. We can handle it."

IVs were soon dripping into Mama's and Senora's arms as an emergency room doctor arrived. The young man with thick glasses grabbed the chart nurses had begun compiling.

"Are they going to be okay?" Jake asked.

"Their condition isn't critical," the doctor said. "They should recover quickly once the antidote begins to work. Who else took the drug?"

"I did," Jake said.

"Then let's get you prepped. You need the antidote as well."

"But I'm fine," Jake said.

"Maybe, maybe not," the doctor said, "You're here. Can't take any chances."

Almost an hour had passed before Mama and Senora began to respond to the antidote. Jake was drinking coffee and wishing for gin when Mama's eyes finally popped open.

"Where are we?" she asked.

"Hospital emergency room," Jake said.

"Did we all react to the drug?"

"Just you and Senora. They gave me the antidote in an abundance of caution."

"Did we manage to channel Madam Aja?"

"Yes. Wyatt is lost in time and needs our help."

"What can we do?" Mama asked.

"Madam Aja explained it to me. I'm not sure I fully understand what she meant," he said.

"Give me the short version," Mama said.

"We have to rain on someone at a birthing facility in New Orleans's Seventh Ward."

"Are you being facetious?"

"Sorry," Jake said. "At best, Madam Aja was cryptic. She implied Aura would know what to do."

"Has Angie located her?"

"Not yet," Jake said.

Senora was coming to, blinking and popping her jaws as she tried to unplug her ears.

"Are you okay?" she asked when she saw Mama Mulate.

"Yes," Mama said, "but I'm never drinking Old Crow again for as long as I live.

## Chapter 30

The last thing I remembered was grabbing Aura's arm before she pulled the trigger of an ancient flintlock pistol and blew off Felix François's head. When I found myself sitting at the bar of La Fée Verte, I wondered if I shouldn't have let her.

Aura was standing beside me, her arm resting on my shoulder. Ben and Doris were sitting beside us, and Yvonne was behind the bar polishing a glass. It was as if we had never left.

"What were you thinking?" I said. "Every planter at the meeting was packing. You could have gotten us both killed."

Ignoring my rebuke, she said, "We're screwed now. What are we going to do?"

"I had no choice. I was reverting."

"Damn it to hell!" she said.

I raised my hand to get Yvonne's attention. "I heard a quote some author supposedly said about absinthe. Do you know it?"

"Oscar Wilde," she said.

"Please say it for me," I said.

"Just for you, cutie pie. Wilde said, 'After the first glass of absinthe, you see things as you wish they were. After the second, you see them as they are not. Finally, you see things as they really are, and that is the most horrible thing in the world.' At least that's pretty close to what he supposedly said."

"How many absinthes have I had?"

"Who's counting?" she said. "Ben's buying your drinks.

"You've had two," Aura said.

"Then bring me another," I said.

Ben was listening to our conversation. When Yvonne glanced at him, he nodded and raised his index finger. It didn't take a rocket scientist to tell Aura wasn't happy with the attention Yvonne was heaping on me as she began preparing my green cocktail.

"You want another one too, sister?" Yvonne asked.

Yvonne didn't like Aura's answer or her snarky smile. "I'll drink some of Wyatt's."

I was hoping the absinthe would transport me back to Moonmont Plantation. This time, I intended to go alone. After drinking some of the cocktail, I slid the glass in front of Aura.

"All yours," I said. "I have to go to the bathroom. Take my stool while I'm gone."

I didn't make it to the bathroom before I found myself more than two-hundred years in the past. This time, I wasn't at Moonmont Plantation.

Aura had finished the Absinthe cocktail when she realized Wyatt hadn't returned to the bar. Nothing could hide her dire expression as she stared down the hallway.

"What's wrong?" Ben asked.

"Wyatt. I'm worried about him," she said.

"Hey, these green ghosts will do that to you. Wyatt probably passed out on the toilet."

"Not funny," Aura said. "Will you check on

him for me?"

"He hasn't been gone long. Give him five more minutes," Ben said. "Yvonne, bring us four more."

Yvonne was more than happy to comply. Mesmerized by the cocktail creation ceremony, Aura forgot about Wyatt. The thought returned when she was lightheaded from her latest absinthe cocktail.

"Will you check on Wyatt now?"

"Sure," Ben said. "I need to use the facilities anyway."

Doris leaned across Ben's vacated stool. "I can't believe Wyatt won't even consider my generous offer for the old pendant he has. Will you talk to him for me, try to convince him? There's a reward in it for you."

Aura had no intention of convincing Wyatt of selling Doris the pendant. She saw no reason, however, to bother explaining why."

"Sure," she said.

Ben returned shortly. "He's not in there," he said. "Maybe he went outside for a cigarette."

"Wyatt doesn't smoke," Aura said.

"Then maybe he got a phone call. Probably didn't want to share his conversation with everyone in the bar."

"Maybe," Aura said. "I'm going to have a look around."

Aura gasped when she stepped outside and took her first breath of warm August air. After walking the length of Pirate's Alley, she retraced her steps, glancing in the bathroom hallway before returning to the stool.

"Did Wyatt come back?" she asked.

"Sorry, babe," he said.

"Thanks for the drinks," Aura said. "I have to find him."

Not bothering to look back, Aura left the little bar. In her heart, she knew Wyatt had returned to

Moonmont Plantation. Thinking maybe she was wrong, she headed through the suddenly crowded French Quarter toward Bertram's bar on Chartres.

Mama, Jake, and the entire crew had descended on Bertram's. Bertram was in Cajun heaven as he dispensed one drink after the other. Mama and Senora had both survived their datura overdoses and were doing their best to keep up with Jake and Colley's cocktail marathon. When Aura came through the door, the crowd at the bar elicited a communal cheer. Carlos began filming as everyone applauded.

"Is Wyatt here?" Aura asked.

"We were hoping you'd know where he is," Jake said.

"I fear he's returned to Moonmont Plantation," Aura said.

"Where is that?" Mama asked.

"Felix François's sugar plantation on the German Coast."

Mama's hand went to her mouth. "Not in 1811 New Orleans, I hope."

"Yes," Aura said.

"How do you know?" Jake asked.

"I was there with him."

"How did he manage to travel through time?" Mama asked.

"I found Wyatt at a little bar on Pirate's Alley called La Fée Verte. He was drinking absinthe cocktails."

"Wyatt doesn't drink," Mama said.

"Trust me; he was drinking. He had the pendant Madam Aja gave him. He somehow had the idea absinthe would transport him to the past. He was right."

"How is it you went with him?" Jake asked.

"His body began to flicker. I could see he was

disappearing, so I grabbed his arm. He has this crazy idea he can change time."

"Might not be so crazy," Jake said.

"What?" Aura asked.

"Aura, this is Senora. She is Madam Aja's daughter. We almost lost our lives channeling the old voodoo woman. She gave us some valuable information."

"Such as?" Aura asked.

"There's a birthing clinic in the Seventh Ward. Something is happening there that could change the course of time."

"Like what?" Aura said.

"Madam Aja called you Aura Lea. She said you would know."

"I am Aura Lea. I have no clue what she was talking about."

"Bradley's waiting in the limo," Jake said. "Angie found the location of the birthing clinic. Bradley will take us there."

"Bring me back a po'boy," Bertram said.

"There's a po'boy shop in the Seventh Ward?" Jake said.

"One of the best," Bertram said. "Mama knows where it is."

"I've been there dozens of times," Mama said.

"Me too," Senora said. "Maybe an oyster po'boy is what we need to shake off the effects of the datura."

"Give me your camera, Carlos. I think I've found a new calling," Jake said.

"You don't have to do that, Boss Man," Carlos said.

"You're job's safe. I'm on a roll," Jake said. "Everyone have a party on me while we're gone. Maybe we'll have something to celebrate when we return."

The Seventh Ward, between the Fairgrounds and Faubourg Marigny, wasn't far away. Like most of the city, it had suffered greatly during Hurricane Katrina. Now, both new condos and hundred-year-old shotguns, camelbacks, and Creole cottages filled it.

Caribbean-influenced teals, greens, purples, and blues colored many of the homes. Though much of the area had experienced gentrification, some of the population still lived in conditions of near-poverty. They found the birthing clinic in one of these pockets. Bradley pulled to the curb and helped the group exit.

In a house on a narrow lot, the little clinic was freshly painted, though white instead of pastel. There was a reception area inside the front door. A stern black woman, dressed in a skirt of azure decorated with yellow half-moons, glanced up from her magazine when they entered.

"Help you?" she asked.

"We're here to film the birth," Jake said.

"You made it just in time," the woman whose nametag said Veronica told him. "Follow me."

Mama held her hand near her mouth and spoke in Jake's ear. "Guess we don't have to worry about HIPA regulations."

"You ladies wash up," Veronica said. "We may need your help."

"I don't know anything about delivering a baby," Aura said.

"Well, honey chile, it's time you did. Never know when you might need to know."

Mama and Senora were grinning as Aura washed her hands in the sink.

"Water's not even hot," she said. "And they probably reuse the gloves."

Mama cracked up when Senora said, "What gloves."

Three people occupied the birthing room: a young woman in bed, her legs spread wide and in obvious pain, a man who looked just as distressed as he held her hand, and a young black man with cornrowed hair that reached to his shoulders.

A tie-dyed smock cloaked the young man. He had a palm on the young woman's knee and was instructing her on how to breathe. He looked every bit as distressed as the woman preparing to give birth.

"I'm Jake Huntington, Doctor. We're here to film the birth."

The young man turned, grabbed his head, and collapsed to the floor. Colley knelt beside him, trying to revive him.

"Jimmy ain't no doctor. He just got into med school," Veronica said. "You ladies will have to deliver the baby. I gotta go watch the front door."

Senora rushed to the bed, hugged the man, and then massaged the birth mother's shoulders a moment.

"Don't worry," she said. "Me and Mama Mulate will deliver your baby."

"You a mambo?" the man asked.

"I'm not, but Mama is," Senora said. "You're in good hands."

The man's smile was weak. At least it was a smile. Mama and Senora began coaching the woman, calming her and preparing for the imminent birth. Aura was standing by the man who looked strangely familiar to her. He continued holding his wife's hand. Aura could see one of his hands was missing, the bandage over the stub bloody.

Jake was having a blast filming the birth. Mama and Senora were too busy helping the woman deliver her baby to notice the man's recent injury.

"Push, baby, push," Senora said. "It's coming. Deep breaths and push."

Mama was rubbing the young woman's

shoulders as she swabbed her forehead with a damp cloth. Too busy staring at the man with the bloody stump, Aura wasn't watching. He briefly turned away from the birth when Aura spoke to him again.

"Charles Deslondes, is that you?"

"How do you know my name?" he asked.

"I think I knew your great-grandfather."

The young man had no time to respond to Aura's words as the baby was being born.

"It's a boy," Senora said. "He's perfect."

Both Charles and his wife began sobbing. Mama helped Senora with the newborn and then deposited it in his mother's arms when he started to cry. Charles bent over his wife, their expressions soon consumed with smiles of happiness.

"Who are you? How does she know my name?" Charles asked.

"I'm Jake Huntington, the Cryptid Hunter. You're going to be on an upcoming episode."

Charles turned to Aura. "Who are you, and how do you know me?"

"It's complicated," Aura said.

Before Charles could ask more questions, his wife handed the newborn to Aura.

Aura said, "I think he needs a diaper."

"If you don't mind me asking," Jake said. "What happened to your hand?"

Charles's frown said it all. "Lost it at the factory in a punch press. Don't know what I'm gonna do now with a new son."

While Mama and Senora looked for a diaper, the new mother clasped her husband's hand.

"It'll be all right, baby. We'll make it somehow."

Charles buried his head in his wife's ample breasts. "Oh, Priscilla, I'm so sorry."

"You got nothing to be sorry about," Priscilla

said. "Be proud. You got a beautiful new son, and you still have your job."

Jake could tell by Charles's look that something was wrong.

"Priscilla, this is Mama, Senora, and Aura. I'm Jake. Mama and Senora will take care of you and the baby. Aura and I need to have a few words with Charles in the hall."

Charles's eyes were red as he followed Aura and Jake through the door.

"Didn't the factory take you to the doctor?" Jake asked.

"They would have, I'm sure. Priscilla was having the baby. I needed to get here."

"Damn, the accident just happened?"

"About three hours ago," Charles said.

"What's the name of the factory?" Jake asked.

"Orleans Mobile Construction Company."

Jake had his cell phone out. "Angie," he said. "I have a problem."

Aura found a coffee pot and gave Charles a cup along with two aspirins.

"We need to get you to a hospital," she said.

"I can't," he said. "I don't have the money."

Jake caught the last of the conversation. "The factory put your severed hand on ice. My assistant Angie has arranged to have it reattached at the nearest hospital."

"I can't afford it," Charles said.

"Trust me when I tell you you're not going to pay a penny. New Orleans Mobile Construction will pay. I promise you."

"I'll lose my job."

"Good," Jake said. "I'm opening a studio in New Orleans. I need lots of new hires I can trust. You just convinced me you deserve to be one of them."

"I get lots of overtime at the factory," Charles said.

Jake patted his shoulder. "I have a feeling you're going to be very happy with the money I pay you."

They heard the siren of an approaching ambulance. "I can't leave Priscilla and my son," Charles said.

"You won't have to. They're coming with you. You have the best healthcare now."

"You sure about this?" Charles asked. "You don't even know me."

"I know you better than you can ever imagine," Jake said. "You started on the Huntington clock ten minutes ago."

Angie wasn't far behind the ambulance. "I'll accompany them to the hospital and make sure everything goes well," she said.

Mama, Senora, Jake, Veronica, and the young intern watched the ambulance leave with Charles, Priscilla, and their newborn son.

"I want to contribute," Jake said.

"Wonderful," Veronica said, pulling a donation slip out of a drawer. "We take any amount from a dollar on up." Veronica's eyes grew large when she read the figure on the check Jake handed her. "You must have made a mistake."

"No mistake," Jake said. "I'm donating one hundred thousand dollars. A few requirements."

"What?"

"I want to be on the board of directors. You're going to need a bigger facility and money for salaries. How much do you and the young man make?"

"We don't make nothing," Veronica said. "We are volunteers."

"Why aren't there more people in the world like you?" Jake said. "My assistant, Angie, will be back in touch after she takes care of Charles and Priscilla."

"You know Charles?" Mama said when they exited to the sidewalk.

"He's Charles Deslondes. His ancestor led the slave rebellion of 1811," Aura said.

"That explains it," Mama said. "Deslondes's captors chopped off both his hands."

"Damn," Jake said. "I hope the hospital has good surgeons."

Mama patted Jake's shoulder. "Some of the best in the world," she said. "If Madam Aja was right, I believe there's a good chance we just changed the course of time."

"Where to, Boss Man?" Bradley asked.

Jake was already dispensing martinis and gin. "Back to Bertram's," he said.

# Chapter 31

The third absinthe worked as had the first two, returning me to antebellum Louisiana. This time, I wasn't in the bedroom of the Moonmont Plantation.

It was dark. I was naked, looking for something to wear in the middle of a driving rainstorm. As lightning raced across a darkened sky, I saw wet clothes hanging from a line behind a slave shack. It didn't take me long to realize why someone had left their clothes in the rain. I grabbed a wet shirt and a pair of pants off the line.

There was uneaten food on the table of the first shack I entered. It didn't matter what had caused everyone to leave. The sound of a weapon firing returned me to reality, and I stepped back into the rain.

I trudged toward the dark outline of a large house looming in the distance. When I reached it, I was knocked to the ground by a frightened man bursting through the door. He was bleeding, our collision leaving my shirt sticky with his blood.

Whatever wound he had hadn't affected his running ability. He'd disappeared into the darkness of the trees surrounding the plantation when three men followed him out the door. I was quickly grabbed and slapped in the face.

"He is not Andry," one of the men said. "Let him go."

"Where is he?" another man asked me.

"He ran toward the trees," I said.

Two men started away in the direction I had pointed. The third man was Charles Deslondes.

"Who was it?" I asked.

"Manuel Andry," Deslondes said. "Someone alerted the plantation we were coming. Andry was the only one here."

"He was bloody," I said.

"Louis cut him with a cane knife."

"Who is Andry?" I asked.

"The owner of this plantation and the leader of the local militia. There are weapons and uniforms in his basement. We were hoping to dispatch him, keep him from alerting the militia."

"What now?" I asked.

"He is badly injured. My men will find him. Even if they do not, he will likely die in the woods from loss of blood. Come inside. We were wondering where you were."

"I'm here now," I said.

Deslondes nodded and tapped his fist against my chest. I followed him up the porch steps and into the house. A dozen men, including Joffrey, were waiting for us. Joffrey seemed surprised to see me.

"Wyatt, where have you been?"

"I was delayed," I said.

My stilted explanation seemed to satisfy him. "And Andry?" Joffrey asked.

"Escaped into the woods, the men are chasing him. He won't get far," Deslondes said. "Let us see what is in the basement."

Torchlight cast moving shadows on the stone

walls of the basement. The floor was damp, and the underground room mostly empty except for a rack of muskets, a hundred rounds of shot, and black powder. There were also a dozen militia uniforms. Deslondes began doffing his wet clothes and donning a regal blue captain's coat complete with epaulets.

"These uniforms will gain us stature," Deslondes said. "Put them on."

Joffrey and I soon looked like real soldiers. The dry clothes felt better than had the wet slave outfit, though I wondered what price the momentary comfort would cause me to pay.

"What happened during the meeting with the American emissary?" Deslondes asked.

"It grew contentious," I said.

"Are the Americans on their way here?" Deslondes asked.

"Not that I know of," I said. "At least it wasn't discussed."

"Then get some sleep," he said. "The revolution has begun. When dawn arrives, we will head to New Orleans. Freedom or death," he said.

"Freedom or death," the men in the basement repeated.

The toe of Joffrey's boot nudging my ribs awoke me. Numbness in my shoulder slowly disappeared as I dragged myself off the hardwood floor and followed him out the door. The rain had ceased, a crowd gathered around the porch.

Dozens of men and women, all dressed in the garb of slaves, awaited the appearance of Charles Deslondes. Most, their faces reflecting universal resolve, brandished pitchforks or cane knives. A cheer rippled through the motley crowd when Charles Deslondes, dressed in his royal blue uniform jacket, walked through the front door of the Andry Plantation. After halting on the porch, he raised his arms until the gathering grew silent.

"I am grateful you are here. Freedom without commitment is a fool's fantasy. Today, we begin the journey to regain ours. There is no in-between, only freedom or death."

"Freedom or death," the crowd chanted.

"Now, the time has come for us to march to New Orleans. Men and women, just like you, achieved freedom in Mother Haiti. Are we as one?"

The universal voice of the crowd had only grown stronger as they continued to chant. There was no white stallion. Deslondes seemed just as regal when he mounted an old brown nag and trotted away toward the plantation's front gate. Dozens of former slaves followed, I among them. As Deslondes had said, the revolution had begun.

We'd gone no more than a mile when the shoes I was wearing began rubbing my feet raw. The farther we marched, the more people joined us. We found the next plantation deserted. Deslondes ordered us to set it ablaze.

Many people cheered as the beautiful antebellum mansion burned. Rubbing my aching feet, I sat beneath a large tree. A man in a broad-brimmed hat and wearing spectacles as thick as the bottoms of soda bottles tripped over my foot. Grabbing his arm as he lunged forward, I managed to break his fall.

"You okay?" I asked.

"Didn't mean to step on you," he said. "I'm about half-blind."

"No problem," I said. "I was stretching my leg out and didn't mean to trip you."

"I been tripping over things all my life," he said. "Weren't your fault. You thirsty?"

"Parched," I said.

The man sat beside me at the base of the giant tree and handed me his canteen.

"I just filled it up at the well and drank my fill from the ladle. Have some."

"Thanks," I said.

"I'm Pinkney. Who are you?"

"Wyatt," I said. "Glad to meet you, Pinkney. Thanks for the water."

"Everybody just calls me Pink," he said. "What's the matter with your feet?"

"Shoes are too small," I said.

"Trade with me," he said.

"I can't take your shoes," I said. "I'll get by."

"I got the opposite problem," Pink said. "Mine are too big for me."

"You sure?"

"It'll be an even swap. I got an extra pair of socks on trying to make these things fit. Trade me, and I'll throw them in."

"Pink, you're a godsend. Now, if I just had something to put on my blisters."

I took the socks and started to put them on. "Wait just a minute," Pink said.

He reached up to a low-lying limb of the tree and plucked a half-dozen leaves. Placing them on a flat rock, he began grinding them with the butt of the knife.

"Rub your hands in the sap and wipe it into your sores."

I did as he said. "I don't recognize this tree. What is it?"

"Gingko. Come from China. Some people say the leaves are poison. They ain't. They'll heal your sore feet."

"Hope you're right about that," I said. I pulled on the thick wool socks and then the shoes. "You're right. My feet already feel better. Pink, you saved my life."

"Not me," he said. "Was whoever had you sit under this big old ginkgo tree."

"You believe in angels?" I asked.

Pink smiled for the first time. "That's the only way I made it long as I have. I been beat twice."

"I saw a man beaten almost to death not long ago. Are you okay?"

"Made me kinda crazy in the head," he said. "Other than that, I'm good to go."

"How do those shoes fit?" I asked.

"Perfect," Pink said. "Thank you."

"No, thank you. You saved my life."

"You think this revolution gonna work?"

I didn't want to admit I already knew the answer to his question.

"Hope so," I said.

"What kind of weapon you got?" Pink asked.

"Pitchfork."

"I got a musket, ten rounds of shot, and a full powderhorn. Trade me."

"Can't do that," I said.

"I couldn't hit the broadside of a barn," Pink said, "Trade me. Maybe you can kill a slaveowner for me."

We had traded shoes and weapons. Pink's canteen was almost empty.

"Where's the well?" I asked. "I'll fill your canteen."

Pink pointed in the general direction of the burning plantation belching gray smoke from its collapsing roof. When I returned, he'd reclined against the ginkgo tree, his eyes closed. Frightened chickens were cackling as some of our party chased them. I handed Pink his canteen.

Our march soon continued again down the dusty road. More men and women joined our numbers, growing to perhaps five-hundred. We encountered no plantation owners, militia, or American soldiers. Though I knew the revolution was doomed to fail, I didn't know how or when. It left me filled with apprehension.

Even in Louisiana, January days are short.

As the light began to fail, we had by my count burned or partially burned four plantation homes, several sugar houses, and acres of cane standing in the fields. We encountered no resistance. Word spread through the group that we had killed a French planter who'd refused to leave his home.

There were a few farm wagons in our procession. When we made camp for the night, several heavy pots wore set over a fire and a tasty stew made from chickens and vegetables. Pink waited beneath a tree while I stood in line for two bowls of the stew.

"Best tasting food I ever ate," Pink said.

He laughed when I said, "I'm so hungry, I could eat the backend of an alligator."

"How are your feet?"

"Your potion did the trick. What about yours?"

"Fine," he said. "I'm ready to walk another twenty miles."

"I doubt we walked quite that far, though it felt more like forty."

"Say, Wyatt, you haven't smiled much since I met you. How's all this gonna end?"

I had to tell another lie. "No idea. You married?"

By now, it was dark, an owl hooting nearby. Pink waited until we heard the beating of wings before answering me.

"No wife, no kids, no mama, no daddy, no brothers or sisters."

"I'm sorry," I said.

"Don't be sorry," Pink said. "If you got nobody, then you got no one to mourn for and nothing to lose."

"That's a cynical way to look at things," I said. "If you have no one to love, how do you know how it feels?"

"I had a dog once," he said. Hearing the catch in his voice, I decided against replying.

"Ever heard of Bolthole?" I asked.

"Me and every slave on the river. Not many people know how to get there."

"I do," I said.

"You thinking of running?" he asked.

"Maybe. Want to come with me?"

Pink used an index finger to raise his glasses to his forehead. He closed his eyes and slowly shook his head.

"I ain't done much of nothing in my life. I been so scared since I heard about the revolution. I have no friends or anyone else to talk to about it. Yesterday, I just decided that whatever happened to me, it's better to die a free man than to live forever as a slave. You go, Wyatt. I'm staying."

"Pink, you have a friend now. I'm not sure about anything except that I'm probably here for a reason. I'll be marching with you when the sun comes up."

"Wyatt, I got a bad feeling about tomorrow. If things turn bad, get yourself to Bolthole."

"If it does, I'll take you with me."

## Chapter 32

My arm was still asleep when I awoke the following morning. Though my uniform was damp, the giant tree against I'd propped had protected me from the rain. Pink, resting against the other side of the tree, was also awake. My stomach growled, and the raw onions tossed to us by a passing man did little to change the rumblings.

Horses were snorting as participants in the insurrection began chequing up on the dirt road in front of the burned-out plantation. Before dawn had broken, we were marching toward New Orleans to the beat of a dozen drums. Pink was beside me.

"Feel okay?" I asked.

Pink said, "Like a pile of warmed-over shit."

"Glad to hear you feel better than I do," I said.

The bad weather wasn't over. Skies continued to darken. I took it as a heavenly sign of what was to come. We were barely a mile up the road from where we had bivouacked when it started to rain, a steady drizzle dampening our spirits.

The drum corp kept cadence with our progress and helped alleviate some of the malaise

I felt when we encountered another plantation's sugar fields. The main house and slave quarters, like the other estates we had passed, was deserted.

The revolution continued to grow, a steady stream of men and women joining us from the forests and fields. The musket resting heavily on my shoulder began to grow wearisome. Pink's words returned me to reality.

"Don't get too far ahead of me," he said. "I'm blind as a bat."

"You can't be that blind," I said.

"You ain't nothing but a moving blur. I can't even see the puddles I keep stepping in."

"I'm trying to avoid them," I said. "Right about now, this whole damn dirt road is becoming a giant mud hole. Hand me your bandanna."

Pink unknotted the red scarf from around his neck and handed it to me. After tying it together with the one I had, I laced it through the loop in my trousers and knotted the end of it.

"Hang on to this. It's the best I can do," I said.

"Just tell me when you plan to stop walking so as I don't run into you and knock you down."

Two hawks, backdropped by angry clouds, circled high overhead as rain continued falling on us. Every step I took, the mud kept trying to suction off my shoes. Wet socks did little to help keep them on. The barrel of the musket sounded metallic when I thumped it with my fingernail.

"I'm thinking about tossing this heavy piece of shit in the bar ditch," I said.

"Don't do that," Pink said. "We're gonna need it before the day's over."

"You sure about that?"

"I never killed nobody in my life. That's why I give it to you," Pink said.

"I've never killed anybody either. Hell, even if I were so inclined, the best I could probably do would be to get off a single shot," I said. "We'd all be better off with slingshots."

"Don't make light of what we're doing," Pink said. "If I had the power in me, I'd kill every one of those sorry bastards."

"I meant no disrespect," I said.

Our fellow insurrectionists were experiencing the same discomforts as Pink and I. They cursed among themselves as their shoes sloshed through the mud. Tears were falling from Pink's eyes when I turned to check on him.

"Wyatt, I got a bad feeling."

"Like what?"

"Like just before the second time I got beat."

"Then let's step off in the bar ditch and get the hell out of here. I've seen some of the other marchers do it already. I told you, I know the way to Bolthole."

"You go," he said. "I can't see shit, and my gut tells me I ain't got long to live. Don't matter none. I'm committed to the cause. I ain't lying when I say, for me, it's either freedom or death."

"Shut the hell up," I said. "For whatever reason, I'm part of this damn revolution. I'm going nowhere except down this muddy road."

Someone up ahead of us was calling to me.

"Rifleman, we need you up here."

"Slow down," Pink said.

"Hang on," I said. "People need us up ahead."

Grabbing Pink's arm, I pulled him along as I picked up the pace. The procession had come to a halt. Something was about to happen. I could see it in the eyes of every man and woman we passed that it wasn't good. We soon reached the front of the procession.

Deslondes was off his horse, his musket raised at something in the sugar cane field to the side of the road. The muskets of the dozen or so riflemen with him aimed at the advancing militia.

Even through the rain that was now falling harder, I could see at what their muskets pointed.

Enemy militia trampled rows of cane as they advanced toward us. It was easy to see their tall military hats above the cane. Gold epaulets decorated their regal blue uniforms.

More soldiers dressed in different, though no less majestic uniforms followed behind them. Probably American regulars. Though we had them outnumbered, they had many more swords, muskets, and pistols.

Our drums had grown silent, my heart beating fast as I raised my musket.

"Hold your fire," Deslondes said. "They are still too far away. Wait until they are within range."

The militia advancing toward us had yet to raise their weapons. When they were within the length of a football field, people behind us began to sound an alarm.

"They are behind us," the voice said.

"Jacque," Deslondes said. "Drop back and protect our rear."

One of the riflemen lowered their weapon and hurried to the rear of our assembly. I'm no military man and had never been in a battle. I could see the advancing soldiers had us outgunned, probably ten to one.

"Do not fire until I give the word," Deslondes said.

The arms of the man beside me trembled as he held the heavy musket in a firing position. The militia moving toward us had yet to raise their weapons. When a horse behind us whinnied, the frightened man pulled the trigger of his musket. Every man in line except me followed suit.

Our volley, hitting not a single target, fell short of its mark. The French militia was rapidly closing the distance between us. They were in range before we had time to reload our weapons.

"Fall back and regroup," Deslondes said.

We were all turning to obey Deslondes' orders when the French militia opened fire. People beside me dropped as hot lead shredded bodies. Both horses and insurrectionists began reacting to the ensuing massacre. Jacque came running through the crowd.

"They have us surrounded," he said.

"Then we fight them with what we have," Deslondes said. "Are you with me?"

Many of the men and women had held their ground. "Freedom or death," they called as one.

By now, the French militia had reloaded their weapons, hot lead whistling past my head and killing more of our troops. I had a round in my musket, and I drew a bead on the militia leader riding a white stallion. When I squeezed the trigger, the ensuing blast knocked me on my ass, busting my lip. Deslondes was waving his saber, imploring his men not to run. Many didn't, raising their pitchforks and cane knives and charging behind Deslondes across the cane field.

The frontal assault was futile. The French militia was well trained and had already reloaded their weapons. Bullets continued shredding our troops as I dragged myself out of the mud. One of them hit the man beside me. It was Pink, holding his chest as he gasped and collapsed. I hurried the short distance to him on my hands and knees.

"They got me, Wyatt."

Blood billowed crimson from the wound in Pink's chest as he lay at my feet in a heap. I turned and dug my musket out of the mud. As screams of the dying echoed in the distance, I reloaded the heavy weapon. When I glanced up, I realized I'd missed the man on the white horse. His insignias marked him as an officer. Maybe if I could bring him down, the leaderless militia would turn and run.

Holy hell was breaking out all around me, our revolutionary army screaming bloody murder as bullets ripped their bodies. I aimed and squeezed the trigger. I didn't miss, my shot knocking the man off the back of his white horse.

It didn't matter. American regulars were moving in front of the militia, still engaged in hand-to-hand fighting with Deslondes and his band of revolutionaries.

I glanced around at the human carnage surrounding me. Blood was pooling in the puddles, and those still alive were groaning in agony. A drummer boy stood tall, continuing to beat his drum until a bullet struck him in the head. He was dead before he hit the ground

By now, the militia had brought in their bloodhounds, the beasts baying as they chased fleeing patriots through the marshes, swamps, and cane fields.

French and American soldiers were among us, using their sabers to skewer bodies and chop off heads. I found a bloody cane knife and stabbed it through a man's thigh when he came to finish Pink and me. He fell to the muddy road, screaming and clutching the blade protruding from his leg.

It was then, as if by an act of a benevolent god, the skies grew almost instantly dark as a sudden downpour, accompanied by crashing thunder and blinding bolts of lightning encompassed the bloody battlefield. Under cover of the deluge, I grabbed Pink and dragged him to the bar ditch. He was smaller than me but heavy enough that I was having trouble pulling him.

"Holy hell!" I cried out.

Water filled the ditch beside the road. Louisiana is flat, and the water wasn't exactly rushing past us. Still, it was fast enough that a tree branch banged into my temple, almost knocking me out. A hundred feet from the battle site, I dragged us out of the bar ditch and began looking for an escape path.

We somehow made it to the swamp, and I pulled Pink into the water with me. Behind us, the sounds of dying horses, men, and women chilled my soul.

The storm halted as quickly as it had begun. The sun momentarily came out from behind dark clouds, the bay of bloodhounds informing me they were tracking us. We had to lose their scent somehow.

Pink was no longer moaning. Pulling him up out of the water, I realized his wound was more than serious. Blood was beginning to spurt from the wound in his chest. He would bleed out in a matter of minutes if I didn't stop the flow. Ripping off my shirt, I stuffed it into the billowing wound.

It mattered little. If I were unable to pick up the pace, the bloodhounds would soon be on us. The thought of being torn apart by a pack of angry dogs was the last way I ever thought I would die. I took Pink's head in my arms.

"Pink, if you can hear me, you gotta hold your breath."

Not waiting for an answer, I ducked beneath the water, pulling him with me.

How far I managed to swim underwater, dragging Pink, I'll never know. I was spewing water and air out of my mouth and nose when I surfaced. I could still hear the dogs in the distance. Putting my fingers to Pink's neck, I thought I felt a pulse, though ever so slight.

He didn't respond when I said, "Pink, are you still alive."

I didn't know how much water he might have swallowed while we were submerged. As he had already lost too much blood, I dared not squeeze his chest. The cold water revived him, and he opened his eyes.

"Take another breath, Pink," I said before submerging again.

This time, when I reemerged, I was gasping for air. Blood was coming out the corners of Pink's mouth. It concerned me but at least let me know he wasn't dead.

The dogs had lost our scent, as I could no longer hear them. With great difficulty, I climbed out of the water, somehow managing to drag Pink out with me. He was still alive, though barely.

I wasn't sure I remembered the way to Bolthole. Something other than my recollection was going to have to get us there. Supporting Pink as best I could, I started ahead through the swamp.

## Chapter 33

My mind and body were beyond exhaustion when we reached Bolthole. Although it was beginning to grow dark, there was enough light to see the village was much bigger than I had perceived the night Joffrey, Aura, and I had first visited it.

More than a village, it was a thriving community on a bayou that led downriver to the Gulf. A hundred or more frame houses and other structures formed a fishing community bordering a burgeoning bayou.

Pirogues and fishing boats lined the banks, nets drying in tall racks. Cajuns were part of the community, and children of both black and white parents began following us. Two men finally took Pink from me. A large black man with a gaping scar across his face put his arm under my shoulder.

"Need help, brother?" he asked.

"More than you can imagine," I said. "Is it Bolthole?"

I smiled for the first time in many hours when he said, "The place to be when there ain't nowhere left to run."

"Who are you?" I asked.

"Scar," he said.

"I mean your real name."

"My slave name was Robert Thompson. I chose Scar as my new name. It defines who I am and where I've been."

"What about Pink?"

"He being cared for. If the good Lord wants him to live, he will. You look pretty horrible, likely feel even worse. Gonna get you some rest and something to eat.

The little town was alive with men, women, and children. Scar helped me through the cloth door of a cabin. It's never frigid in Louisiana though a chill had penetrated the very being of my soul. The scarred man seated me in front of a roaring fireplace. A woman brought me a bowl of gumbo. I downed the entire bowl and then rubbed its cracked ceramic against my forehead.

"Thank you," I said. "You saved my life."

"I'm Zinnia."

"Pleased to meet you, Zinnia."

"Hand me the bowl, and I'll get you more gumbo."

"Thank you," I said again.

Zinnia was a middle-aged woman who seemed too attractive to be the wife of a man with such an ugly scar on his face. She must have read my thoughts.

"Some people have visible scars," she said. "Others have scarred souls. I prefer the visible ones."

"You're an angel, Zinnia. If everyone thought that way, the world would be a better place."

Too hungry to wait for her reply, I put the warm bowl to my lips. Zinnia draped an orange Afghan around my shoulders.

"Believe me," she said. "I'm no angel."

"I'm Wyatt. So sorry to interfere in your life."

"You ain't the first stray dog that husband of mine has drug home. You won't be the last. Can I get you something else?"

"I'm good. That was the best gumbo I've ever eaten."

"We got more oysters, redfish, and other seafood than we can eat around here," Zinnia said. "Mama taught me how to make gumbo forty years ago."

"I saw the pirogues. Do Cajuns live here?"

Zinnia nodded. "Cajuns, Indians, and former slaves. We call our tribe 'The People.'"

She smiled when I said, "You're a tribe?"

"Tribes ain't nothing more than like-minded folks," she said. "They ain't gotta be the same color. Sure you don't want another bowl of gumbo?"

I shook my head. "My stomach's full, and the crackling fire in your hearth feels wonderful. I can hardly keep my eyes open."

"Then don't. I'll cover you with one of my mama's quilts, and we can talk again tomorrow."

"What about Pink?" I asked.

"Falala is with him," she said. "The best healing hands on earth. Now, close your eyes and get some sleep."

The aroma of biscuits baking and bacon sizzling in a skillet revived me from a fitful dream. No matter how intoxicating the aroma, I fought the urge to open my eyes and face reality. The flames from the hearth were too comforting. Zinnia didn't allow my denial as she patted my cheeks until I opened my eyes. When I did, she handed me a cup of hot coffee.

"Fresh biscuits, scrambled eggs, and bacon. You hungry?"

"Starved."

Scar was introspective, neither he nor Zinnia

conversant as we ate breakfast.

"Something wrong?" I asked.

"Your uniform," Scar said. "A militia uniform."

"Charles Deslondes was also wearing a uniform. We got them the night before last when we raided the Andry place. I was here three nights ago. Joffrey and I met with Deslondes and your council of elders."

"You're white. You could be a spy."

"If you think I'm a spy, why did you treat me so well instead of just locking me up?"

"Because we don't know for sure. We're meeting with the council after breakfast."

"For what? To put me on trial?"

"Bolthole must be protected. If you're a spy, you'll never be allowed to leave."

"How are you going to know?" I asked.

"You aren't the only one from the revolution seeking asylum here. There are others."

"What about Pink?" I asked. "He'll vouch for me."

"Pink can barely see and would have no way of knowing if you are a spy."

"What am I here to learn? I already knew how to find this place when Joffrey brought us here the other night."

I began regretting my question almost before it was out of my mouth. In Scar's mind, I could be infiltrating Bolthole to scout defenses and firepower."

"Betrayal," he said.

"How am I going to prove I'm not a spy?"

Scar shrugged off my question. "We better go. The council be waiting for us."

We were soon in the cabin where Joffrey, Aura, and I had met Charles Deslondes. Lionel, Chief of Bolthole, John, and Paul sat in cane chairs in a semicircle in front of the fireplace.

They didn't offer me a chair.

"I'll just put it to you straight," Lionel said. "Are you here to spy on us?"

"I've been with Charles Deslondes since we took the Andry place. One of Deslondes bodyguards injured Andry with a cane knife though he still managed to escape. He was the local militia leader and had a cache of weapons, ammunition, and uniforms in his basement."

John rubbed his bony old hand through his snowy white hair.

"So you took one of the uniforms to wear?"

"Not just me," I said. "Deslondes wanted us to wear the uniforms to instill confidence in the rebels."

"Uh-huh," John said.

A film of sweat on Paul's bald head glistened in the flickering light of the fire.

"What happened to Charles and Joffrey," he asked. "Why aren't you with them?"

"I was never asked to act as one of Deslondes' officers. I don't understand why I'm under suspicion. Joffrey and Esther both spoke for me."

The three men exchanged knowing glances.

"How do you know Esther?" Lionel asked.

"What difference does that make?"

"She is the person who told Joffrey you are a passeblanc."

"And?"

"You lied to us. You're not a passeblanc."

"Esther says I am," I said.

"We have our spies," John said. "Some of them in New Orleans. We had your history checked at the Notarial Archives. You ain't black."

"Hell no, you ain't black," Paul said. "You're whiter than a French whore's tittie."

"Tell us your story," Lionel asked.

They waited as I drew a breath. "Don't lie to us," John said.

"You wouldn't believe me if I told you," I said.

"Try us," Lionel said.

Lionel had painted me into a corner. I couldn't tell them I was a time traveler searching for a missing moonstone. They wouldn't believe it and would probably have me hung."

"Esther contrived the story about me being a passeblanc because she knew I would be helpful to the revolution. She knew you would never trust me if I were white."

"That's part of the problem," Lionel said. "Esther herself is a spy. Someone alerted Andry about our impending attack. Everyone except Andry had deserted the plantation before Charles arrived."

"That someone was Esther," Paul said.

"How can you be so sure?" I asked.

"She the mistress of Felix François. She had the trust of everyone in the revolution, and she confided everything she learned to François. She betrayed us."

"Even if what you say is true, what does it have to do with me?" I asked.

"She would not have bothered providing you a cover story unless you was complicit."

"I'm not a spy," I said. "I was in the battle like everyone else. Why would I have risked being killed?"

"You're white. You're wearing a militia uniform. How do we know you didn't kill some of our people yourself?"

"I wasn't the only person who participated in the battle that made their way here. Scar told me so. Surely, some of them saw me and know I wasn't fighting for the enemy."

Lionel, John, and Paul huddled near the fireplace. I couldn't hear their whispered conversation. When they ended the discussion, Lionel motioned Scar.

*Cycles of the Moon*

"Round up the men and women who came here from yesterday's battle."

"All of them? They's a dozen or so."

"Everyone," Lionel said. "We'll wait on you."

We waited until Scar returned with the combatants who had managed to escape through the swamp and find their way to Bolthole. As they crowded into the room, I counted a dozen men and two women. None of them was wearing a militia uniform.

"I'm Lionel, Chief of Bolthole. Thank you for your bravery. Does any of you recognize this man?"

"I seen him yesterday morning," a young man with sideburns and a mustache said. "I throwed him and Pink an onion for breakfast."

"Anyone else?"

A murmur pulsed through the group. "We all seen him," a woman in a yellow dress said.

She smiled when John asked, "How can you be sure?"

"He white," she said.

"It didn't bother you a white man was marching with you dressed in a militia uniform?" John asked.

"All the officers dressed the same way," a man said. "We was told he was working for General Deslondes and that he a passeblanc. Hell, General Deslondes himself is whiter than he be."

"Did any of you see him do anything unusual?" Lionel said.

"Like what?" the woman in yellow asked.

"You tell me," Lionel said.

Lionel, John, and Paul's eyes all focused on the man with the mustache and sideburns when he spoke.

"I seen him do something," he said.

"Then don't just stand there, man. Tell us," Lionel said.

"He killed the American captain," he said.

"Impossible," Paul said. "We was told we killed none of the enemies."

Paul's words upset the group, and they began grumbling among themselves.

"That's a lie," the woman said. "General Deslondes and his officers killed a dozen or more of those French bastards."

"They were fighting hand-to-hand," a man said. "We could see it from the road. Some of us went to help. We was getting the best of them until the Americans began backing them up."

"Then how did you manage to escape?" Lionel asked.

Every man and woman in the group pointed at me.

"He held his fire until the American officer charged us," the woman said. "He drew a bead with his musket and blew the bastard off his white horse."

"It put the French and Americans in disarray until we was able to escape. Even General Deslondes got away."

The group stared at the floor when Lionel said, "General Deslondes escaped?"

"We think he was captured," the man with handlebars said.

"Are you sure this is the man that shot the American captain?" Paul asked.

"He was helping Pink, and that's why he wasn't up ahead with the others," the woman said.

"He tied bandannas together so they wouldn't get separated."

"Don't lie to me," Lionel asked.

"Hell, Chief, look under his coat and see if it ain't still there."

Lionel was no more than a step away from me. When he lifted the tail of my coat, he found the two red bandannas still hanging from the loop in my pants.

"Then you're not a traitor," Lionel said.

"Traitor? Hell, Chief, that man's a hero. He saved every one of our lives."

"The French and Americans killed forty-five or fifty of us," the woman in yellow said. "If it wasn't for him, we'd all be dead."

A nod punctuated Lionel's stern expression, and he rested his right hand on my shoulder.

"Son, I got no earthly idea why a white man was in the middle of our revolution, but I'm grateful to you. You're welcome to stay here forever if you like, and while you're here, you got the run of the place."

## Chapter 34

My time in antebellum Louisiana was running short. Though I still had no idea where to find the missing moonstone, I had one more task to perform in Bolthole before leaving forever. Falala met me at the door of the cabin.

"I was wondering when you would come," she said.

"I wasn't sure I was. How is Pink?"

"Healing," she said.

"Can I see him?"

"Of course you can."

Falala pulled back a curtain revealing a cot occupied by a man covered with a green wool blanket. It was Pink. He opened his eyes when Falala spoke.

"You have a visitor," she said.

Pink's attempt at a smile quickly turned to tears as he grasped my hand.

"We lost, Wyatt."

Squeezing his hand, I said, "I'm leaving Bolthole today. Before I go, I have something to give you I found in the mud."

"What?"

I'd fished Pink's spectacles out of a puddle before running from the bloodhounds. They'd been in my shirt pocket since abandoning the battlefield. I put them on him and adjusted them around his ears. He grabbed my wrist and pulled me closer to his face.

"I don't even know what you look like," he said.

My face was six inches from his when he released his grip. Falala was standing beside us.

"I'll never see you again. Now, I'll never forget your face."

"You will see him," Falala said.

We both stared at her, waiting for an explanation. She didn't give us one.

"Will he be okay?" I asked.

"Before too long, he'll be shucking oysters and trying to chase off the single women living here in Bolthole. If I were you, I'd worry more about yourself than Pink. You have a narrow path back to where you came," she said. "God speed."

"Can you tell me the way to Moonmont?"

"Follow the tip of your nose," she said.

I didn't bother saying adieu to anyone else in Bolthole, and set out through the swamp. Daylight fails early in January. I was soon wading through creepers and vines amid total darkness. My spirits lifted when I entered a clearing and saw Moonmont in the distance.

I found the plantation abandoned, all the slave shacks empty. I thought I saw a light inside the beautiful old plantation building. When I reached the kitchen through the darkened hallway, I found the light source and two people I knew. It was Shug and Miss Peach.

"That you, Wyatt?" Shug asked.

"It's me. Where is everyone?"

"They gone," she said.

"Joined the revolution," Miss Peach said.

Something that would have smelled wonderful even if I wasn't half-starved, was cooking on the hearth. Miss Peach soon had a hot bowl of beans and cornbread in front of me. When Shug produced a bottle of French wine and poured me a glass, I decided to worry about my alcoholism later.

"Where is Esther?" I asked.

"She gone to New Orleans with the master," Shug said.

"What are you two going to do?"

"Guess we wait here till everyone return," Miss Peach said.

"If there's no one else here," I said. "Let's check Felix's office."

Shug and Miss Peach had big grins as we entered Felix's regal workplace. They watched as I rummaged through his desk drawers. Finally, I found what I sought.

"You want your freedom?" I asked.

"We got no place to go," Shug said.

"There's plenty of work in New Orleans," I said. "Here's Felix's seal. I'm an advocat. I can make it happen."

I found some paper and had soon penned letters of freedom for Shug and Miss Peach. After forging Felix's signature, I witnessed the document with mine. The two twins were now free people of color.

"You're free," I said.

"Then let's celebrate," Miss Peach said.

Shug cracked another bottle of wine when we returned to the kitchen. The weather had grown chilly. Crackling flames in the hearth warmed the kitchen and made it seem like a half-acre of heaven. I was already drunk from the wine and didn't care.

"I'm looking for a moonstone," I said.

"Like the one's in Maurelle's magic pendant?"

Shug asked.

"Yes. Joffrey had the pendant. One of the moonstones was missing."

"Esther has it," Miss Peach said. "She took it with her to the townhouse in New Orleans."

Shug began to cry, and Miss Peach quickly joined her.

"What's the matter?" I asked.

"So many of the people we know joined the revolution," Shug said. "It failed. The planters have rounded up many of the slaves not killed in battle."

"Where did they take them?" I asked.

"Downriver to the Destrehan Plantation," Miss Peach said.

Shug burst into tears. "The planters are going to execute everyone we know."

I put my arms around the two young women and hugged them to me.

"Let's drink more wine," I said. "Sometimes the only way to face reality is with an addled brain."

Shug and Miss Peach were still asleep when I left Moonmont the next morning. It was still dark. The rain had finally stopped, and a waning moon lighted my way as I trod down River Road. I don't remember how many bottles of wine we had drunk. It didn't matter. The events of the past days and the casualties of war had prevented me from becoming intoxicated. My addiction was a curse. Tonight, it had proved a non-factor in my life.

Before dawn, I stopped by the side of the road, falling asleep against a tall tree. When I opened my eyes, I was looking into the barrel of a pistol.

Two men dressed in blue coats with gold epaulets stared down at me. Both appeared young, probably in their early twenties. The mud on their coats, pants, and boots tipped me that they were both battle-hardened and would have little compunction in killing me on the spot.

"On your feet," the man with the pistol said.

His partner had a musket. Though I thought about it, I had little chance of making a run for it without taking a bullet in the back.

"I'm one of you," I said. "We have nearly the same uniform."

"The rebels stole many uniforms and were wearing them when we encountered them."

"But I'm white," I said.

"Then you're a deserter. Either way, you're coming with us to the Destrehan Plantation."

The soldier with the pistol kept it trained on me while his partner tied my hands behind my back. They were both on horseback and led me down River Road with a rope around my neck.

I'd visited modern-day Destrehan Plantation for the first time when I was five. It's haunting, beautiful, and steeped in time. 1811 Destrehan was quite different. It was a working plantation occupied by French sugar barons who owned hundreds of black slaves needed to toil in the many cane fields.

The planters were wealthy beyond belief, and the slaves doomed to a life of endless toil, strife, and beatings. When we turned into the road leading to the iconic plantation, I got my first sense of the inequality that existed during the slave rebellion.

The French planters had quelled the insurrection of 1811 and had chosen Destrehan Plantation to conduct their trials. The titular judge sat behind a desk on the front porch of the plantation. Members of the French Militia and American soldiers from the post in New Orleans were standing at attention as a black man, his hands tied behind his back, stood before the judge.

A prosecutor dressed in a dark robe espoused the crimes of treason and insurrection the slave had committed. The man had no counsel. The judge took little time to deliberate.

The trial, such as it was, was short, taking only the minute or so it took for my two captors to walk me past the outdoor setting where the trial was occurring. By the time we reached a barn around back, and they had secured me in a makeshift jail cell, we heard a volley of musket fire.

Thirty men occupied the pen with me. One of them was Joffrey. He shook his head when he saw me.

"I thought you must have deserted us," he said.

"Pink and I escaped and made it to Bolthole."

"Why are you not still there?" Joffrey asked.

He shook his head again when I said, "Stupidity, I guess. I stopped by Moonmont. Shug and Miss Peach were the only ones there."

Joffrey's expression was grave as he stared up at the barn beams. "Are they okay?"

"I drafted documents of freedom for them and forged Felix's name."

"François will never let that stand," he said.

"I'm sure lots is going on in New Orleans. Maybe they'll be able to disappear into the population. What's happening here?"

"Monkey trials," he said. They have executed sixteen of us since early this morning." All of the people with us were men. All of them were older, some of them crippled or infirm. "The planters can not afford to execute able-bodied men and women, and most returned to their masters."

"You're not old or infirm," I said.

"Neither are you. I expect as ringleaders we

will receive special punishment."

"Did Deslondes survive?"

Joffrey nodded. "He has unique hell to pay for his part in the revolution. The planters will make his death a spectacle."

As we watched, guards appeared and dragged away one of the old men in the pen with us. We could hear the sounds of the ongoing prosecution and the prosecutor's distant voice as he laid out his case against the hapless defendant. Every man in the cell, including Joffrey and I, flinched at the angry blast of musket rounds executing the unlucky insurgent.

"The men do not receive a proper burial," Joffrey said. "Their heads are chopped off with an ax and then placed on a pike. A man brought in earlier said severed heads displayed on pikes go all the way to New Orleans. That is not the worst of it," he said.

"What?"

"They set the headless bodies on fire, and kick the smoldering remains into the ditch."

"That's illegal," I said. "Code Noir requires that even slaves receive a Christian burial."

"You forget Louisiana is no longer a French colony. Americans have no such law."

The planter's tribunal was nothing if not efficient. Another man was soon dragged out of the pen and led around front where the judge and prosecutor awaited him. Everyone flinched again when the death volley rang out. One of the old men began tapping out a cadence on the wall of the barn.

"Freedom or death," he said.

The other men soon joined in the chant.

As the hours passed, soldiers led the men in the pen with Joffrey and me away to their deaths.

"They are saving us for last," Joffrey said.

"For what reason?"

"They have something special awaiting us," he said.

"Like what?" I asked.

"Torture," he said. "Steel yourself. Our deaths will not come easily. By dawn, we will be dead, our bodies burning and our heads stuck on the end of a sharp pike."

## Chapter 35

Few people know the moment they are fated to die. The old men in the pen knew both when and how their lives would end. Joffrey and I also knew. The stress it wrought was paralyzing. When six men entered the enclosure, I realized for me that agonizing moment had arrived. What happened next seemed almost like a ritual.

Two of the soldiers pointed pistols at us while the others tied our hands behind our backs. Heavy leg irons were attached, and a rope around our waists bound us together. The sun was setting as the armed guards led us from the pen, hobbling to the tribunal where judge, prosecutor, and hundreds of spectators, including slaves and soldiers, awaited.

While the other executions were only the prelims, ours was the main event. The crowd to witness our trial was much larger than earlier. Half the people were slaves, there to witness an event so horrifying it would prevent them from ever rebelling again. I could see by the look in Joffrey's eyes he was thinking the same thing.

Soldiers and slaves formed a semicircle

around the large porch of the plantation home, Joffrey and I forced to kneel on the ground with our backs to the judge. It meant only one thing. Our fate was already decided. The memory of Samuel's beating resonated in my mind. That Joffrey and I were about to be made examples terrified me.

The judge sat behind his desk cloaked in a black robe. Though he had no wrinkles and looked to be in his forties, his hair was long and snowy white. The prosecutor was a small man with a deep bass voice. It echoed against the barn in the distance.

"These men are guilty of treason and sedition. They helped plan the unsuccessful revolt the planter's quickly quelled. They aided and abetted this doomed rebellion that had every intention of marching to New Orleans and overthrowing the legal government there."

Two soldiers dragging a man around the corner interrupted the prosecutor. The man wore no shirt, the raw welts on his back and shoulders, a testament to a beating he had already received.

"That man is Charles Deslondes," the prosecutor said. "His monstrous plot must be duly punished. Your Honor, Deslondes has already confessed to leading the slave revolt. What say ye?"

"He must die a death as heinous as the crime of sedition and treason he perpetrated," the judge said.

When the judge pounded his gavel on the desk, soldiers began preparing a pyre near the semicircle center. They proceeded to saturate it with coal oil. After preparing the pyre, soldiers led Charles Deslondes to the center of the semicircle. Like Joffrey and I, heavy leg irons restricted his movement, and his hands tied behind his back.

Swollen shut were Deslondes eyes, his lips bleeding. After having him kneel in the center of the semicircle, a militiaman tossed a bucket of cold water in his face. It seemed to revive him.

Someone untied Deslondes' hands, attaching single ropes to each of them. When two men carried a log into the arena and placed it in front of Deslondes, he began to struggle. Men grabbed his shoulders while others pulled his hands across the log. A muscular man with an ax and black hood over his head entered the arena. Realizing what was about to happen, Deslondes continued to struggle.

Though he refused to cry out, he recoiled in agony when the axeman lopped off his right hand. He was near unconsciousness from loss of blood when one of the militiamen doused his head with another bucket of water.

There was no fear in Deslondes' eyes, only resignation. He continued to struggle until the axeman lopped off his left hand. An officer with the militia entered the semicircle, his blue uniform and gold epaulets pristine. As the rapt audience watched, he pointed the pistol at Deslondes right thigh and pulled the trigger.

A collective moan echoed through the crowd as a guttural cry escaped from somewhere deep in Deslondes' chest. Blood began gushing from the wound, soaking his brown pants. The officer shot him, point-blank in the other thigh. A soldier doused him with another bucket of water as the pyre in front of him was ignited. As the flames lighted the darkening sky, four men lifted Deslondes by his arms and legs and tossed him on the burning pyre.

People witnessing the scene were crying, some wailing at the top of their lungs. Even the militiamen seemed in shock. Deslondes refused to cry out as flesh began to bake and fall off his body.

"His head," the judge yelled. "Take his head before he dies and place it on a pike."

The axeman used the handle of his ax to position Deslondes head over a burning log. When he lopped it off, it rolled across the semicircle. One of the militiamen kicked it back into the circle. Another man speared it with a pike and raised it in triumph over the crowd.

Though not a religious person, I had closed my eyes and began praying. Joffrey was doing the same. As we awaited our fate, I heard the prosecutor directly behind me speaking to the judge.

"I have received a message from Felix François. He wants to deal with these two himself."

"Can we let him do that?" the judge asked.

"François is the most influential planter on River Road. He has the ear of the American magistrate."

"Dare we let him take them?" the judge asked.

"I think we have little choice."

The judge summoned the French officer who had shot Deslondes in the thigh from point-blank range.

"Disperse the crowd," he said. "These two have been summoned to New Orleans."

Although relieved, we had dodged Deslondes' fate, and I couldn't help but wonder what François had in store for us. Soldiers herded Joffrey and me to a sugar wagon, placed on our knees, and lashed to the four corners of the bed. The wagon continually jostled us as it bumped its way down River Road to New Orleans. About every mile, we passed a head on a pike. There were also smoldering bodies on the sides of the road. The severed heads were grotesque though not nearly as repulsive as the smell of human flesh wafting in the January breeze.

We were mostly silent until I said, "Maurelle's magic didn't save you or the revolution."

"We were doomed by the missing moonstone."

"What happened to it?" I asked.

"Someone who wanted the revolution to fail popped it out of the pendant?"

"Who," I asked.

"Someone close to Maurelle and me."

"Esther?"

"She is the only one who could have done it," he said.

"Was it she who took the pendant from Maurelle?"

"I took it. Maurelle never allowed anyone other than me to touch the magic pendant. Not even Esther."

Joffrey nodded when I said, "But you trusted Esther enough to leave the pendant with her."

"I thought she was as passionate about the revolution as I. She had a different plan. In the end, she betrayed both Maurelle and me for her self-interests when she took the moonstone from the pendant."

"You think Esther still has the missing moonstone?" I asked.

"What difference does it make?"

"If we returned it to the pendant, it would again be magical."

"Maurelle now knows I betrayed her. I pray Felix has not taken vengeance on her."

"You love Maurelle?"

"I have had many women in my life. None of them ever moved me like Maurelle. She is the only true love I will ever know."

"Maybe she feels the same," I said.

Joffrey didn't answer as we had reached the back gate of the Old François Place. Abel, the gatekeeper, lowered his eyes, refusing to look at Joffrey as the driver guided the wagon through the gate. When we reached the stable, Felix was waiting for us and led us at gunpoint to the courtyard of the townhouse.

Torches were burning and illuminated two holes Felix's slaves had dug. Six house slaves looking thoroughly cowed were also in the courtyard. Joffrey's shoulders trembled when he saw the lifeless body in one of the holes. It was Maurelle. Her eyes were closed. Even in the flickering torchlight, I could see the blood coating her back where her wings had been.

"You killed Maurelle?" Joffrey said.

"She betrayed me," Felix said.

"You cut off her wings," Joffrey said. "How could you be so cruel?"

Felix didn't answer Joffrey's question. "Cain," he said. "Bring me the hatchet." The bald twin of Abel, the gateman, handed his master the hatchet.

Joffrey collapsed when Felix smashed the butt end of the hatchet against his temple.

"Untie his hands," Felix said.

When Maurelle's diamond wedding ring flashed in the torchlight, I realized what Felix was about to do.

Joffrey was unconscious when Felix chopped off his ring finger and tossed the disembodied digit into the shallow hole where Maurelle lay. That the hatchet needed sharpening was apparent as Felix began using it on Joffrey's hand and then his neck. The house slaves and I watched in horror as Felix finally succeeded in chopping off Joffrey's head.

"Put it on a pike and take it to Place d'Armes for display. Toss his body into the other hole. Even in death, they won't be together." Cain didn't immediately react to the command. "If you do not wish to have your body added to the graves, then you will carry out my order. Now!"

"Madam Maurelle is not yet dead," Cain said.

Felix pointed his pistol at Cain's head and pulled the trigger, the blast knocking him into the hole with Maurelle.

"Does anyone else want to join him?" Felix said. None of the remaining house slaves answered. "Then cover the dead."

As slaves began shoveling dirt on top of the bodies, I awaited my fate. Finally, Felix stood before me, the barrel of his pistol pressed against my forehead.

"If you wish to die now," he said, "your death will be more horrible than Joffrey and Maurelle's. If you perform a legal matter for me in the capacity of my advocat, I may show you leniency. Your choice."

"What legal matter?" I asked.

"I am divorcing Maurelle effective immediately. The document is already prepared. You only have to sign it."

Felix didn't bother untying my hands or removing the leg irons as he led me into the Old François Place to his upstairs office. After sitting me in a chair, he untied my hands, the barrel of the pistol pressed into my spine. When my hands were free, he retied my left hand to the chair.

Felix's pistol pointed at my head as I stared at the divorce decree on the desk.

"Just sign it," he said.

Felix handed me the beautiful writing instrument he had given me. His pistol was touching my forehead as I took the pen and prepared to sign the document.

Felix's left hand rested on the desk. Instead of using the pen to sign the decree, I stabbed it through the back of his hand. Felix shrieked in pain, the pistol bouncing across the floor.

Someone was there to pick it up. It was Esther.

Felix continued to scream in agony as Esther pointed the weapon at his head and pulled the trigger. All the house slaves and I recoiled when the blast sent Felix tumbling backward. Cain's brother Abel was behind her with the hatchet, and she used it to chop off Felix's head.

"Put it on a pike and take it to Place d'Armes," she said.

"Madam Esther," one of the house slaves asked. "What will we do with the Master's body?"

"He's no longer your master. Advocat Thomas will prepare papers freeing all of you. Take the monster's body to the river. He does not deserve a Christian burial."

The house slaves began obeying Esther's orders, one of them untying me. They had no key for the leg irons and used the dull hatchet to free me.

The big cat I'd seen the first time I'd visited was Esther's pet. He paced the room as the slaves completed their gruesome task and left the study carrying Felix's body.

"I am giving all the slaves their freedom. I have been in contact with Shug and Miss Peach. They showed me the documents you prepared for them. I used them as a template to create documents of freedom for everyone."

For the next hour, we signed and witnessed the documents Esther had prepared.

"There is no document for you," I said.

"I do not require papers," she said.

"Joffrey said you removed a moonstone from Maurelle's magic pendant."

"I was of a different mindset when I removed the moonstone. I regret my actions and all the death and misery it caused."

"Why did you do it?" I asked.

"I loved Joffrey but found I was unable to

betray Felix. I did not want to see Moonmont burned or Felix killed. If Joffrey had the magic pendant, the revolution might have succeeded. I could not take the chance it would."

"What about me? Why did you tell Joffrey I was a passeblanc?"

"It was Felix's idea. He was insanely jealous of Joffrey and suspected him of colluding with the insurgents. You were Felix's friend and advocat. He planned to talk with you about spying on the slave insurrection for him."

"He never did," I said.

"Events began occurring too swiftly. There was no time."

"You say you loved Felix. You just killed him," I said.

"And now I have nothing left."

I hadn't noticed the gold cup on the table until Esther lifted it to her lips

"What are you drinking?" I asked.

"Hemlock."

She drained the deadly poison. "What did you do with the moonstone?" I said.

Esther's body was shaking, her eyes beginning to dilate. Her mouth hung open, a tongue swollen and raw protruding from her quivering lips. Opening Felix's desk drawer, she removed something and handed it to me before collapsing dead to the floor. It was the missing moonstone.

When I glanced at the brilliant crystal, I noticed my arm was beginning, like an old filmstrip about to end, to flicker and fade. The moonstone wouldn't travel through the time vortex, and I looked for someplace to hide it.

Esther's cat was pawing at something beneath a table. It was a mouse hole. I had only just managed to shove the moonstone into the hole when the wall disappeared.

## Chapter 36

When my eyes popped open, I was sitting at the bar in La Fée Verte, Yvonne's surprised expression informing me she had never expected to see me again.

"Where did you go? Your girlfriend looked all over for you."

"Thanks for keeping the pendant for me. I need it now."

"I don't have it," she said.

"Where is it?"

"I didn't think you were coming back, so I sold it to Ben and Doris," she said.

"You did what?"

"They offered to transfer a hundred thousand dollars into my bank account. It was more than I could pass up. I'll split it with you," Yvonne said.

"How long have they been gone?" I said.

"Just walked out." Bounding off the stool, I rushed to the door. "What about the money?" she asked.

I didn't bother answering her.

As I hurried out the door of the little absinthe bar, I saw Ben and Doris hailing a cab at the intersection of Pirate's Alley and Royal Street. I was yelling and running toward them when a taxi pulled to the curb. I watched them drive away.

"Wyatt," I heard someone call.

It was Aura, her head stuck out of the passenger seat of Jake's limo. I quickly joined her.

Pointing at the disappearing vehicle, I said, "Bradley, follow that cab."

Needing no other orders, Bradley squealed away from the curb. The cab, moving slowly down the narrow roads of the French Quarter, turned on Orleans Street. Bradley went with him, quickly pulling to the bumper of the slower-moving vehicle.

"Now what?" he asked.

"Force him to the side of the road."

Bradley didn't ask questions, bumping the cab as he laid on his horn. The suddenly terrified cabbie stepped on the gas. Aura and I held on as the big limo swerved through moving cars and pedestrian traffic. We raced past Bourbon and Dauphine with no mishaps. When the cab ran the Burgundy stop sign, Bradley went with him, not stopping when he clipped a car's fender.

The cabbie didn't slow down when he reached N. Rampart, barely averting a collision with an oncoming trolley. Bradley slammed on the brakes and slid sideways to keep from broadsiding the public transportation vehicle.

The rubber from the limo's tires was smoking as we u-turned onto N. Rampart. The limo's engine was more than a match for the fleeing cab. We caught it just after passing the St. Peters intersection. With the limo's nose in front of the cab, Bradley forced it off the road, onto the sidewalk. I jumped out of the car before it had come to a complete halt.

I opened the backseat door of the cab as Ben hurriedly exited the other door. Bradley was big but also fast as a cat. After chasing Ben a hundred yards, he brought him down with a flying tackle. I knew by Doris's purse in Ben's hand where I would find Maurelle's pendant. Snatching the bag, I dumped its contents on the sidewalk. And there it was. With the pendant secure in my hand, I started back to the limo.

"Thief!" Ben called. "Stop that, man."

Cars were moving slowly on the major thoroughfare, rubbernecking as we reached the limo. Aura was wrestling with Doris, who was using her phone, trying to call 9-1-1. Snatching it away from her, I heaved the phone into the street.

"Where to?" Bradley asked when we were again in the front seat of the limo.

"The hell out of here before the police arrive."

Tires squealed, and rubber burned as Bradley powered away.

"Quite a tackle back there," I said.

"I played linebacker at Alabama," he said, "and a few seasons with the Tennessee Titans."

He laughed when I said, "You could have had quite a career in NASCAR."

"Maybe, if I wasn't six-six and didn't weigh 250 pounds. I did do a few movies as a stunt driver."

"Take us to the Old François Place, and keep an eye out for the police."

"You found the missing moonstone?" Aura asked.

"I know where it is," I said. "Bradley, park on a side street. The cops will be looking for the limo and swarming the Quarter before long."

"If we go to jail, Boss Man will bail us out."

"Of that, I have no doubt. Doesn't matter because we have something important to do first."

Bradley parked in the alley behind the Old François Place, fences and tall trees making the limo almost invisible from the road.

"Want me to come with you?" he asked.

"We're good. Wait here for us," I said. "We won't be long."

The alleyway led us to the back of the Creole townhouse. We found the back gate unlocked. As we walked past the stable, I thought of Joffrey and Abel, trying but failing not to let it bother me as we entered the front door of the Old François Place.

It had rained while I was off time traveling, the mildewed rug leading up the stairs wet and slippery. Clutching Aura's wrist with one hand, I gripped the railing with the other. Abandoned for more than a century, the hallway and pictures on the walls had faded with time since last I'd visited.

The door to Felix's office, swollen by time and humidity, refused to open until I gave it a firm yank. The room was drastically different than I remembered, and I wondered if the moonstone was still where I'd left it.

The flocked wallpaper covering the hardwood walls was faded and sagging. Moths had eaten holes, and mouse droppings littered the rugs. Vandals had ransacked the furnishings now laying smashed and strewn across the floor.

"I last saw the moonstone in this room. I hid it before returning to the present," I said.

"Find it, and let's get out of here. It stinks, and it's giving me the creeps."

"I can't see what I'm doing," I said. "Open the curtains and let in some light."

Aura waded through the trash on the floor to open the frayed and faded curtains. When she returned, she handed me an inscribed gold cup.

"Check this out," she said. "Looks and feels like solid gold. Can you read what it says?"

"Esther and Felix, January 1811."

"What does it mean?"

"Last time I saw Esther, she used that cup to poison herself with hemlock. Before she did, she told me she and Felix were married."

"How did he get out of his marriage with Maurelle?" Aura asked.

"Murdered her. At least he thought he did. He must have married Esther the same day he chopped off Maurelle's wings."

"What a deceitful monster," Aura said. "What was Esther doing in New Orleans?"

"We don't have much time," I said.

"Then tell me the short version."

"Esther had the hots for Joffrey and felt betrayed by him and Maurelle. She was also the only person Maurelle entrusted to handle the magic pendant. She removed one of the moonstones before giving the pendant to Joffrey."

"What about Esther and Felix?" Aura asked.

"Their relationship was complicated. All the house slaves looked up to Esther and obeyed her. Because of this, Felix used her to get what he wanted. Esther allowed it because she coveted the power their relationship provided her. She ended up loving Felix, and he loved her as much as he was mentally able to."

"Then why did she turn on him?" Aura asked.

"Joffrey. When Felix killed him, she realized the price of betrayal."

"Felix killed Joffrey?"

"Like I said, long story. I'll tell you when we have more time."

"It blows my mind Esther killed Felix the same day she married him," she said.

"Murder, suicide," I said. "Let me find the moonstone, and then let's get the hell out of here."

Time and the elements had taken a hard toll on the old house. Going to my knees, I began moving the debris that had accumulated against the wall. When I exposed the mousehole, I drew a breath, hoping the mice hadn't moved the magical stone. They hadn't. It was still there, just as I had left it some two-hundred years before.

"Hurry up," Aura said.

"Just a minute. I need to reattach the loose moonstone."

Aura watched as I held the moonstone in one hand, the pendant in the other. I needn't have worried as the moonstone, and the pendant started to glow and then melded together in some celestial magnetic attraction. The room burned with a heavenly brightness when the missing moonstone rejoined the magical pendant.

"Eureka!" I said.

Without speaking, I led Aura down the stairs, out the front door to the back gate. Jimi Hendrix's song *Purple Haze* was blaring from an open window when we reached the limo. After lowering the volume on the radio, Bradley unlocked the passenger door for us.

"Turn it back up," Aura said. "I can't think of a more appropriate song to listen to right now."

Bradley cranked the volume and waited for me to tell him where we were going.

"The anthropology lab at UNO. And keep an eye out for the cops," I said.

"Yes, sir, Boss Man."

"While you're at it, call Jake. If he and Mama are back from Tulsa, tell him they need to join us ASAP if they want pictures of a lifetime."

"Maybe we should wait on them," Bradley said.

"Not gonna happen," I said. "The Absinthe Fairy has been waiting for two centuries. I don't intend to keep her waiting a minute longer than necessary."

Bradley eased out of the alley and then followed a circuitous path to UNO. He parked the limo near the anthropology building and exited with us.

"I've been part of lots of strangeness since coming to work for Jake. I'm sensing this one is about to top them all."

The hallways were empty and we encountered no one on our trip through the building. We found the door to the anthropology lab locked. The knob glowed when I held the pendant to it and then began to turn. Hinges creaked as the door opened wide to permit our entrance.

The magic worked again for the door to the refrigerated room. Aura uncovered Maurelle's naked body. When I handed the pendant to her, she clasped it around Maurelle's neck. A mist of green began filling the room. It glowed with ephemeral light and swirled over Maurelle's body.

Her eyes slowly opened, and she rose to a sitting position. The stubs of her wings became pink and then crimson. Gossamer wings unfurled from the stubs and were soon fully six feet across. Her green eyes were limpid when she clutched my hand.

"Thank you, Wyatt," she said.

"I brought your daughter with me," I said. "Aura is the one who clasped the pendant around your neck."

Maurelle and Aura, tears welling in their eyes, embraced for what seemed an eternity. Maurelle began to levitate, her green gossamer wings slowly fluttering as she flew from the refrigerated room.

"Wait," Aura said.

Maurelle ignored her until she reached the pile of Joffrey's bones lying on a display rack. When she touched his bones, they began to move and then to reassemble into the virile young man Aura, and I had known. He had no missing parts. When I handed him the diamond ring, he slipped it on his little finger.

"I have questions," Aura said.

"And I have answers," Maurelle said. "I lied to you. It was Felix who chopped off your wings and threw you over the railing."

"I'm not dead," Aura said.

"Join us in the magic forest. It is where you belong."

Joffrey was smiling as a man possessed. He saluted me as he and Maurelle levitated toward the ceiling. It was then Mama, Jake, and his crew burst through the door. Darkness filled the anthropology lab until someone had the presence of mind to turn on the lights.

Jake glanced at me. "What just happened?"

"Redemption," I said.

"You can tell us about it later. Someone else besides Bentley called us while we were at Bertram's. They were on their way there, and I suspect you might be interested in seeing them," Jake said.

"Who?"

"Charles Deslondes, his wife and newborn child."

## Chapter 37

Dozens of people trying to get a glimpse of the Cryptid Hunter crowded Bertram's. A man both Aura and I recognized was at the bar beside an attractive young woman with a baby. Bertram was in the middle of the action, probably telling tall Cajun tales.

Since leaving the anthropology lab at UNO, Mama hadn't let go of my arm. Though Jake and Aura seemed jealous, Mama, my closest friend, didn't care. I was just as glad to see her and happy to be alive. Jake shouldered his way through the crowd to fetch us drinks.

The man who I thought I recognized was talking with Jake's crew. It was either Charles Deslondes or else his doppelganger. His swollen hand was black and blue, though it looked as if it was completely functional.

"Am I seeing things, or is that Charles Deslondes?" I asked.

"It's him," Mama said.

"Is there something you need to tell me?" I asked.

"When we thought we'd lost you in time, I summoned Madam Aja," Mama said.

"You saw Madam Aja?"

"Senora, Jake, and I took datura to summon her."

"You didn't," I said. "Datura is poisonous."

"We did. Senora and I overdosed and had to go to the emergency room. Jake has a castiron stomach and only got a little loopy."

"What did Madam Aja say?" I asked.

"That time is like a river. She advised us to visit a birthing clinic in the Seventh Ward for answers."

"Hmm!" I said.

Jake had returned from the bar, his arms filled with drinks. He'd caught the last of Mama's words.

"What happens in the past affects the future, and vice versa," he said. "Charles was at the birthing clinic, his wife Priscilla in labor. Mama and Senora delivered the baby."

"What's up with his hand?"

"Severed that very day by a punch press in the factory where he worked. He went to the clinic instead of the hospital."

"But he has a hand," I said.

"The people at the factory put it on ice. Surgeons were able to reattach it."

"Thanks to Jake," Mama said.

"I have to talk to him," I said.

Deslondes was all smiles, pumping Jake's hand when we reached him through the crowd. He and Mama exchanged a fist bump.

"Charles, this is Wyatt Thomas. You met Aura at the clinic."

"Your face is familiar," Deslondes said. "Have we met?"

"Many years ago," I said. "Is this your lovely bride?"

"I'm Priscilla," she said.

"Your baby is beautiful," I said. "What's his

name?"

"How did you know he is a boy?" she asked.

"Isn't he?"

"His name is Pinkney," she said. "We call him Pink."

When I started to speak, I had to choke back tears.

"Something wrong?" Charles asked.

"One of my dearest friends was named Pinkney. A wonderful man as I know your beautiful son will be."

Seeing my distress, Aura pushed me to the bar. Bertram was waiting with a glass of lemonade.

"You okay, Cowboy?"

I downed half the lemonade before answering him.

"I am now."

Jake and his crew had wrapped the episode they'd come to New Orleans to shoot. Bertram was happily dispensing alcohol, the party just beginning when Aura pulled me aside.

"I can't stop thinking about what Maurelle said about the magic forest."

"It's not that far up the road," I said. "Bradley's sober. I'll bet he'll take us."

"I hate to leave. The party's just beginning."

"And will still be going full steam when we return," I said.

Aura and I were soon leaving New Orleans, heading upriver in the limo's front seat.

"Sorry to take you away from the party," Aura said.

"It's my job," Bradley said. "I love it, and Boss Man pays me more than I deserve."

He nodded when I said, "No, he doesn't."

The spot where Moonmont once stood was now little more than a field of grass waffling in a gentle breeze. Bradley found a place to park and opened the door for us as we stepped out of the limo and started toward the grove of tall trees in the distance.

"Hey," he said. "Want me to come with you?"

"Please wait for us," I said.

"Will you be okay?" Aura asked.

He was grinning when he said, "A lot of Hendrix music and a little weed is all the company I need. Call if you need me."

In the middle of August, Louisiana was hot. When we reached the edge of the forest, I'd already unbuttoned my shirt.

"Do you remember the way to Falala's?" Aura asked.

"Not really."

"Then how will we ever find it?"

"Follow our noses," I said.

"Look at the butterflies. They're all over the place."

Two hawks circled high overhead, their wings barely moving. Something behind a blackberry bush rustled the vegetation. It was Grishorn, the chupacabra. Tears were in Aura's eyes as she ran to it and hugged its vast neck.

"Grishorn, I've missed you so."

We followed the beast through the forest until we arrived at Falala's cabin. Joffrey was sitting in a rocking chair on the porch, smoke rising in gentle puffs from the cigar he was smoking. He waved at us. Falala opened the door of the cabin and also waved. A tiny green fairy flitted out of the trees and rested on Joffrey's shoulder. As we watched, the cabin melted away as if it were never there.

"A mirage," Aura said.

"Maybe. Let's get back to the limo."

"Not yet," Aura said. "We have unfinished business."

A grove of trees surrounded by a thick carpet of green grass lay beside a bucolic brook. Aura was tossing off her clothes and almost naked when she reached the trees.

"Hurry," she said. "I've already waited too long."

Before I could respond, an electrical crackle caused me to turn around toward the direction from where we had just come. It was Aura. At least it looked like her. She was naked, her blue-toned gossamer wings fluttering in the breeze.

"Thank you," she said.

"For what?" I asked.

"For returning me to my home."

"Are you Aura?" I asked.

"I'm Aura Lea."

"Then what about Aura?"

"I was part of her until you rescued me. She was never a fairy."

Aura Lea began to rise into the air. "Wait," I said. "I'm not sure I understand."

"Yes, you do. You are a Traveler and rearranged some of the water of time for us."

Before I could question her further, Aura Lea continued to levitate. Then, in an explosion of multicolored fairy dust, she disappeared forever. I stared at the sky until a voice called to me from under the trees. It was Aura.

"Where are you?" she said. "Get your clothes off and join me."

When I reached Aura, I was naked. She was lying on her stomach, and I could see her vestigial wings were gone. After dragging my fingers through her hair, I saw her ears were no longer elfin. The next hour was like a dream you never want to end. When it did, Aura rolled onto her back.

"Wyatt, I've had a blast here in New Orleans, but I hate the humidity. I have another job offer.

I'm going to take it."

"Oh?"

"My passion is Egyptology. My new position will take me to Africa. It's my dream job, and I can't turn it down."

"I'll miss you."

"We'll see each other again," Aura said. "Who was that you were talking to?"

"A fairy," I said.

Aura rubbed my chest with the palm of her hand. That's what I love about you. You're always making up things to lighten the moment. What did your fairy say?"

She punched my arm when I said, "It's complicated."

"Give me the short version," she said.

"Tell you later. There's a celebration waiting for us in New Orleans, and I'm in desperate need of a glass of lemonade."

End

# Book Notes

Though *Cycles of the Moon* is fictional, most of its historical details are accurate. The largest slave insurrection in America occurred in January 1811. Charles Deslondes led the revolt. As horrible as the description of his death was, it's how it happened.

The French sugar farmers didn't coddle plantation slaves. They toiled their entire lives. There were no families because the imminent heartbreak of separation was too great. Black men and women wanted their freedom and suffered beatings and torture by their owners to prevent them from having it.

Though Bolthole is fictional, such places existed, often deep in the swamps where even bloodhounds could no longer follow the scent. Whites and blacks are all human, and there were many liaisons, even marriages between the two races.

The French were cruel though perhaps not as much as the Americans who gained control of the region following the Louisiana Purchase. Code Noir was an actual law created by Louis XLV, the French emperor known as the Sun King. Because of Code Noir, many slaves became free people of color and a force in the melting pot that is now New Orleans.

I hope you enjoyed *Cycles of the Moon* as much as I enjoyed writing it. Covid-19 rocked my world in 2020, and this book took me almost eighteen months to complete. I can only hope the chaos we've all experienced during the pandemic has served to put a dramatic edge on an important historical event that deserves to be told and retold.

I hope you like Wyatt Thomas, my moody private investigator. If you do, please consider leaving a review and reading the other books in the French Quarter Mystery Series. You may also like my Paranormal Cowboy Series that includes Ghost of a Chance, Bones of Skeleton Creek, and Blink of an Eye.

I want you to be the first to know I'm beginning a new series called Cryptid Hunter. Jake Huntington, a prominent character in Cycles, is the protagonist. In my next book *Vodou Nights,* Jake and Mama travel to Haiti, a mysterious country I believe is near the ancient continent of Atlantis. I hope you will consider reading it when it's finished.

Thanks for being a fan. Without fantastic readers like you, my stories would be little more than morning fog wafting across a forgotten lawn before disappearing forever into the Great Unknown.

# About the Author

Born on a sleepy bayou, Louisiana Mystery Writer Eric Wilder grew up listening to tales of ghosts, magic, and voodoo. He's the author of fourteen novels, four cookbooks, many short stories, and Murder Etouffee, a book that defies classification. His two series feature P.I.s adept in the investigation of the paranormal. He lives in Oklahoma near historic Route 66 with his wife Marilyn, two beautiful dogs, and one remarkable cat.

www.ingramcontent.com/pod-product-compliance
Lightning Source LLC
LaVergne TN
LVHW040039080526
838202LV00045B/3408